T0152557

GIRLS NEXT DOOR

LESBIAN ROMANCE

Edited by Sandy Lowe and Stacia Seaman

Girls on Campus

Girls Next Door

Visit us at www.boldstrokesbooks.com

GIRLS NEXT DOOR

LESBIAN ROMANCE

edited by

Sandy Lowe and Stacia Seaman

2017

GIRLS NEXT DOOR: LESBIAN ROMANCE
© 2017 BY BOLD STROKES BOOKS. ALL RIGHTS RESERVED.

ISBN 13: 978-1-62639-916-7

"Neighbors" by Elizabeth Black appeared in *Vamps* (Torquere Press, 2009)

THIS TRADE PAPERBACK ORIGINAL IS PUBLISHED BY
BOLD STROKES BOOKS, INC.
P.O. BOX 249
VALLEY FALLS, NY 12185

FIRST EDITION: JUNE 2017

THIS IS A WORK OF FICTION. NAMES, CHARACTERS, PLACES, AND INCIDENTS ARE THE PRODUCT OF THE AUTHOR'S IMAGINATION OR ARE USED FICTITIOUSLY. ANY RESEMBLANCE TO ACTUAL PERSONS, LIVING OR DEAD, BUSINESS ESTABLISHMENTS, EVENTS, OR LOCALES IS ENTIRELY COINCIDENTAL.

THIS BOOK, OR PARTS THEREOF, MAY NOT BE REPRODUCED IN ANY FORM WITHOUT PERMISSION.

CREDITS
EDITORS: SANDY LOWE AND STACIA SEAMAN
PRODUCTION DESIGN: STACIA SEAMAN
COVER DESIGN BY JEANINE HENNING

CONTENTS

CUPCAKE

Georgia Beers

Okay, full disclosure: I do not enjoy yoga. I go, yes. Three times a week. I need to. I have to. At thirty-three, I'm not getting any younger and my muscles aren't getting any more flexible. Plus, I have an office job, and sitting on my ass all day long doesn't do much to keep me fit. My mother is always telling me I have to keep moving as I get older. Granted, she is a woman who never stops. Ever. If I could bottle an eighth of her energy, I'd be good to go for years.

Anyway. Yoga. Yeah. It's not my favorite. I have terrible balance and it takes great effort for me not to fall over in the middle of class during any given pose. I've gotten better, but I don't really put in the effort needed to become good at it. I go because I have to. The yoga studio is a good size and located in one of those large buildings downtown, populated by offices on the top three floors and retail shops on the ground. I can walk there from my office, which is nice, as I don't have to find parking. Also of note: Next door to the yoga studio is a cute little place called Cherry on Top. That's the other reason I must go to yoga: Cherry on Top is a cupcake shop, and I can't seem to stay away.

Today is Monday, and class is no different than any other day. My muscles are still trembling as I roll up my mat and wave to Gina, the instructor who I'm pretty sure is determined to kill me one of these days. I always wave so as to stay on her good side. I can't tell you how many times I've almost shouted, "I don't bend that way!"

in the middle of class. It's only that everybody *else* seems to bend that way that keeps my lips sealed shut. Yeah, with her long legs, perfect bubble butt, and disturbingly cheerful instructor voice, Gina is a certified sadist. I'm sure of it.

The class is pretty big, given it's the 5:30 one. We've all come from our offices, changed out of our business suits and heels in the locker room and into Spandex in the hopes of having an ass like Gina's one day. Most of us know our chances are slim, but we try anyway. I throw my towel over my shoulder and take a slug from my water bottle. Another advantage to this time of day is most of the women (and two men) in my class head home immediately, though some of them do what I do and hit Cherry on Top. They buy boxes of cupcakes to take home to the families, I imagine. I like to hang out. Still in my yoga clothes, I sit at Cherry on Top's little counter next to the display case. It's almost like a bar, with five red vinyl-covered stools.

"Well, hello there, Belle." She calls me that because the first time I sat down at her "cupcake bar," I was reading a book. She asked if I'd ever seen *Beauty and the Beast*. I basically laughed and said something along the lines of "duh," and she's called me Belle ever since.

"Hi, Katie." I take a seat on one of the bar stools.

"I've got a new one today. You game?" Her blue eyes sparkle with approachability. You can't not like Katie. She's cute and friendly and cheerful and you just…want to be around her. I love to listen to her talk. I enjoy watching her work as I sit on my stool and eat my cupcake. When it's not busy—like tonight—I really like just talking to her. About anything. About nothing.

"Always." This isn't the first time she's tried a new flavor on me. I love when she does that.

Katie glances back at me, her deep blue eyes scanning down, then up what she can see of my body. "Yoga's doing you good." She turns her back—which I am thankful for, I can feel the heat in my face—and it gives me a chance to look at her. She's small. I'd put her at maybe five-two, but with a solid frame. She does yoga, too, though we've never been in a class together, and I think it's been much more beneficial for her. She looks solid, muscular but in a very feminine way. Her hair is light brown, just past her shoulders, and she's wearing it down today. Most days, she'll wear it in a high ponytail, which allows me a really great view of her neck. She's dressed in snugly worn jeans and a blue T-shirt, a white apron tied around her waist. Her small hands move quickly, spreading frosting over a light-colored cupcake, then very carefully—and artistically, really—shaving a spiral of peel from an orange and sticking it into the white frosting. I am perfectly content to just sit and observe. Whenever she turns my way, I flick my gaze elsewhere. Can't have her thinking I'm some creeper staring at her all the time. Even though I kind of am. (Staring. Not a creeper.)

At this point, I'm guessing you've probably figured out what I *really* like about Cherry on Top. Subtlety has never been a strong point for me.

She holds up the cupcake, and that pop of orange really makes it look pretty. It's in a silver wrapper and it just looks…classy. Not bad for a cupcake. Once she's satisfied, she nods once, sets it on a small plate, grabs a Diet Coke from the cooler behind the counter, and slides it all in front of me.

"Triple Citrus," she says by way of explanation. Then she moves down the counter to take care of a woman from my class. She wants a dozen cupcakes and tells Katie to "surprise her" with the combination.

Katie has never watched me try her new flavors. I think it makes her nervous, though it's not like any of them have ever been awful. I was not a fan of the peanut butter and jelly cupcake, but that's just me. Peanut butter isn't my jam (no pun intended) and I told her so, but the shadow of disappointment on her face was almost too much.

I swipe a finger through the frosting and taste. It's got a very subtle hint of citrus and it's hard to pinpoint whether it's orange, lemon, or lime, but it's delicious. I carefully unwrap the cake and break it in half. It's a perfect size; not too big, not too small, fits right in my hand without overflowing. I pop a piece into my mouth and savor. The citrus is stronger in the cake, its tang surprising my taste buds in the best of ways.

Katie rings the woman up and sends her on her way. Then she looks at me, a hint of trepidation on her face. I grin and give her a thumbs-up. The relief in her expression is so obvious I almost laugh.

"This is delicious," I say around a mouthful of cake. "One of your best."

"Yeah?" She returns and leans her forearms on the counter. "Orange, lemon, lime, and a teeny bit of grapefruit in there."

"So…quadruple citrus."

"Technically. But Triple Citrus sounds better."

"True. I never thought I'd say this about a cupcake, but it's almost refreshing."

A smile breaks across her face and my day is made. She raps her knuckles on the counter. "Excellent. I'll put a batch out tomorrow morning." And she's off toward the small whiteboard on the wall where she jots a note in purple marker.

Early mornings are when she's busiest. I've only been here once before work, and I won't ever do that again. The line was massive, and despite having one of her two employees helping her out, Katie could barely register my presence. I'm pretty sure I pouted like a ten-year-old girl.

I take another bite, then a swig of the Diet Coke. "I hope my yoga instructor doesn't come in here and see me eating this. She lives to try to make me tip over in class." Katie laughs, and it's something I adore so much about her. When she laughs, she *really* laughs. Like, throws her head back and just lets it loose. Unabashedly unashamed.

"I'm sure that's not true," she says.

"Oh, it's true. Trust me."

People are milling about in the hallway outside, some from my class still exiting and heading home, others meandering in for the 7:00 class. Cherry on Top isn't busy, so Katie props her elbows on the bar and gazes at me with those eyes.

"So, Belle, how was your day?"

And that's another thing about Katie. When she asks you a question, she seems to really want to know the answer. She seems really interested in what I have to say. Of course, I could be projecting. I am, after all, a customer, and it would simply be good business for her to keep me coming back for my three-times-a-week sometimes-more-than-one cupcake and soda. Maybe she's like this with every customer. Right now, with that face looking at me, I couldn't care less about them.

I know. I know. I might have a slight crush. *Slight.* I'm aware.

"It was okay," I say honestly. "How about yours?"

"Well, that sounds less than convincing, but I'll let your not-very-subtle subject change slide for right now. My day was good. Lunchtime was busy. And I'm working on another new flavor."

"Oh?"

She nods. "It still needs some tweaking. You can be my guinea pig when I'm ready to share it."

"That's what I'm here for." Our gazes hold for a beat longer than necessary, and I pop the last bit of my cupcake into my mouth. "All gone." I hold up my empty hands.

She laughs that laugh and closes her hand over my forearm. "I like you, Belle. I'm glad you're here." And before I can absorb the feeling of her grip or her words, she's sidling down the bar to take care of one of the two guys in my yoga class who has decided he needs a cupcake more than I need to talk to Katie. I silently grumble at him as he says something I can't quite make out and she laughs. He's done this before, taken her attention away from me, and I've decided I hate him just a little. Or maybe quite a bit. I try hard not to glare at him, especially as he is obviously flirting with her. I fail miserably and, as she laughs at something he says, I am once again reminded of the dangers of crushing on a most-likely-straight girl.

I narrow my eyes in the guy's general direction, try to make his head explode using just my mind. Sadly—and unsurprisingly—it doesn't work.

Yeah, just a *slight* crush.

❖

So, by now I'm sure you're wondering why a charmer like me doesn't have a girlfriend. That's a good question, one I try not to ask myself all that often, mostly so I don't drive myself insane. Or make myself cry. I guess the standard, very, very clichéd answer is that I just haven't found the right girl yet. I date. Of course I date. I'm attractive enough, have a good job, I'm smart, I'm funny. My bestie, Morgan, would tell you I'm a catch, that any girl would be lucky to have me. Apparently, Any Girl is having some trouble finding me.

"I don't know why you don't just ask her out," Morgan was saying now. We rarely talk on the phone, but when I'd texted her that it was Cupcake Night, as we call it, she had too much to say for typing and called me instead.

"Because I don't even know if she plays on our team, Morgs."

"One way to find out."

"Yeah, that'd go over well. 'So, Katie, I notice you seem to enjoy my company here in your cupcake shop, and I wonder if you'd also enjoy it in the bedroom.'"

I can almost hear Morgan roll her eyes. "Yeah, that's exactly the right approach." She scoffs. "Go with that."

I make a sound of frustration and change the subject. "How's work?"

"It's great. I can get you in. I know it."

Morgan and I met three years ago when I started working at my current company. When the owners sold to a larger conglomerate six months ago, Morgan took the opportunity to flee to a competitor. Which turned out to be a smart move, as the rest of her department was laid off three weeks later. The reality is, I could be let go at any time, but I'm not so good with change, so I'm sticking it out. For now. "I know you can. I have it filed in the back of my mind."

"All right, I'm gonna say something now." Morgan's tone has changed, cluing me in to the fact that I am probably going to hate the words about to come out of her mouth. I brace myself. "You need to learn to make a move, babe. You let yourself…stagnate. You know? You won't look into changing jobs, even though you know they're going to lay you off eventually. That's just a matter of time. You like this girl. You *like* her. I know you. And you won't make a move there either. I mean, what's the worst that happens? She says, 'Sorry, Charlie, I don't swing that way, but you're swell. Let's be friends.' What's wrong with that? At least you'd know."

She seems to run out of steam then and we're both silent for a few beats.

"Are you mad?" she asks softly.

"No." I'm mostly telling the truth. Nothing she said is off base, but nobody likes to have a giant mirror held up in front of their face either, you know?

"I just…think you deserve more." She pauses, and I picture her collecting the right thoughts, the right words to say. "You're an amazing woman. You're smart and you're funny and you're pretty and you're sexy."

"Hey." I slide a joking lilt into my voice. "Back off, lady."

Morgan laughs, as we both know I'm not her type. Because I'm a girl. "I'm just saying that any company and any woman would be lucky to have you. I don't think you feel the same way, and you should. That's all."

"This is why I keep you around, Morgs." And then we're back to casual conversation and I'm relieved. We talk a bit longer and finally hang up.

Morgan is right on all counts. I hate to admit it, but it's true. I hate change. I always have. I am not a go-getter. I like stability and routine and things that I can predict, and I don't think there's anything wrong with that. I know people who like to shake up their world every once in a while. They move often or take impromptu vacations or switch jobs at the drop of a hat. Those kinds of things make me twitchy. Which is not to say I can't be spontaneous. I can. I just like to…plan it out first.

Romeo, the handsomest calico cat on the planet, hops up onto the couch and settles himself on my lap, preventing me from moving for at least the next forty-five minutes. "It's a good thing I planned on watching TV, pal." He looks at me and yawns, bored with me. Both of us know I'd never move him anyway. He kneads my sweatshirt and yoga pants (ow) until he's comfortable, and I turn up the volume on *Bones* because I can't hear it over his ridiculously loud purring.

❖

I don't know what Morgan did.

Did she conjure something?

I need to call and ask her. But that will have to be later because right now, I'm busy. Darren, a security guard I say good morning to every single day of the work week, hovers awkwardly over me while I clean out my desk. There are four of us, and we've all been laid off on this sunny Tuesday morning. We are packing up our meager personal effects while a uniformed guard watches to make sure we don't steal a stapler or mouse pad.

It's nothing personal. I know this in my brain, but my heart and, more than that, my ego is taking a beating. We look like criminals. Like we've been caught stealing corporate secrets and selling them to the highest bidder. The rest of the office is trying not to watch, but it's hard, like driving past a car accident without looking. I get it. I went through the same thing when the last batch of people were let go. Your facial expression shows a mix of sympathy and relief, and no matter what you do, you can't manage to mask it because all you can think is "Thank God it's not me." It's sad and embarrassing and emotional and awful and I pack as fast as I can, throwing framed photos, stress-relieving gadgets, and my coffee mug with the picture of Romeo on it into the banker's box they gave me. I just want to get out, get away from the stares and the scrutiny and the pity. Most of all, the pity.

To my right, I can hear sniffling coming from the adjacent cubicle. Maggie was also laid off, and while I plan on holding in my tears until I'm alone, Maggie has no such intention. She's been crying openly since she started packing. Behind her, Cliff is the opposite. He's angrily throwing his belongings into his box. Things are breaking—you can tell by the sound—but I think he's beyond caring. His brow is furrowed, his ruddy face red with anger, and he's been muttering for a good ten minutes, the occasional swear word popping out, crystal clear among the garbled sentences.

Darren walks me to the elevator, then rides down two floors with me, both of us feeling so awkward we have no idea what to say to each other. In the lobby, I stop at the front door and take a deep breath, my banker's box held at my waist. The other elevator car dings its arrival and I know Maggie's in it. I don't want to deal with the rawness of her emotions right now or I'll lose the tentative grip I have on my own.

"You take care of yourself, Ms. Vaughn," Darren says quietly.

"You, too, Darren."

I step out into the daylight. It's a weird dichotomy: On this mentally gray and foggy day, the weather is sunny and bright, a pleasant seventy degrees with the kind of crystal-blue sky that makes you stop in wonder at the beauty of nature. I put my box in the trunk of my car, slide into the driver's seat, and drop my forehead against the steering wheel.

I don't know what to do or where to go.

That lasts for…I have no idea how long. When I lift my head from the steering wheel, nothing has changed. The sun is still shining. I'm still parked between a blue minivan and a black SUV. I'm still unemployed. I yank the door handle to hurl myself out of the car, suddenly oppressed by the recycled air and my own self-pity. Before I can figure out where I'm going, I'm pushing through the glass double-doors that lead into the little shopping plaza next to my building that houses the yoga studio.

And Cherry on Top.

It's late morning, so Katie's early rush has passed. She has an employee during business hours, a kind-looking woman named Ruthie who has a super-pleasant smile and works surprisingly fast for somebody as old as my grandmother. When I walk in, Ruthie is arranging colorful cupcakes in the display case and I can see Katie farther back, spooning batter into cupcake pans with an ice cream scoop. When she glances up from her work and sees me, I'm pretty sure her face lights up as she smiles. Pretty sure…

I take a seat on one of the stools with a great sigh of relief. Ruthie approaches me, but Katie intercepts her with a gentle hand on her arm.

"It's okay, Ruthie. I've got this one."

I smile at Ruthie, who nods and returns to her display case.

"Hey, Belle. To what do I owe this surprise visit?" Katie glances at the clock on the wall. She wipes her hands on her apron, then lays her forearms on the counter to look me in the eye. "You're not taking an early yoga class, are you?" She makes a show of looking for my gym bag. I sit at her counter in my black slacks, pale yellow silk top, and black heels, looking every bit the businesswoman. Except now, I have no business.

"Nope," I say quietly. "No yoga clothes."

"Too bad. I'm partial to the capri-length black pants and the purple tank top."

I'm momentarily speechless as she holds my gaze. I clear my throat and manage to ask, "You are?"

"Definitely. Though the blue top with the white stripes runs a close second." Katie grins at me as I sit slack-jawed. "So, what's going on? This is an usual time for you to be here, and don't take this the wrong way, but you don't look so good. You're really pale." Before I can answer, she's got her palm pressed against my forehead, then the side of my face. "Are you sick? You're not coming down with something, are you?"

Her concern is so genuine, the feel of her hand so warm on my skin, that I feel my eyes well up. Which immediately mortifies me. I turn away quickly, but Katie sees before I can cover.

"Oh, God." Without a word, she grabs a blueberry cupcake from the display, pops it on a plate, and slides it in front of me. "What is it? What happened?" When I don't answer, she looks around, then moves to the end of the counter and lifts up a little flap I never really noticed. She extends her arm. "Come with me."

I'm barely holding myself together, but I stand and obey her.

"Ruthie, we're going to the office for a minute. Hold down the fort for me?"

"You got it, boss."

Katie grabs my hand in hers, snaps up my cupcake with the other, and tugs me along behind her until we're in a very small office I'd never noticed before. It's tucked in a back corner. She closes the door behind us. The office is tiny, barely big enough for a small desk and chair, a second chair, and a four-drawer filing cabinet. A laptop sits open but sleeping on the desk. I'm pretty sure if I stretch my arms out, I can touch both walls at the same time. Despite its diminutive size, the office is neat as can be. Katie maneuvers me to the chair in front of the desk, makes me sit, and sets my cupcake down in front of me. Then she perches one butt cheek on the edge of the desk and looks at me intently. I feel like those blue eyes can see right into my heart, my soul. I swallow hard, never having felt anything like it, and my eyes fill again.

"Talk to me." She brushes some of my hair off my forehead. "Tell me what's going on."

I look down, swallow again a couple times, force myself to get it together. The last thing I want to do is lose it in front of this wonderful, shockingly sexy woman who's being so kind. I don't want her thinking I'm some sort of dishrag, weak and useless. After a moment, I feel more in control. I take a deep breath, look back up at her, into those eyes.

"I got laid off this morning." I say it quietly, understanding that it's the first time I've actually said it out loud. I'm impressed that my tone is more matter-of-fact than it is pathetic. Point for me.

Katie gives a little gasp. "Oh, no. Oh, Hayley, that sucks. That *sucks*. My God, I'm so sorry."

I blink at her, focused on only one thing, only one word. "You know my name."

"Of course I know your name."

"I've never told it to you. Have I? You've never asked and I don't think I've ever told you."

"You haven't. I found out on my own."

"How?"

"I asked around."

I blink some more. "You asked about me?"

"Mm-hmm."

We sit there, looking at each other and grinning, and it suddenly doesn't feel like one of the worst days of my life any longer. Which is weird because, let's face it, I'm still jobless. I have a mortgage, a cat to feed, bills to pay. But something about having all of Katie's attention focused solely on me seems to make the entire world feel like a better place. Which is *so* weird.

"Well," I say. Because what else can I say?

Another moment of silence passes before Katie slaps her hands on her jean-clad thighs. "Okay. Here's what we're going to do." She moves behind the desk, opens a drawer, and pulls out a fifth of vodka and two coffee mugs. As my eyebrows go up in surprise, she pours a shot into each mug, hands me one. "I keep this handy for bad days. I think today qualifies." Mug held in the air, she says, "To the next chapter." Bringing her eyes to mine, she adds softly, "Because you know there is one." And it might be me, but that line seems kind of...loaded.

I touch my mug to hers and we down the shots, grimacing as the vodka burns its way down our throats.

"I didn't say it was good." Katie laughs.

"Because you'd have been lying." I cough as I speak, feeling my eyes tear.

"Next, you're going to eat that cupcake."

"I am?"

"Mm-hmm. Cupcakes make everything better. Why do you think I do what I do?" She breaks the cupcake in half, then breaks one half in half and hands it to me. "Also, the blueberry pairs really well with the vodka. How I know this shall remain unspoken." We eat together, our eyes never leave each other, and she's right. The sweetness of the blueberries chases the hot tang of the vodka nicely. When I nod, her expression seems to say, *See? You should listen to me more often.*

She settles against the desk closer to me. Much closer. I can smell her scent: sugar, fruit, but something else that's not of the bakery...something spicy, something uniquely her own. "After that, you're going to go home and change, then come back here and pick me up. You'll take me to the grocery store, where I'll get ingredients for dinner. Then back to my place so I can cook for you and we can discuss your next steps." A sexy darkness has settled into her gaze, and it's hard for me to look at her without squirming. In a good way.

Somehow—totally unlike me—the first thought I have actually pops right out of my mouth before I can stop it. "You're kind of bossy."

Surprisingly, she isn't offended. Instead, she raises her

eyebrows. "You have no idea." And before I can even comprehend what's happening, she's leaned forward, her fingertips under my chin, and she's kissing me. It's soft and tender and sweet, but there's something underneath, a hunger, a promise of more. As she pulls back, I'm startled to see her face flush a light pink. She visibly swallows, then whispers, "I've wanted to do that for weeks now. *Weeks.*"

I can't seem to do anything other than sit there with a goofy grin on my face, thinking that, despite having been laid off this morning, I may have just hit the mother of all jackpots. Not about to let it slip through my fingers, I stand up, step right into her space, take Katie's face in my hands, and kiss her again. Not softly. Not tenderly. Not sweetly.

Her mouth is hot and tastes like blueberries with a hint of alcohol. I delve my tongue in for a little more before slowly pulling away and leaning my forehead against hers, both of us breathing raggedly.

Katie rolls her bottom lip in and bites down. "Okay, that was…" Words seem to escape her.

"I've wanted to do *that* for weeks," I say quietly.

"Glad to know we're on the same page." Her blue-eyed gaze shifts up to meet mine. "Feel any better?"

"Why? Did something bad happen today? Because I can recall nothing before these past five minutes."

That makes her smile. I love to see her smile and want to recreate it any chance I get.

"Nah. But something really, really good happened."

"*That*, I am aware of." My arms are still around her waist, and I interlock my fingers at the small of her back. She's small, but she's warm and solid, and I wonder how I ever got by without holding her like this.

"Good." As she says it, a loud crash sounds from outside the door, obviously a stainless steel bowl falling to the hard floor, and Katie's shoulders come up as she grimaces.

"I'm okay," comes Ruthie's muffled voice, and we both chuckle.

"I need to get back to work. I've got a huge order to fill." The obvious regret in her voice makes letting go of her totally okay, though when she rubs her thumb across my bottom lip, I have to think twice.

I nod. "I'll go home and regroup. Catch my breath. Absorb." Meeting her eyes again, I add, "Everything."

Katie's smile lights up the room. "You do that. Come get me at six?"

"I will." And I kiss her once more, softly, and the knowledge that kissing every inch of her body is suddenly a distinct possibility floods my system with heat.

As Katie puts her hand on the doorknob, she turns back to me and lays a gentle, comforting hand on my upper arm. "Hayley? It's going to be okay."

Her expression is warm and kind, and I give her a smile back as she squeezes. I snatch up the remaining cupcake—no way I'm not eating the rest of that heavenly delight—and follow her out of the office. Once in the open kitchen area, she gives me a wave, winks at me (causing a pleasant fluttering in my stomach), and heads over to help Ruthie with whatever batter she's mixing. I let myself through the counter and walk toward the door. My grip on the handle, I turn back and Katie looks up, catching my eye, and I know beyond a shadow of a doubt that she's right.

It's going to be okay.

I push through the door, pop the remaining blueberry cupcake into my mouth, and head into the next chapter of my life.

GUILTY PLEASURE

M. Ullrich

The first time I heard about Samantha Sanderson was during an awkward "welcome to the neighborhood" conversation with her parents as they helped me unload boxes from the U-Haul. I don't recall the exact course we took through multiple topics, but somehow we ended up on how I'm single, a lesbian, and how their college-aged daughter was a lesbian, too. Even though the conversation with this middle-aged couple was awkward in and of itself, I was at least a little grateful that they didn't assume I knew her because of our shared orientation. They told me how they'd known about Samantha's preference for girls since grade school, even when *she* didn't, and had to act surprised when she had *finally* come out in high school. I laughed when it was warranted. It was easy to talk to these bright, cheery people, even if they did contrast with my usual quiet, broody self. It gave me good reason to be content in my choice of new home. Starting someplace new in your early thirties isn't easy for anyone, especially an androgynous lesbian. If I had worried about landing in a neighborhood where I'd feel unaccepted, those worries were squashed. I had hit the neighbor lottery with the Sandersons.

I settled into my new home quickly and easily. My new job was great, and the Sandersons seemed to know just when I was feeling a little lonely, and they would offer to have me over for dinner. It was nearly perfect until spring break rolled around. That's when Samantha came home from school. I knew she was trouble the moment I saw her. She was the type of woman who would distract you every day for the rest of your life.

I was checking on tulips that were sprouting up defiantly through the chilled soil. The previous owners must've planted the bulbs, and to my surprise it looked like my planters out front would be filled with the color in no time. I was looking around at the bare trees that lined the streets when she caught my eye. A leggy strawberry-blonde jogged up the Sandersons' front path. Her yoga pants clung to her full thighs, and even though the rest of her was hidden under an oversized sweatshirt, I knew her curves didn't stop there.

"You must be Andy." When she spoke it surprised me. She had a throaty, raspy voice that I knew would narrate every sexy dream I would have from that point on.

"Excuse me?" Pretty women make me dumb, I'll admit it, and Samantha didn't qualify as just pretty—she was drop-dead stunning. I eyed her curiously, and she tossed her long ponytail back and forth as she laughed.

"I'm Samantha." She jogged across the small patch of lawn that separated my house from her parents' home. Well, I suppose it was her home, too. "My parents have mentioned you a time or two." She eyed me up and down, and I was suddenly very conscious of how I looked: short hair that had been styled by my pillow, wrinkled pajama pants, and a hooded sweatshirt I've had for longer than I care to admit. She smiled at my silence, and I damned her for having beautiful eyes, too. The kind of eyes I saw myself falling into, deep, and that was as unexpected as it was unwelcome.

"Andrea," I corrected so unnecessarily that I even annoyed myself, "but yeah, most people call me Andy." I kept my hands drawn close to my sides because Samantha's eyes were soft enough to be called a temptation. I didn't need to know whether her skin was just as dangerous. "Nice to meet you." I turned away as casually as I could and started to retreat, but dammit, I still heard Samantha's sultry voice say that she hoped to see me again soon.

There was no immediate second meeting, I actually didn't see Samantha again until she came home for the summer, when I was bringing my beat-up garbage cans to the curb around the same time she was waiting for her ride. Gone were the workout clothes, and instead she looked like she was dressed for a night out on the town, one that would inevitably lead to a very satisfying night in bed. If our age difference wasn't obvious before, it certainly was now—my night was ending just as hers was beginning.

"Hey there, neighbor!"

I know I grimaced slightly when she called out to me, mostly because I wanted to avoid a conversation. Almost enough to climb into the trash can.

Let me set one thing straight, I don't feel comfortable ogling women. I want to be better than all the jerks that objectify and stare, but sometimes I can't control the gravitational pull of a short black dress. I can easily ignore cleavage, and toned arms are something I can admire innocently, but a nice ass wrapped perfectly in a short dress will forever be my downfall. So when Samantha turned back to her front door to check that it was fully shut, my jaw met the pavement. Her long, toned, and tanned legs were on display and led straight up to the most perfect ass I had ever seen; more than a generous handful, definitely muscular, and so firm that I could easily imagine myself coming against it. My cheeks flushed, and I knew the instant Samantha turned around I had been caught staring. Her salacious smirk clued me in. I didn't bother to wave before making my awkward retreat.

I made a promise to myself that night: I would avoid Samantha at all costs. Did I think anything would happen between us? No. But I didn't want to risk the only friendship I'd forged in my new neighborhood by coming across as a creepy pervert with regard to their daughter. Samantha, however, had other ideas.

She started showing up out of nowhere at the most inopportune times over the summer. Once when I was washing my car she suddenly appeared at my back offering to help. I screamed, she laughed, and then I declined the offer—which was very difficult considering her short shorts and my hatred for washing cars, but I made a promise. I could swear she looked disappointed when she headed back inside, but I have an active imagination. The next time was when she insisted on helping me bring in my groceries. I only had five bags, but three were already in her hands before I could refuse the offer.

"Wow," she said as soon as she stepped into my home. "You've really changed this place. I remember how dark it was when Mr. Mattsson lived here. This is nice." Samantha spoke the whole time she followed me into the kitchen, which was a relief. I muttered a small thank you when she set the bags on the counter. I know it was probably rude, not offering a drink or snack, but my mind was focused on getting her out of my space because honestly, she looked very good and very comfortable right where she stood. "You're very quiet." Her observation went unacknowledged by me, out of spite or stupidity, I'm not sure which, but it's probably the latter.

"Okay." Samantha giggled, and I wanted to kick myself in the mouth for smiling in response. "My parents are having a barbecue this weekend and wanted me to invite you. That's why I was heading over here. I hope you can make it." She stood so bashfully in the middle of my small kitchen, hands in the back pockets of her jeans and staring at the floor, I was helpless.

"I can. I mean I will." I cleared my dusty throat. "I'll be there. I love barbecues." I offered up the words and immediately regretted them. They were just as good as "I carried a watermelon"—I groaned inwardly at the *Dirty Dancing* reference Samantha was surely too young to understand.

"Great!" She seemed genuinely pleased, and I was genuinely surprised. Her smile was brilliant and my heart skipped a beat. I was screwed. I'd be lucky if I could contain myself to just having a crush on her. "I'll see you Saturday at four, Andy who loves barbecues." Samantha left with a wink, and once the door shut behind her I exhaled heavily. Great, she had jokes, too.

How dare she intimidate me in my own home?

❖

"Andy is in construction, isn't that right?" Mrs. Sanderson was delightful, but it irked me she felt the need to include me in every conversation. Her friend's leaky faucet was hardly a good segue to construction jobs.

"I'm an architect, but I've always preferred the hands-on side of the business," I answered, even though all I honestly cared about was getting another burger and beer. I wasn't lying when I said I love barbecues. Babbling? Yes. Lying? No.

"Architect? Really?" I heard Samantha before I saw her. I had actually started to believe that she wouldn't be caught dead at her parents' small get-together. I was wrong.

"Yes, sweetheart, she's working on the new bank in town."

"Interesting." Samantha eyed me curiously.

"Not really." I tried to end the personal conversation there, but Samantha wasn't having it.

"Construction doesn't surprise me. It explains how this," she motioned up and down my body, "looks so good." My blush set my face aflame. I would've sworn I was on fire.

"I said the same thing!" Mrs. Sanderson nearly squealed. Like mother, like daughter, apparently. Samantha shared a bright smile with her mother before her eyes settled on me again. "I thought for sure she spent hours at the gym, but I was wrong." Mrs. Sanderson wasn't helping matters.

"I'm surprised you got that much out of her, Mom, I've yet to hear her manage more than a few words." Samantha was teasing me. I knew it, she knew it, but somehow no one else in the circle could see the small horns sprouting out from her gorgeous head.

"Andy?" Mrs. Sanderson looked at me in surprise, and all I could muster up was a weak shrug. "She's a chatterbox!" I looked down at my empty bottle and hoped that with enough prayer I could manage to just disappear.

"Need another drink? I'll walk with you to the cooler." Samantha looped her arm in mine and led the way. I looked back to the small group. They were all oblivious to my desperation to be called back.

"Talkative with one Sanderson woman and completely silent with the other. What's that all about?" Samantha reached into the cooler and fished out two dripping bottles. I admired her denim-clad backside momentarily before accepting the offered beer. I screwed off the top with the hem of my T-shirt and took my first sip to buy some time. Apparently my days of avoiding Samantha were over. I waited for the sizzle of the carbonation to leave my tongue before smiling slightly and speaking.

"Closer in age, more in common, I guess?" I could feel myself start to give in and wanted to play along, but deep down I knew I shouldn't.

"So you're a fan of daytime talk shows and scrapbooking, too?" Samantha followed my lead, opening her bottle with the hem of her tank top, but she made a show out of it by lifting the material an extra few inches to reveal her abdomen. I noticed the slight glimmer of a navel piercing. I shook my head both to answer her question and to clear my less-than-innocent thoughts away.

"Work, life, gardens—all that boring stuff." Samantha wasn't buying my answer, and I didn't blame her. After another mouthful I answered truthfully. "Your parents are very warm and welcoming. It's been nice getting to know them and making a friend in the neighborhood."

"I'll be your friend," Samantha offered, but the way her lips wrapped around the mouth of her bottle led me to believe we had different definitions of "friendship."

"Samantha." I nearly laughed and stuttered my next words out. "I-I'm sure you have plenty of friends your age—"

"Maybe I'm looking for older, more experienced friends."

What could I say to that? Thankfully, a commotion by the entrance to the yard stole everyone's attention. Turned out Samantha's parents had invited an old friend of Samantha's without her knowledge. The reunion was sweet and long enough for me to make a quick exit. With a few thank-yous along the way, I was safely on my side of the lawn once again.

That night, I took a stiff drink onto my small, covered front porch to sit and think. Not about Samantha, no—there was no reason to give much thought to the young woman who enjoyed torturing me. I wasn't wondering where a continued conversation would've taken us. There was no reason to daydream about what it would feel like to twirl her silky hair around my fingers or the chill that would travel down my spine as she tugged at my hair while I buried my face between her legs. No, the tranquil evening was made for deeper thoughts than those.

Muted giggles caught my attention from next door, and I looked over to see Samantha and her old friend rushing toward an SUV parked at the curb. They both climbed into the backseat, and my stomach dropped as very familiar motions came to life behind the windows. Whoever this old friend was, she was making quick work of Samantha's tank top and bra.

The night was dark and the streetlights obscured my view with their glare, but I could tell when Samantha was grinning. I knew when her head was thrown back, and my own breathing changed when I noticed her motions become erratic. I'm not usually one for voyeurism, especially when the star of the show is Samantha, but I couldn't tear my eyes away. My clit was swelling and the wetness that pooled between my legs was getting uncomfortable. I considered the darkness one last time before I unbuttoned my jeans and slipped my hand beneath the waistband of my underwear. It didn't take long. I stroked myself into a frenzy and came before either woman exited the vehicle. I was quick to orgasm thanks to thoughts of Samantha and what it'd be like to be pressed into a backseat with her, pressed against and burrowed deep inside her, feeling her breath against my neck and pinning her down as I made her come over and over again. My imagination is a wonderful thing. At one point, I even imagined Samantha's eyes locked on mine as I shivered through the last of my tremors.

I waited for them to make their getaway before I made my way back inside for a shower and a sleepless night.

❖

"Am I too forward, or do you not find me attractive?" I dropped my briefcase and jumped when Samantha and her damn raspy voice snuck up behind me. I'd just gotten home from a long day at work, and this was not something I was in the mood for.

"Samantha." I tried to contain my frustration, but the most I dialed it back to was a lengthy sigh. I left my keys hanging in the door as I turned to her. She stood there in a tank top and short skirt. Her outfit just made me angrier. It also scattered my brain a bit. "Wh-what are you talking about?" Playing dumb had seemed like a good idea, but I should've chosen my question more carefully.

"I've been trying, very obviously, to show you that I'm interested in getting to know you. *Intimately.* I added that last part just to make sure I'm not being too vague." She crossed her arms. That made her look even younger and more stubborn. I had to rub my temples thanks to the headache that had been lingering behind my eyes all day.

"Don't do that!" Samantha tugged at my wrist. "Every time I try to talk to you, you make it so difficult." Just then, a woman with a small terrier trotted down the sidewalk. I turned back to my door and threw it open.

"Come on." I ushered Samantha in, and the moment I shut the door her lips were on mine. Sweet, soft, and determined. I gave in for a minute, letting myself get lost in the feel of Samantha's mouth and the scent of her fragrant hair surrounding me. I kissed back, and I knew I should be embarrassed, but I'm only human. I tore myself away and backed up a step. Samantha looked so absolutely frustrated then that I had to smile.

"You are stunning." I started in a higher-pitched voice than usual. Arousal does that to me. After a dry cough I managed to get my voice back under control. "I would have to be crazy not to find you attractive, but you're my neighbor, and your parents are very kind people that I'd prefer not show up on my doorstep with pitchforks wanting my head for what I've done to their daughter!" She started laughing at me, but I pressed on regardless. "This is my home now. It matters to me what my neighbors think."

"I'm not going to go home and tell my parents. I mean, unless there's something to tell them."

"It's not just about that! You're a kid—"

"I'm twenty-six." That surprised me. Samantha must've noticed that, because she started to get cocky and advanced. I stepped back cautiously. My living room seemed a lot smaller then. "I took a few years off before I started college to help take care of my grandmother." For just a second, her predatory façade slipped, and I caught a glimpse of a young woman I wouldn't mind getting to know better.

"It's not a good idea," I said weakly.

"But you're attracted to me, and I'm attracted to you." It was still odd to hear her say she was attracted to me, even though it was made obvious by her ongoing advances. She stepped closer again. No more than a foot separated us, and my resolve weakened further.

"You're attracted to me?" I needed to echo Samantha's words, just to hear them again.

"I am." She reached out and grabbed my hand. "I think this quiet, mysterious, boyish thing you have going on is so fucking sexy." She didn't release my hand before fingering the collar of my shirt with her free hand. "Tell me you don't feel this, too."

I was feeling a lot of things at the moment, and horny was definitely at the top of the list. My eyes closed involuntarily as Samantha caressed my inner wrist. "I do, but…"

"But nothing." Samantha pulled me toward her.

"What happens tomorrow?" I needed to ask, even though I didn't care much for the answer. I had a feeling that Samantha felt the same, since she laughed.

"Whatever we want."

"What about a few weeks from now when I'm sitting across from your mom while she insists on feeding me? When she brings you up in casual conversation and this is all I can think of? I'll be twisted inside."

"Forget about it."

Did she just say to forget about it? "Forget about it?" I asked with a tilt of my head as if to understand her better, much like a dog.

"Block the memory." Samantha smiled slyly. Her plump, pink lips looked delicious. "Eat your meal, talk about plants and the weather, and forget you ever fucked me." She chuckled, and the rasp in her voice added such smoke to it that my knees gave out just a bit. I swallowed thickly, and in an instant the lump of anxiety in my throat was gone, along with my resistance. I advanced and pinned her against the wall next to my TV, lifting my arms and positioning my elbows on each side of her head. I'd been unaware of our difference in height until then. My two-inch advantage was delightful in this moment.

"You think it'll be so easy to forget?" My words came out as a whisper against her lips. Samantha smelled so good and looked even better with her lips parted in a wanton invitation. She must've been surprised by the sudden shift in my demeanor because it took her longer to respond than usual, but she recovered quickly.

"No, not for me. I'll think about it often—especially when I make myself come at night." She leaned up slightly. I felt wisps of her hair against my cheek before she whispered into my ear, "Like you did the night of the barbecue." I tried to pull back, but Samantha held firmly to the front of my shirt.

"You saw…?"

"I did." Samantha ran her palms up my neck and started to pull me forward. I was embarrassed, weak, and incredibly turned on. "And I knew then that I not only wanted you but I needed you. God, all I could think about was being on my knees—" I cut her off by pressing my lips to hers. We'd talked enough, now I needed to feel and taste and hear the noises she'd make as I gave her what she wanted.

Our second kiss was heated. It ebbed and flowed from firm to soft. I explored the cavern of her mouth and reveled in the feel of her velvety tongue entwining with mine. Samantha's lips were a marvel. If I wasn't so goddamn wet and swollen, I could've spent the night sucking on her succulent lower lip just to hear the way it caused her breathing to change. Maybe another time, but it wasn't the night for just kissing.

My attention was torn away as I felt Samantha's delicate hands mapping out my back, then my sides, and then slipping up the front of my shirt and tracing my abdomen. A comical whimper escaped me when Samantha's short nails scraped against my skin.

"You like that, huh, stud?" She really needed to stop talking. And I made her.

I lifted Samantha slightly and brought her over to the couch. I gently tossed her down and made quick work of the flimsy excuse for underwear she had on beneath her pleated skirt. I bit roughly just above her knee before trailing my tongue up her thigh and diving into her waiting pussy. Samantha was soaked, and sweet, and oh so divine. Her squeal of surprise only added to my pleasure as I lapped at her juices. I traced her glistening outer lips with the tip of my tongue before parting them and delving deeper. I felt Samantha's long fingers weave into my short hair and tug gently every time I neared her exposed clit, but I wasn't ready for that yet. I wanted to savor the build-up and the way Samantha grew wetter against my mouth when I tongued her hood.

Samantha's pussy was beautiful: pink and ripe for the eating. I enjoyed every delightful second of tongue-fucking this woman I barely knew. I might not have known her favorite color, but I did know what it was like to feel her pulse quicken from the inside.

"Andy..." Samantha's whine was music to my ears. All it took was hearing my name from her sinful mouth to make me sink my fingers into her, curling just enough before withdrawing them and plunging in once more. She cried out and palmed her own full breasts. There was a light sheen of sweat covering her face, and I watched as every bit of pleasure played out in her expression. This Samantha was absent in the car the other night. This Samantha was someone I knew I'd never forget. "Stop staring and make me come!" Her demand was delivered with a smile, and I jumped into action.

I leaned forward, took her swollen clit between my lips, and sucked hard. She convulsed slightly and I continued to work her pussy with both my fingers and mouth, bobbing my head enough to alternate between friction and suction until Samantha's hips began to move erratically. She came seconds later with a loud, shrill cry. I laid my head on her stomach as she started to come down.

"Mmm...I knew you'd be good."

I couldn't contain my laugh at that. "I bet you say that to all the old ladies you pick up." I crawled up her body and placed a gentle kiss to her lips. Samantha looked radiant with her strawberry-blond hair stuck to her damp, reddened face. Magnificent, really.

"Yeah, so old." I squealed when Samantha grabbed my ass roughly and pulled me into her. "And for the record—I don't do this often." I saw something in her eyes, an honesty and maturity she seemed to hide so well.

"Even if you did, it's none of my business." I spoke the truth, and I felt at peace with it. I'd take whatever Samantha was willing to give me.

Samantha contemplated my words briefly. "It's not, but I wanted you to know." The weight of her words slipped away as she turned her attention to the button on my pants. Which was a relief because I was ready to combust. "May I?" Samantha asked while dipping her index finger under the waistband of my underwear. I felt it graze my trimmed hairline. A shock seized my clit and I pushed against her hand.

"Please." I was never above begging with any lover. "It won't take long."

"The first time," Samantha said with a smile that was so fucking sexy and confident. "But I plan on making you come all night long." She ended her promise with a firm, long caress along my turgid clit, making an abrupt and fully expected orgasm rush over me. I rode out the pleasure against her hand, and just as the waves began to subside, I collapsed on top of Samantha. She started tracing lazy patterns across my back, over my shirt. The peace was broken by her giggles.

I leaned up and asked, "What's so funny?" I was self-conscious then, assuming she was laughing at how quickly I had come.

"I'm sorry." She sputtered her apology breathlessly. "A couple days ago my mom told me I should find a nice woman like you. I'm not sure if this was what she had in mind, though."

I groaned and buried my face in her neck. The musky scent of her sweat turned me on all over again. I started grinding slow circles between her legs. "Go out with me?" I whispered the request directly into her ear. I didn't want to look at her if she was going to reject me.

"I thought you'd never ask." Samantha erupted in girlish

giggles again as I started to assault her neck and chest with kisses. "Hey, Andy?" She pulled me up by my hair.

"Yeah?"

"Welcome to the neighborhood," Samantha said with such a soft, genuine look in her eyes, I just knew that I had found the perfect home.

HOOPER STREET

Anna Larner

As streets go, Hooper Street wasn't much of a looker. Rows of terraced houses bunched together like a set of teeth in a mouth that rarely smiled. White PVC windows, like the white of the eyes of someone gasping for air, stood out starkly against the red brick. The occasional hanging basket, with brash pansies gaudy and out of place, only seemed to make things worse. And there was an unsettling thin breeze, stalking the street half catching the air, like the breath of the dying.

You wouldn't set out to live in Hooper Street; you would likely just find yourself there. For it was neither city nor suburb; but something in between, a gap if you will, where if you were not careful your hope and ambition might disappear, unnoticed.

So, unsurprisingly, it is not the first place you would expect to find love. Like a daisy growing in a drainpipe it would simply have no business being there.

Abbie Lawrence had no business being there.

It was a Tuesday when I first met Abbie. I know it was a Tuesday because that's the day in the week the bin men come, whipping up an instant storm of sound as their hungry lorries hiss, jaws grinding, and the empty bins wheeled down the street rumble like passing thunder.

I remember that I was trying not to dwell on why bin day had become a highlight of my week, when over my left shoulder I heard a voice, like a bird on a branch chattering away for a reason unknown to mankind.

"I love getting rid of my rubbish. It's so—I want to say cleansing, but that makes me sound like a hippie, doesn't it?" Abbie said, as she swung her rubbish bag merrily into the bin with a satisfied sigh. "Although, you know, I think I would have liked to have lived in the sixties. Peace and love, and all that."

I risked a reluctant glance in the direction of the chatter, hoping that somehow it wasn't directed at me. It was. *Crap.*

"I'm Abbie. Your new neighbour. Okay, that's an obvious thing to say, isn't it? I mean if I wasn't your new neighbour, then I would be trespassing in your actual neighbour's front garden. But I'm not. Trespassing, I mean. I *am* your new neighbour." My new neighbour's voice trailed off. She looked down.

I dropped my rubbish in the bin, wincing as the glass and tins knocked heavily against the plastic, and closed the lid. I turned fully to face Ms. Chatty Knickers, took an audible deep breath, and bolstered myself to say, "I'm, Jem. Erm…welcome to Hooper Street." I really did try my best to sound enthusiastic. But as we all know, trying your best is rarely good enough.

Abbie held an outstretched hand towards me. I looked at it longer than was polite before shaking it once, firmly. I would like to think I smiled, but I probably didn't.

"Jem, that's an unusual name," Abbie said. She hadn't stopped smiling, and now her eyes shone and sparkled, somehow reflecting light on what was the dullest of days.

I gave her sparkling eyes maybe a day or two at most, and her smile no more than a week before Hooper Street worked its magic and snuffed them both out.

I could have explained that Jem was short for Jemima, and that Beatrix Potter had a lot to answer for, not to mention my parents. But to be honest, I hoped that my silence to her question would signal the end of our chat. *Nope.*

"Your hands are lovely and warm. My hands are always cold." Abbie rubbed her hands together. "They used to call me Mittens at school because I used to wear them all the time. I much prefer mittens to gloves, although, you know, you can't do that much in them." She frowned.

I looked at my watch, blatantly. It was clear she was lost in thought, I guessed about what you couldn't do wearing mittens.

"Like typing." Abbie beamed.

I was right.

"Or playing a piano. Erm, or riding a bike—actually, no, you could ride a bike." She mock held handlebars and pressed on pretend brakes, just to see. "Yes, that would work. Or—"

"Put your hand over someone's mouth to stop them talking," I suggested. "They'd be perfect for that, wouldn't they?" As contributions go—harsh.

"Oh yes!" she said enthusiastically, and then it had dawned on her that I was telling her to shut up, and I watched as she dropped her eyes once again to the floor.

I ignored the sudden ache in my heart.

Being mean didn't come naturally, although, truth be told, neither did being friendly. "Well, it was really nice to meet you." I turned without looking at her and went inside.

I sensed that she was still standing there, no doubt bleeding from the emotional stabbing I'd just given her. I felt like a shit. I was shit, a life-hating, cynical arsehole. I wasn't proud of this, because, well, I wasn't proud of anything. *Oh for fuck's sake...*

I opened my door and stepped back onto the street to find Abbie sitting on the wall of her front garden. I say "garden," more a dedicated space for bins and weeds than a horticultural triumph. A few doors down someone had placed a bench in theirs. I have no idea why, as the spaces were more of a soul trap than a sun trap. I'd never seen anyone sit on that bench, not even the motley band of neighbourhood cats who picked their way nervously around it.

Abbie was plucking out the debris of moss from between the broken bricks in the wall. It almost looked like she was weeding. *Weirdo.*

I don't know whether it was guilt, or even worse, an affliction of conscience, or—madness, probably, but nonetheless I shook my head, took a deep breath, and asked, "So…you want some coffee?" As invitations go—charmless.

Abbie turned and smiled broadly. I felt myself blush.

"Yes! I'd love that," she said. "Thank you."

I watched as she clapped her hands together with glee. I regretted my invitation immediately.

"Oh, perfect. I've made a Victoria sponge," Abbie said, excitedly. "Do you have jam? That's the only thing. I haven't had time yet this morning to make any."

Really? Who makes their own jam? Are you for real?

Even if she noticed my incredulous expression, she continued, "I was going to get sugar. But if you have sugar…we could make some jam together. What do you think?"

It was best she didn't know what I was thinking. Let's just say I didn't know how a quick coffee became a home-baking morning.

"You know," I said as gently as I could manage, "I've only time for a quick coffee. Work, and everything."

I looked quickly away. I knew enough by now to know that her pretty face, with its cute, bunny-like nose, would be all hurt again. Her round, trusting chestnut eyes would reveal her wounded heart. And there it was again—that funny pain in my chest.

Thankfully, we were momentarily interrupted by another neighbour a few doors down, who was dragging her bin, like a dead body, onto the street. She looked tired. In fact, that was the best way to describe the residents of Hooper Street—tired and all that went with being tired for too long.

Abbie waved and called over, "Hello! I'm Abbie." The neighbour looked as horrified as I felt. Abbie had obviously not got the memo that read "under no circumstance do the residents of Hooper Street say hello to each other or make any attempt, accidental or otherwise, to be friendly. We do not need to know each other's names; it is not expected or required."

The neighbour, without smiling, nodded awkwardly and shuffled indoors.

"It's not you," I said, with an apologetic tone. I lied—it was her. "It's just, well, it's Hooper Street."

Abbie frowned. "I don't understand."

"Yeah, it's hard to explain." And it was. In that moment, I couldn't be the one to tell someone who still believed in neighbourliness, in life, that there was no point in that belief. No point to anything. I must have gone quiet, drifted off for a second, because I was surprised to feel Abbie's hand on my arm.

She said, tenderly, "Well, you can explain it to me over coffee. Yes?"

"Sure." We shared a smile this time. It struck me in that moment that it had been a long time since I had shared anything with anyone.

❖

"So how long have you lived here?" Abbie asked, seated on my kitchen stool, swinging her legs, as she looked around my home.

I felt a sting of embarrassment. My home, if that's what you could call it, made minimalism look indulgent and frilly.

"A while," I confessed. "I know it's a little bare. I rent it, so…I guess I didn't plan to stay as long as I have." It occurred to me that I couldn't remember the last time I made a plan.

I handed Abbie her coffee, and she caught me looking at my watch. She looked down again. My rudeness clearly knew no limits.

"So what do you do for a living?" she asked the floor.

"I work from home, doing statistics—boring really. For insurance companies, risk and…stuff, you know." I shrugged.

Abbie's eyes widened with delight. "I love statistics!"

Something told me she would. I doubt there was much this girl wouldn't love.

"I mean, what are the chances of you and me meeting?" Abbie asked, smiling again.

I was beginning to understand she did the smiling thing a lot. I found myself hoping her lightly freckled cheeks would soon ache, forcing her to stop. I shrugged again in reply.

"I mean, it's got to be, what, a million to one, I bet you? Maybe a million million," she suggested, taking a sip of her coffee and frowning.

I guessed she was trying to work it out.

"Is that a billion?" she asked.

I was right.

"Or—" she continued.

"So what do you do?" Impatience had got the better of me, plus, let's face it, she was working out the answer to an unanswerable question that nobody had asked.

"Oh, I'm a self-employed graphic artist. People pay me to draw stuff."

"Cool." I was impressed, and a little relieved that her ink-stained hands weren't from colouring in for fun. From what I'd seen so far, I wouldn't have put it past her.

It made sense that she was arty. Her tousled shoulder-length brown hair was streaked with pink, and her black jeans and T-shirt were splattered with paint. She smelt of patchouli oil and… I realised I was staring and quickly took a slug of my coffee. "So what brought you to Hooper Street?" I asked, bracing myself for a winding tale of woe.

"Oh well…"

Here we go.

"I've always wanted to own my own home. And, well, the ones in the suburbs were too expensive, and it seemed to be only flats in town. I'm not very keen on flats. I don't know, they seem a bit temporary, don't they? I wanted to make a home. And then I found this lovely place on the internet…"

Okay, you must have bought it without visiting. Gotcha.

"And I came to see it, and I loved the area, and I thought—perfect."

Blimey.

"I saw you as well, actually," Abbie said, blushing. "You were on your way out. I said hello but I don't think you heard. You looked really hot." She looked down and sipped at her coffee.

Two things were surprising about her statement. Firstly, that she had considered Hooper Street to be "perfect." *Loony*. Secondly, she considered me to be "hot." I felt my cheeks tingle. *Hold on, did she mean hot or* hot? *Are you flirting? Nah. Sweaty, I'm guessing she meant sweaty.* After all, I'm always rushing, why and what for I don't quite know. Other than, for far too long, I've always had the sense that I'm late for something or someone.

"So how about you?" she asked, a smile teasing at the edges of her mouth.

"Same, I guess, without the perfect bit." I left out the fact that some trollop had broken my heart and I hadn't cared where I lived, as long as it was miles away from her.

I hadn't meant to go quiet.

"Well, I'll let you get back to it." She slipped off the stool. "Have a good day, and…it was nice to meet you."

Why? I've been shitty to you. I managed to mumble a guilty "Good-bye." *For God's sake, would it hurt you to be nice, just for once? Just for today?*

Just as she was closing the door behind her, I heard myself say, "It was nice to meet you too, Mittens."

She beamed a smile at me, her eyes shining once again, picking up the light that the room had lost long ago. "You can blow a kiss with mittens better than with gloves, you know," she said, with a wink. And with that she blew me a kiss, and I swear I felt it land where my heart used to be.

Loneliness is a funny thing, and I don't mean funny ha ha. It is insidious, stealthy. One minute it's a treat to have your own space, and the next it's achingly awful. You lose your natural sense of balance. Everything means too much, or perhaps worse, too little. You make poor choices—sleep with the wrong people for the wrong reasons, or sleep with no one for the wrong reasons. You become too loud or too quiet. You overcompensate. You tell yourself you're fine, that in some way this is a choice, that you've won some ethical something, when in truth all you feel is loss. And then you worry that you'll forget how to be with someone. You worry that you won't be able to do the girlfriend thing ever again. You worry too much, too often, day and night.

I didn't mean to lie awake thinking about Abbie Lawrence. Worrying that despite her saying it had been nice to meet me she probably thought I'd been colder than her hands in winter. It was ridiculous therefore to wonder what it would be like to kiss her, to feel her body naked against mine. To imagine the curve of her breast, the softness of her thigh. I didn't mean to see her face each time I closed my eyes. She was just the over-chatty annoyingly friendly neighbour, right? Let's face it, she was Disney World and I was Hooper Street, and that was that.

I had just managed to settle myself with that idea when my doorbell rang, frightening the life out of me. It was ten thirty. Nothing good rings your door at ten thirty at night.

Wrapping my bed sheet around me, I drew the curtains back just enough to peer down at my front step. *What the...?*

Pulling on jeans and wearing my T-shirt back to front so the label irritated my neck, I rushed downstairs and opened my door.

Abbie held up a cake tin towards me and said, "I *know*, I know it's late. But I was bored and so I made jam. And then I thought of you and wondered whether you were bored too. So I thought... well..."

My expression must have been surprised verging on *what the fuck*, for she quickly said, "I don't mind if you want me to go." The hurt bunny was back. "Yeah, it now seems like a weird idea. I'll go—"

"Wait. It is a weird idea. Yes." I glanced down the street. It was empty. "But now you're here." I shrugged. "And you've got cake." I stepped aside.

"Should we have decaf coffee?" Abbie asked excitedly. "Do you have decaf? I don't drink decaf, as a rule. I mean, it's weird, isn't it? How do you make a naturally caffeinated thing decaffeinated? I mean, it's like taking the stripes off a tiger or the sticky out of glue or..."

She was doing the thinking thing again.

"The fruit out of jam?" I offered, hoping to steer her towards the reason for her visit.

"Yes! That's great. The fruit out of jam. I like that." She was smiling at me.

I couldn't smile back. All I kept thinking was that a few moments ago I was fantasizing about kissing her, touching her...

"I talk too much, don't I?" Abbie asked, the sparkle in her eyes dimming.

I had upset her yet again with my silence. "*No.* Well, yes. But in a good way. A happy way." I think I then managed a reassuring smile. *Okay, when did I start believing happy was good?*

"It's when I'm nervous, you see," Abbie said, biting her lower lip. "I always talk too much. I can see people's eyes glazing over, their feet shuffle impatiently. But I can't seem to stop."

I remembered how dismissive I'd been to her. I felt sure my eyes had glazed, my feet had shuffled. I felt bad. She was lovely. Weird. But really lovely.

"I'm sorry if by being mean I've made you nervous," I said, accompanying my sincere apology with a blushing smile.

In reply, Abbie slid a slice of cake across the breakfast bar. I watched her take a large bite out of hers. I matched her with an equally huge mouthful. We giggled with greed.

Talking with her mouth full, Abbie said, "You *were* mean."

I stopped chewing, holding the cakey mixture, doughy, like guilt, in my mouth.

"But I kind of guessed it might be because you were sad. Are sad." She wiped her mouth on the pretty gingham napkins she had brought. "After all, happy people aren't mean, are they?"

"No, I suppose not."

"So I forgave you, particularly when you invited me for coffee. And, well, when you called me Mittens. I liked that." She took another bite of cake, and mumbled, "Do you have a nickname?"

To her credit, she hadn't asked why I was sad. She hadn't pried, and I liked her even more for that.

"Do I look like I have a nickname?" I shook my head at the thought.

Abbie frowned.

Oh no, she's thinking of one.

"Yeah, I don't need one, Abbie. Thanks."

Abbie kept frowning.

"Really, when I say I don't need one, I mean I don't want one. Okay? Abbie?" I suppressed thoughts of Jemima Puddle-Duck.

"Absolutely." Abbie nodded, distracted.

I could tell she was still thinking of one. And she was.

"Sad eyes."

Any nickname with the word "sad" in it wasn't good.

I raised my eyebrows. "Sad eyes? Really?"

Abbie nodded. "You have sad eyes." She reached across and brushed my fringe aside as if she needed to see my eyes more clearly.

A terrible urge to cry tightened my throat.

She stroked my cheek and then brushed her thumb over the corner of my mouth. "Sad eyes with jammy lips."

I stood up, wiping at my mouth with the back of my hand. I would have cleared plates had we used any. "Coffee, then? Yes?"

Abbie nodded. She looked at me as if she was trying to work something out, before turning away to press at fallen crumbs with her forefinger.

"I don't have decaf coffee," I said. I couldn't help but smile. "Just the strong stuff to keep us both up all night." I hadn't meant to be suggestive.

Abbie laughed. "That sounds fun." She walked over to me. The kettle clicked. She was blushing and smiling, with those eyes that shined. "Really fun." She tucked my T-shirt label inside my collar.

I swallowed, just finding breath to say, "So, erm, earlier, when you said 'hot'…"

Abbie gave a slow nod. "Yes, I meant *hot*. I just thought I'd put it out there. In case…" She slipped her hand into mine, cool and gentle to the touch.

I swear I forgot to breathe, and, in that moment, with her body pressed against me, I forgot to hate the world, and come to think of it, I no longer remembered my hurt. I couldn't quite take in what

I thought was happening, in my kitchen, in Hooper Street, where nothing like this happens.

Okay, so I probably don't need to ask you if you're gay, then. But how did you know...?

"How did you know then about me...? I mean—" I had no moisture in my mouth to finish my question.

I felt Abbie squeeze my hand. "Let's just say it's less what I *knew* and more what I *hoped*."

Hope. The word that mocked me by sticking around longer than it should have done, and upset me when it eventually left.

As if time, in that second, was waiting, pausing for me, I tried to decide whether kissing the girl next door, having only known her for a few hours, whether that would be all right or madness. Surely Abbie would need to ponder on this too, do that thinking thing she did.

Nope. No thought needed, apparently, as she began kissing me, pressing her soft lips against mine, tucking her arms around my waist. "You're so lovely," she kept saying.

I moved my face away. Acid tears rolled down my cheeks. "I'm not lovely. You need to know that. I'm not."

"Surely," Abbie whispered, her lips warm against my ear, "that's for me to decide, not you."

Her kisses were so gentle; they seemed to me what love would feel like if you could feel it, if it touched your skin as well as your heart.

My breath caught, as I felt Abbie's hands softly find their way under my T-shirt. "Your hands feel warm, Mittens," I said, smiling.

Abbie's eyes misted with tears as she replied, "I know."

I wondered how long she had waited for her hands to be warmed against another's skin.

And with a smile that would shipwreck the sturdiest of vessels, taking my hand in hers, Abbie led me upstairs. She commented, a little dreamily, that my stairs had the same number of steps as hers and that we shared the same streetlight that lit the way from landing to bedroom. The same streetlight, in fact, that was soon to bathe our urgent naked bodies in a golden half-light.

❖

Happiness is a funny thing, and I don't mean funny ha ha. It is insidious, stealthy. One minute it's a treat to wallow in melancholy and the next it's achingly awful. You realise all you want is to be happy. And by choosing happiness, you lose your natural sense of balance. Everything feels too good. You sleep with the right person for the right reasons. You become too loud and you don't care. You tell yourself you're fine, because you are. And then you forget how to be with anyone else. You know how to do the girlfriend thing. You love her, all day, and all night.

I woke to see Abbie staring out my bedroom window, wearing nothing but my T-shirt. I yawned, a contented lion's roar of a yawn. "Want some tea?"

"Ooh yes. I've been thinking—"

"Okay." *Abbie thinking or normal thinking?*

"I think I'll buy some trellis for the front, hide the bins a little. I may put a bench in, I mean, now that I've maybe got someone to sit on it with." We shared a smug smile. "It'll be easier to get to know people, as they pass by."

And she did. And we sat, in the cool of the shade, talking to passersby, like it was something that always happened. And the neighbour a few doors down started sitting on her bench. And over time people started to say hello, without being made to.

I learned how to make jam, and Abbie learned that a million million was a billion of a chance that we had met.

Turns out to make a difference, to change a life, or at the very least a perspective on life, you just need one person to be brave enough to be friendly and one person to have enough conscience to let them.

And now we live together, in our home, on beautiful Hooper Street, where the bright white terraced windows gleam in the daylight, like the shining teeth of a broad smile. And the flowers, radiant in their baskets, flutter like the wings of butterflies in the gentle breeze.

Snow Day

Missouri Vaun

Snowflakes the size of silver dollars fluttered past. Well, maybe they were the size of quarters, but they were big snowflakes, and there were lots of them. And now they were coming down in blanket waves. Lane wished she'd worn wool socks and boots. The snow was already deep, and as she crossed campus she could feel icy melt seep inside her low-top Converse sneakers.

Students were piling into cars all around the quad because afternoon classes were canceled in advance of the foot of snow on its way in the next four hours. If she hurried maybe she could get to her place, gather her laundry, and make it to her parents' house before the roads started to ice over.

She held her portfolio under her arm as she carefully climbed the somewhat steep sidewalk and turned the corner toward the old Victorian she called home. Just a couple of blocks off campus, the three-story house divided into apartments was enormous. The walkway had iced over fast and Lane was no more than two strides from the wide front steps when she fell on her butt, hard. She might have been able to catch herself if she hadn't been focused so intently on keeping her portfolio from landing in the snow. She tried to stand but her feet scissored beneath her like ice skates.

Lane braced herself with her hand on the icy surface for balance. She scooted sideways until she could step into the snow-covered grass of the small front yard. Her shoes immediately filled with snow. Laundry would obviously have to wait. She was about to try again for the front steps when her downstairs neighbor, Mia, stepped through the door, waved, and bounced down the steps.

"Mia, wait!" Lane wasn't fast enough. Mia's first step onto the sidewalk sent her into a slide. Lane grabbed for Mia's arm and pulled her toward the snow-covered lawn before she hit the concrete. For an extended moment, Mia whirled her arms in the air as her feet slid back and forth before she toppled awkwardly on top of Lane and they both ended up lying in the snow, along with her portfolio.

Lane felt like she was in a scene from a romantic comedy set in northern Minnesota. Mia had certainly been a reoccurring star of her late-night romantic imaginings, but she'd never thought it might happen in real life. Mia was distractingly gorgeous.

"Sorry! I'm so sorry!" Mia's face was very close to Lane's. Her long dark hair tickled Lane's cheek as Mia tried to push herself up with both hands.

"It's okay, the sidewalk is completely iced over. I fell and I was just about to warn you."

"Your artwork is getting wet!" Mia reached for the portfolio and shook the snow off it.

How did Mia know she was an artist? "Um, thank you." They brushed snow off their clothing, and Mia handed her the black folder.

"I was going to go get some food, but I don't think that's going to happen." Mia looked up at the snow falling even heavier now.

"Yeah, I don't think driving or walking is an option." Lane hesitated for a moment. "I'm sure I've got something I could spare." Her stomach clenched while she waited for Mia to respond. She'd probably said too much, but she'd love to have an excuse to spend a little time with Mia. She'd had a crush on her since the first time they'd bumped into each other in the hallway while checking their mail.

"Thanks, but that's okay."

Shot down. She gave Mia a weak smile. "Well, just let me know if you change your mind. I don't think I'm going anywhere either."

Lane followed Mia back into the house and waved before trotting up the stairs. Once inside her cozy apartment, she tossed her jacket over the back of the futon and opened her portfolio on the table to let the pages inside dry out. Snow had dampened the edges. She'd had a productive day, and looking over the charcoal figure drawings made her smile. The woman who'd posed for their class had beautiful subtle curves.

Lane realized she was starving. She'd skipped lunch and now the weather was too bad to go out. She figured her choices were ramen or mac and cheese. *Hmm, starch or starch?* As she stepped into the tiny kitchen the lights flickered and then went out. She flipped the switch on the wall a couple of times. The power was definitely out. Luckily the small gas stove would light up with a match strike and her second-floor apartment had a working fireplace. She'd be fine if she had to ride out the snowstorm for the weekend. Maybe she'd even catch up on her studio art projects without the distraction of Netflix. She had a design assignment due the end of the following week.

A half hour later, Lane was sampling her macaroni from the end of a large wooden spoon when she heard a knock at the door. She slid across the hardwood floor in sock feet, pot still in her hand, to see who was there.

"Mia?"

"Hi. The power's out."

"Yeah, mine is out too."

"I see you managed some food despite that."

Lane looked down at the steaming pot of mac and cheese she held in her left hand. "A gas stove will still work when the power is out."

"Only if you have matches." Mia smiled.

"Oh, yeah…hey, listen, would you like to come in? I've got plenty to share."

Mia seemed to hesitate for a moment, but then she nodded and stepped inside. She pulled her coat tight. "It's so cold."

"I'll light a fire."

"You've got a fireplace?" Mia's expression brightened.

"Don't you have one too?"

"A non-working fireplace. I guess the owner couldn't be bothered with repairing the chimney all the way down to the first floor."

The instant Lane ushered Mia inside she realized how small her apartment was. The living room was basically the bedroom, outfitted with a futon and throw pillows. Even though the space was small, the fireplace made it cozy, and with the high ceilings and big windows, the light was great for the small studio workspace Lane had set up amongst the bay windows at the front.

"Follow me." Lane led the way to the kitchen and started to spoon two servings into bowls. "If you carry these I'll build a fire and we can warm up while we eat."

Lane was hyperaware that not only was Mia watching her, but she was standing very near in the tiny space, closer than was necessary. The soft floral scent of her perfume invaded Lane's senses. She almost dropped the pot when she felt Mia's warm fingertips against her bare skin. She'd pushed up the sleeves of her sweater while cooking, leaving her tattooed forearms exposed.

"I remember when I first passed you in the entryway I thought these were printed sleeves." Mia slid her finger over the dragon tattoo that encircled Lane's left arm.

"I like dragons." Lane cleared her throat. Every tiny hair on her arm stood at attention under Mia's touch. And for that matter, all the nerve endings up to her shoulder and down her back.

"Did you draw these?"

"Yea…" Lane's voice cracked. She cleared her throat. "Um, yes, I did."

Lane had decided to get the tattoos because her pale skin offered the perfect canvas. And besides, she loved creating pen-and-ink drawings that she could wear. Both of the tattoos that adorned her forearms were rendered in black ink with no color. She felt they balanced her dark hair. She'd been cursed, or blessed, depending on your perspective, with pale Irish complexion, blue eyes, and dark hair. In contrast, Mia's skin was a warm caramel color. She looked like the female lead of the Bollywood films Lane had suffered through with her sister. At least the big dance scenes at the end of every movie were almost worth the wait. Women with long dark hair and brown eyes were her kryptonite.

All Lane knew was that every time she passed Mia coming or going, her heart skipped a beat. Mia would casually fling her hair over her shoulder to say hello. The innocently sexy gesture always sent Lane's heart plunging into her stomach. And now Mia was in her kitchen, wearing skinny jeans that hugged every curve, touching her arm, admiring her dragon tattoo, and about to share mac and cheese in front of a roaring fire. It was like her own little butch girl dream come true.

Mia set the bowls on a table near the futon and returned to the kitchen table to look at Lane's drawings while Lane started a fire. Lane said silent thanks that she had everything she needed to build a fire right at the moment when she needed it most.

"These are really good." Mia held up one of the figure drawings to look at it more closely. "Is it pencil or charcoal?"

"Charcoal. Are you an art major?" She didn't think she'd seen Mia around the Art and Architecture building, but it was a big place, so she didn't want to assume.

"Communications major."

"Oh, that's great." Lane wasn't really interested in talking about course study, but, damn, she sure could use better communication skills right now. She felt tongue-tied and nervous. Pain seared her finger and she dropped the match that had burned down to her skin while she watched Mia study the drawings. She sucked her stinging finger.

"Did you burn your finger? Let me get some ice." Mia abandoned the drawings and retrieved ice from the kitchen. She knelt beside Lane. "Here, just hold this on it for a minute." She cupped her hand around Lane's, keeping the ice against her throbbing fingertip.

Mia's face was so close that Lane could sense the warmth of her skin. Mia opened her clasped hands and gently blew on Lane's injured finger. Lane's heart beat loudly in her ears and she was close enough to sketch the details of Mia's face in her memory. Long dark lashes fluttered against her sculpted cheekbones, and when she looked up at Lane, her eyes were like dark bottomless pools. Lane wanted to dive in.

"Thanks." That sounded lame, but Lane didn't know what else to say.

She was more careful with the next match, and flames were soon licking at the dry wood she'd expertly stacked in the small fireplace. Mia moved to join her on the futon in front of the fire. They sat on either end, legs stretched out and facing each other, and made small talk as they ate. Mia did have a roommate who basically lived at her boyfriend's place. That explained why Lane hardly ever saw her.

As they talked Mia was rarely still, leaning forward to listen, sitting back to laugh as they discussed movies, television shows, or music they liked. Their legs brushed with each motion and Mia laid her hand on Lane's calf while making several enthusiastic comments. Lane's arousal registered an electric jolt with every connection.

Late afternoon had transitioned to evening while they talked. The night had taken on a sort of semidarkness. The snow blanketed every object outside the house, giving the atmosphere around the old Victorian an eerie magical glow, like something you'd expect to encounter in a fairy tale. Mia didn't seem to be in any hurry to go back to her place. Without power or a fireplace, it likely was pretty cold and dark. Mia had lingered after dinner, and Lane was not anxious to see her leave.

Lane noticed the fire ebb. "I think we need a little more wood." She reached around for her shoes to pull them on.

Mia fidgeted. "Maybe I should go. I've eaten your food and kept you talking for a long time. You probably had other plans tonight."

"You don't have to leave. It'll just take me a minute to get more wood from the back of the house." She wanted Mia to stay. Whatever she'd planned to do, she'd forgotten it the instant Mia knocked on her door. "We could have a nightcap. I've got some bourbon. I also have hot chocolate."

"Hot chocolate sounds good." Mia scooted to the edge of the futon and leaned around so that she could see Lane. "If you're sure."

"I'm sure."

True to her word, Lane was back in a flash with an armload of firewood. She dropped it into an old wood-sided box by the hearth and stoked the fire. Flames leapt against the blackened stonework, sparks flew up the chimney. She dusted her hands, admiring her pyro skills.

Lane wasn't sure if it was the fire or her raging hormones, but she was feeling overheated. She needed to lose a layer of clothing. As she pulled her rumpled crewneck sweater over her head, her T-shirt underneath pulled up from her loose jeans that rode low on her hips, revealing the plaid waistband of her boy-style boxers and the tattoo on her lower torso.

"What's that?" Mia leaned closer to examine the tattoo of kissing red lips.

"My girlfriend in high school talked me into that one. She liked to kiss me there." Lane's cheeks immediately flamed hot and she was glad the glow of the fire was the only light in the room. She hadn't meant to reveal that personal detail; she'd blurted it out and she wanted to take it back. Mia was looking at her with an expression she couldn't quite decipher.

Mia slid the bottom of her T-shirt up a little and pressed her lips to the tattoo. Lane inhaled sharply. Mia's hot mouth on her skin was so exquisite as to be almost painful. She wanted to run her fingers through Mia's hair. Instead, she froze, biting her lip, not sure what to do next.

Sure, Lane hadn't dated a lot of girls before, it wasn't like she was an expert, but she'd heard stories from her friends. *Please, please, please don't let this just be about straight girl curiosity.*

Mia stood, their lips only inches apart. Lane leaned in, stopping just short of contact. Mia closed the space. They kissed slowly. Lane delicately brushed Mia's lip with her tongue, and Mia deepened the kiss. Mia's fingertips teased the skin at the hem of her T-shirt, and Lane's stomach muscles twitched under the caress.

Lane moved her hand down Mia's fuzzy sweater and over the mound of her breast. When Lane hesitated, Mia covered her hand and guided it under her sweater. Lane followed Mia's direction. She moved up the gentle curve of Mia's stomach to the satin fabric of her bra. Mia's nipple came to a hard point beneath the sheer fabric.

Mia pushed Lane's shirt up and over her head. Lane tossed her shirt aside and let her fingers drift through Mia's thick, silky hair. Mia wrapped her arms around Lane's waist and pulled her close. Her sweater tickled Lane's rigid nipples as Mia placed butterfly-light kisses across Lane's collarbone and throat.

Lane's libido was revving too fast. She needed to downshift or this would be over in an embarrassingly short few minutes.

"I've been wanting to kiss you since the first time I saw you." Lane spoke softly as she trailed her fingertips down the side of Mia's face.

Mia smiled. "I've wanted to kiss you too." She pulled her sweater over her head, and her long hair sparked with a static charge. Then the blouse underneath was gone. Lane barely had time to take in the silky black bra before Mia reached behind to unfasten and toss it in the heap of clothes at their feet.

Lane's knees threatened to buckle at the press of Mia's breasts against hers. "I could fold the futon down if you, um—" She coughed when her voice cracked and tried again. "If that sounds good to you."

Mia smiled and nodded. Lane made quick work of the futon and tossed the cushions against the wooden arm of the frame. Lane took a seat and looked up at Mia, extending her hand. The intensity of the look Mia gave her liquefied her insides. The only sound in the room was the crackling fire and Lane's heart pounding in her ears. Mia took her outstretched hand, but instead of sitting next to her she straddled Lane's lap and kissed her. Lane felt Mia's fingers combing through the short hair at the back of her head as they kissed.

Mia pushed against Lane's shoulders, and Lane scooted back against the pillows. Mia followed, hovering above her. Strands of her thick dark hair brushed across Lane's torso as she moved.

"What are you thinking?" Mia traced circles in the center of Lane's stomach with her fingertip.

"I can't believe you're here. I guess I wasn't sure you liked girls."

"I like guys and girls, but lately certain types of girls have been catching my attention." Mia kissed Lane and brushed her fingers lightly down Lane's stomach.

Lane shuddered beneath Mia's touch. They had to be close to the same age, but somehow Lane felt like a novice while Mia exuded confidence. It wasn't fair. Lane was the one wearing the boy's jeans. She needed to butch up and take charge of the situation.

She nuzzled Mia's neck and then kissed her way across her collarbone and down to her breast. At first, she just slid her tongue lightly across Mia's nipple, then she took it fully into her mouth. Mia moaned softly and arched against her.

Lane had barely gotten on top of her game when she felt Mia's hand at the front of her pants, unzipping her jeans and pushing inside through the fly of her boxers.

"Oh." Lane had to catch her breath.

"Sorry, my fingers are cold." Mia was partially lying on top of Lane and began to caress her. "Is this okay?" Mia whispered the question.

"Yeah...that feels...good."

"You're so wet." Mia kissed her again. Deeply. Urgently. Her tongue matching the strokes of her fingers against Lane's flesh.

Mia's nipple was hard against Lane's open palm. Oh yeah, Mia had definitely been with women before. She knew exactly what she was doing. Lane pushed against Mia's hand. She was going to climax and they weren't yet fully undressed.

Lane writhed beneath Mia as each stroke drove her higher, closer to climax. And then Mia rolled back, pulling her fingers away to linger just below the waist of her boxers. Lane rolled with Mia and reached for her zipper. She blinked when Mia stopped her. "Oh, I thought—"

"I do, I mean, yes." Mia held Lane's hand in hers. For the first time, her eyes were shy as they met Lane's. "But I have something I want to get from downstairs. You know, if you're up for…toys."

Curiosity, excitement, and a bit of intimidation raced through Lane. This evening was definitely taking an unexpected turn. She tried for cool and nonchalant but was pretty sure she failed. "Yeah, sure, whatever."

Mia grabbed up Lane's T-shirt and pulled it on. "I'll be right back."

Lane lay in stunned silence. She was bare-chested, her fly open, her heart pounded in her ears and between her legs, and she had no idea what Mia had gone to retrieve. The old house creaked with Mia's movements until she returned with a small cardboard box. Lane sat up as Mia dropped to the side of the futon. The firelight flickered warmly, casting their silhouette in shadows against the wall.

"I ordered this for, well, to try out with a woman I was seeing last semester. We were in this great gender studies course, and I was intrigued to try this. But she turned out to be an arrogant jerk, so we never used it." She handed the box to Lane. "I've been waiting for the right person."

Lane opened the box. Nestled in purple tissue paper was a small bottle of lube, a harness, and a very realistic-looking cock. If it was possible for Lane's heart to beat any faster, it did.

"Is this for…I mean, who…?" Lane fumbled over her words.

"I was hoping you'd wear it. I mean, if you want to."

Lane stared at the contents of the box for a long moment, trying not to hyperventilate as images flashed through her brain. Mia beneath her. Her legs open and wanting.

"We don't have to if you don't want to. I just thought—"

"I want to." Lane gave Mia what she hoped was a reassuring smile. "I'll be right back."

Lane made tracks for the bathroom, but it was so dark that she couldn't see a thing. With the small box still in one hand, she rummaged in the closet for her headlamp with the other. She managed to find it, but the strap caught a camping pot, and the entire box of gear fell off the shelf and various items banged and skittered across the hardwood floor.

"Is everything okay?" Mia called from the front room.

"Uh, yeah, perfect. I'll just be a minute." And after a few missteps and adjustments, Lane thought she'd figured out how to properly wear the strap-on.

Lane stepped up on the toilet. She wanted to see herself in the mirror, but the mirror was too high and she couldn't get the right angle. She left her jeans but pulled her boxers on and grabbed a blanket. She almost forgot she was still wearing the headlamp. That would have certainly been an unfortunate mood killer. Sexy coal miner wasn't exactly the look she was going for. She tossed it back into the closet and stepped over the camping debris on the floor.

The apartment was growing cold, so she threw another log on the fire before turning back to Mia.

The blanket was draped around her shoulders but open at the front to reveal the bulge under her boxers. Mia gave her a slow, seductive smile and stood. She slowly lowered her jeans and panties, then removed Lane's T-shirt she'd donned earlier.

Mia was so beautiful that Lane stood, frozen and breathless.

Mia took the lube Lane was holding, tossed it on the futon, and knelt in front of her. She rubbed the shaft of the strap-on through the thin fabric of Lane's boxers. With every stroke, the base pressed against Lane's sex.

"Does that feel good to you?" Mia looked up as she asked.

Lane nodded, words failing her.

Mia started low, kissing the red lips tattoo, then moving her mouth lower as she slowly pulled the boxers down Lane's clenched thighs. In a night of surprises, her next move was the greatest. Mia held the shaft and took the tip of it into her mouth. Lane gasped. The visual alone sent electric shocks to her core. Holy shit. She might come just from watching Mia's erotic display. Every cell in her body was confirming the truth she'd barely been able to imagine before this very minute. She wanted to make love to Mia. Right here. Right now.

Lane ran her fingers through Mia's hair and pulled her back so she could see her face. "Lie back." Lane stepped out of her boxers that had pooled around her feet and drew the blanket over them as Mia settled across the futon.

Lane hovered over her as Mia reached for the lube and massaged some onto the dildo. Lane continued to caress her. Her brain was overloading, her senses exploding with the combination of touching Mia and the pressure of the base of the cock against her center. Blood pounded in her ears. Her face and chest burned.

"Move closer." Mia spoke in a low voice as she guided Lane into position, inserting the tip with her own hand.

Mia inhaled sharply as Lane pushed farther inside. She watched Mia's face carefully.

"Go slow, okay?" Mia wrapped an arm around Lane's neck and put her other hand on Lane's waist.

"How's this?" Lane pushed a little farther, then pulled out slowly and gently eased back in.

Mia kissed Lane's neck. "Yeah, that's good. Really good."

Mia's foot was against the back of her thigh, urging her on as she set a smooth, slow pace. The sensation of having Mia's legs wrapped around her and both hands free to caress her was indescribable.

"Lane, talk to me. You're too quiet. Is this freaking you out?"

Lane stopped moving and looked down at Mia. "No, is it freaking you out? Do you want me to stop?"

"No, please, don't stop. Definitely don't stop." Mia pulled her down and kissed hungrily, sucking Lane's tongue into her mouth. Her eyes glittered in the firelight when they breathlessly broke their kiss. Mia spoke softly against her lips. "I like this a lot. More than I thought I would."

"Mia, you are so sexy. I've wanted to fuck you since the first time I saw you."

"You can do it harder if you want."

Lane held Mia's gaze as she started to move again, increasing the rhythm and depth of each thrust. Mia moaned and clung to her neck and shoulders. Mia's legs tightened around Lane's hips.

"Yes, so good." Mia arched into her.

Lane watched Mia's head drop back. So beautiful. She bit her lower lip and dug her nails into Lane's shoulders. Then she dropped one hand to the harness and tugged it, echoing each thrust.

Lane was struggling to keep the rhythm as the pressure built inside her sex. She wanted to hold out because she sensed that Mia wasn't quite there. Both of Mia's hands were on her ass now, directing the angle of her thrusts.

Lane was so close to the edge, but she cared more about making Mia feel good, giving Mia what she wanted. Mia's head dropped back, eyes closed, so beautiful. Mia dug her nails into Lane's back and she felt her whole body tense as desire swelled deep inside. She continued to thrust, slowly, deeply, then faster. Mia wrapped her arm around Lane's lower back, directing her movement until she sensed they were both at orgasm. Mia's legs tightened around her hips. She felt Mia's body stiffen and shudder beneath her.

Mia cried out and Lane collapsed on top of her, holding her in her arms.

"Oh, my God, Lane. That was amazing." Mia pushed damp hair off Lane's forehead. "Why didn't you say you'd done that before?"

"I haven't. That was a first." Lane already knew she wanted to do it again.

"For me too."

They were both breathing hard, and Lane was sure her heart was pounding loud enough for Mia to hear it. She started to move, but Mia held her.

"No, don't pull out yet. Just stay a little longer."

Lane smiled and kissed her. "I'll stay here as long as you want."

She reached behind to tug the blanket up over them as the fire crackled and snowflakes continued to fall against the night sky. She regretted cursing the snow earlier. Cradled in Mia's arms and between her legs, Lane was anything but cold. Who knew a snow day could be so warm.

KNOCKING ON HAVEN'S DOOR

Brey Willows

Kris rolled her neck to try and work the kinks out. She hated moving more than just about anything in the world, aside from anchovies.

"That's the last box." Reed wiped her sweat away with her forearm.

"Thanks, buddy. I owe you." Kris slapped Reed on the back, genuinely grateful, but they weren't the kind of friends who got all mushy with one another.

"Fucking right you do. Why can't you buy all that lightweight Ikea crap? Did you really have to buy solid oak...everything?" Reed flopped onto her back on the grass.

Kris joined her and stared up at the cloudless blue summer sky. "That other stuff doesn't last. I could give this stuff to my grandkids."

"You don't even have kids, jackass. I'll have to haul it all out again when you die here alone, being eaten by the dust bunnies."

A car pulled into the driveway next door, but Kris didn't look up. She'd meet the neighbors another day, when she didn't feel like she'd swum through a sweat bath. She nearly groaned out loud when she heard the footsteps coming their way. When a shadow fell over her, she shaded her eyes and looked up.

And promptly lost the ability to speak.

The woman standing over her looked like something out of a wet dream. Long, tanned legs were framed in short cut-offs, and a tight tank top hugged womanly curves and what looked like very, very nice breasts. Her thick brown hair was pulled back into a long ponytail and her jade green eyes looked curious.

Reed stared as well, and hissed softly, "Say something, slick."

The woman standing over them smiled. "Hey there. Sorry I arrived too late to help."

"You and me both." Reed started to sit up.

Kris knocked Reed's arm out from under her and stood up first. "No problem, really. I'm Kris, and this is Reed."

"Haven. Nice to meet you both. I hope you guys like it here."

Kris glanced down at Reed, who looked at her with a grin and a raised eyebrow. "No! I mean, it's just me. Reed isn't my...we're not..."

"She's single." Reed stood and wiped the grass from her butt. "As am I." She reached out and shook Haven's hand, her signature come-and-get-it smile playing on her lips.

Haven laughed and inclined her head slightly. "Good to know. Thanks for clarifying." She turned her attention to Kris. "I have to get going. If you need anything, just give a shout. I work from home a lot of the time, so you know, if you need sugar or whatever." She turned away and waved over her shoulder.

Kris and Reed watched her until she disappeared into the house, the screen door slamming shut behind her.

Reed turned to Kris. "I'll buy this house off you right here, right now. Name your price. In fact, fuck that. Let me rent out the room with the window that faces her bedroom."

"First of all, she's way out of your league. Second, she may not even be a lesbian. Third, if anyone is making a play, it's me. I get first dibs because she's my neighbor."

Reed huffed. "Spoilsport. If you strike out, I'm going in. Straight girls are my specialty, if it comes to that, but my gaydar was loud enough to call the fire brigade."

Kris had to admit, hers was pinging pretty damn loudly too, but she wasn't about to admit it to her oversexed and ambitious best friend. "Yeah, well, we'll see. I don't plan on leaving this place anytime soon, so I'll be able to take my time. Hell, she could turn out to be utterly unlikeable as well as unavailable."

"With a body like that, you don't need to like her. Hate fucking can be seriously hot." She sniffed her armpit and winced. "Speaking of, I reek. I'm gonna head home and shower. You going to the club tonight?"

Kris couldn't think of anything she wanted to do less. "Nah. I'm going to shower and hit the sack. I'm wiped."

Reed dug her keys from her pocket and headed for her truck. "Good. Maybe without you there to make me look bad, I'll actually get some tonight."

"The only reason you ever get any when I'm there is because women feel sorry for my shadow."

Reed flipped her the bird as she drove away, and Kris laughed. As she turned to head into her new home, she saw her gorgeous new neighbor standing at the window, sipping a glass of what looked like iced tea, looking at her thoughtfully.

Kris grimaced slightly and gave her a little wave before going inside. *Well, at least there's no pretense of me being refined.*

❖

"God damn it." Kris stuck her thumb in her mouth and dropped the hammer. She'd been putting her bed together, tired of sleeping on the mattress on the floor, when someone pounded at the front door, throwing off her aim. "I'm coming," she yelled when the pounding kept up. She yanked open the door and instantly softened.

"Spider. Prehistoric-sized, furry spider that could eat my dog. I hate them." Haven motioned with her hands, intimating a spider about a foot long.

"You have a dog? Sure. Yeah, okay. Let me get my shotgun."

Haven frowned and scrubbed at her arms like she had the willies. "No, I don't have a dog, it's a figure of speech. Laugh away, just come kill it, please?"

Kris grinned and grabbed her work boot from beside the door.

"Lead the way, damsel in distress." She followed Haven back to her place and looked at her quizzically when she stepped aside at the front door.

"I'm not going in until it's dead. I'll just have to swap houses with you if you can't find it."

Kris rolled her eyes. "Where was it?"

"Over the kitchen doorway. Just waiting to drop down and devour me whole."

I know the feeling. Watching her absurdly attractive neighbor come and go over the past two weeks had started giving her wickedly good dreams. Kris went in and looked over the door. No spider. She glanced around the floor and went into the kitchen. "Jesus Christ!" She jumped backward, hitting her head on a kitchen cupboard. A white spider, easily three inches in diameter, ran across the top of her shoe and scuttled under the cupboard ledge.

"See? That's it. Don't bother, I'll burn the house down and claim insurance. I'll move somewhere too cold for spiders." Haven stood just inside the front door, craning to look at Kris without actually getting any closer.

"That's a bit extreme, I think. Where are your glasses?"

"In the cupboard behind you. Why? You're not seriously going to release it outside, are you? I'll die of anxiety just waiting for it to come back in and take revenge."

Are princesses in towers this dramatic? "I can't get my boot wedged in there, so I need to get it into something so I can take it out of here." Kris grabbed a glass without taking her eyes off the spider, worried it would find a crack and disappear. Then they probably would have to burn the house down. She got down on all fours, reminding herself she was about a trillion times bigger than it, and it probably thought she was ugly too. She managed to slip the glass under it and quickly spin it so it dropped to the bottom with a surprisingly heavy thud. She pressed a plate over the top and headed outside. Haven practically crawled over her couch to get out of the way.

Kris went to the drain next to the curb and shook the spider out of the glass and down into the abyss. "Back to the hell from which you came."

Haven sat on her front steps and Kris sat beside her. "You can keep that plate and glass. Or throw them away. I'll never use them again."

Kris laughed. "It really was enormous. I've never seen one like that."

"Me neither, and I hope I never will again." Haven grinned at her sheepishly. "Thanks for doing that. It's such a cliché, me running next door because of a spider."

"I'm a big fan of clichés. Sometimes there's nothing better."

A convertible BMW pulled into Haven's driveway, the kind of car that made a lot of sense in Southern California. Kris watched as four extremely hot, very lesbian-looking women got out and headed their way.

Haven smiled at them and waved them over. "Hey, guys. This is my neighbor, Kris. Go on in, I'll be there in a minute."

The women said hello and filed past, and Kris looked at Haven, who just smiled and stood up. "Well, I'd better get to work. Thanks again."

"Anytime. Just let me know when there's another spider-dragon to slay."

Haven gave her a small, suggestive smile. "I have a feeling there will be others."

Kris went back to her place and tried to concentrate on putting her bed together. *What kind of work necessitates five insanely hot women in a house?* Various ideas came to her, none of which she'd actually vocalize. If Reed had been there, she'd have asked outright, but Kris wasn't so forthcoming. She finally got the bed together and put on her favorite light blue Egyptian cotton sheets with the matching blue and white checked bedspread. Reed said it was too girly, but Kris loved the calm it radiated.

"Hey!"

The screen slammed shut and she heard Reed's heavy steps in the kitchen.

"I brought pizza and beer. It's no fun going out without you, so if the mountain won't come to Mohammed…"

Kris grabbed a fresh black tank top and headed to the kitchen. Reed looked her over as she pulled it on over her sports bra.

"Damn, dude. If you were my type, I'd be all over you. As it is, please don't ever show anyone those abs while I'm around because you'll make me look like a bloated marshmallow."

Kris shrugged and grabbed a piece of pizza while Reed opened their beers. "If you'd go to the gym with me, you wouldn't have to worry about it." She ran her hand through her hair and realized it was touching her collar. She couldn't remember when she'd last had it cut, and now it was going to drive her crazy, the way it always did when it got too long. She blew a strand out of her eyes.

"I didn't say I don't like being a bloated marshmallow. I just don't need people seeing it right away."

They settled on the couch and Kris put on some cheesy action film Reed handed her. During a lull in the story, Reed said, "Hey, how's it going with the hot neighbor? Any movement?"

"Nah. It's not like I've had a lot of time. Between work and unpacking, I haven't been around a lot. I saved her from a spider earlier today, though, and you should have seen the women who are over there now."

Reed hit the pause button. "Tell me."

Just as Kris was about to try and describe Haven's friends, they heard laughter. Reed jumped up and went to the window. She looked over her shoulder at Kris. "Seriously."

"Right?" Kris joined her at the window and they watched as Haven gave all four women a hug and a kiss. One of them, a tall, short-haired woman, gave her a lingering kiss before Haven pushed her away, laughing.

"Damn. Girlfriend?" Reed leaned on the windowsill.

They watched as the woman then turned away and headed to the BMW with the others. They waved to Haven as they drove off.

"Who knows?" Kris sighed. "But apparently she's out of my league, too."

Reed flopped back into the overstuffed chair. "You're so

clueless. I think that's one of the things women love about you. You're employed and you have a car. For a lot of women, that's enough."

Kris laughed and hit play, ending the conversation. She had a feeling Haven wasn't just any woman. If, and when, the time came to ask her out, she wanted to be ready.

❖

You can do this. Don't be a weenie. Kris wiped her palms on her jeans for the umpteenth time. Finally, she knocked. It had been well over a month, and she couldn't get the girl next door out of her head. She convinced herself that if she got to know her, she'd know they weren't compatible and she could stop daydreaming about her. Every time Haven smiled at her, every little conversation they had, every time she heard her laugh, it made her want to know more, and she wondered if she was putting Haven on some libido-coated pedestal. Incredibly hot women came and went from her place all the time, and Kris wanted to know what that was about. Between her attraction and her curiosity, she was becoming obsessed. It was time to deal with it.

"Hey, Kris."

Kris swallowed against the knot of anxiety in her throat. "Hey, Haven. I was wondering, would you like to have dinner with me?"

Haven leaned against the door frame, her arms crossed. "Are you asking me on a date?"

"Yes. Unless you say no, in which case I was just going to offer you leftovers as a neighbor."

Haven turned and grabbed a lightweight coat hanging next to the door, as well as her keys. "I'm starving. Where are we going?"

Kris's stomach dropped. "Now? I mean, sure, yeah, okay. Now is good. I could eat." She nearly tripped as they headed to her truck. "Thai?"

"I love Thai."

They settled into the truck, and Kris headed toward her favorite restaurant. She glanced over at Haven, who was tapping her fingers to the music. She looked amazing, in boyfriend-cut jeans rolled at the ankles, cute little Vans, and a flowy white tank top that was just see-through enough to show the outline of her lacy bra. Kris felt her clit twitch and returned her attention to the road. They pulled into the parking lot a few minutes later. She felt every moment of the awkward silence between them, even though Haven looked slightly amused.

They were seated next to a softly falling water feature, and Kris appreciated the way the light highlighted Haven's beautiful eyes.

They picked up their menus, and Haven said, "I was beginning to think you weren't ever going to ask me out. In fact, I was beginning to think maybe Reed was your type after all."

Kris nearly choked on her water. "Good God, no. Reed and I have been friends since high school. Even if she was my type, and she's not, I know her too well to ever go there."

Haven set her menu down and leaned forward slightly. "So what is your type?"

Kris licked her lips, wondering why the water wasn't helping her sudden case of dry mouth. "You. I mean, I like femme women. Soft, afraid of monster spiders, lacy underwear."

"How do you know I'm soft, or that I like lacy underwear?"

Kris glanced down at Haven's top and then flushed, mortified. When Haven started laughing, she relaxed and could breathe again.

"You're really easy to mess with." Haven reached across the table and put her hand over Kris's. "I like the way you look at me."

The waiter came and took their order, and Kris tried to steady herself. *It's another human. You talk to them all the time.* But the moment she looked at Haven, that thought fled and was instantly replaced with the nerves of a teenager on a first date.

"Tell me about your name?" *Small talk is good. Start there.*

Haven looked slightly surprised, but nodded. "My mother came from a really tough background. Bad parents, poor, all the rest of it. When she got pregnant with me, it gave her a reason to get out and try to make it on her own. She didn't want to raise me where she'd grown up. She always said I was her safe haven, and as long as we were together, she knew she'd be okay."

Kris took a moment to process that, and felt her eyes well up a little. "Wow. That's really beautiful. Are you still close?"

Haven shook her head slightly. "Cancer. Five years ago. I miss her every day."

"Damn. I'm so sorry." Kris felt awful for asking, and wished she could pull Haven close and hug the sadness from her expression.

"It's okay, really. Tell me about yourself?"

And so it went, with more small talk about families and where they'd grown up, what states they'd lived in and what countries they'd visited. "I'm a physicist at the university. Mostly research no one else understands or cares about." Kris smiled to show she wasn't bitter about it. "What do you do?"

Haven stared at her for a long moment, as though debating what to say. "Are you sure you want to know?"

Kris laughed. "Well, when you put it that way, I have to know. Are you CIA?"

"Not exactly." Haven took a long sip of her Thai iced tea, her gaze never leaving Kris's face. "Would you consider yourself liberal?"

"Well, yeah. I guess."

Haven grinned mischievously. "Then maybe one day I'll tell you."

Kris looked at her disbelievingly. "Seriously?"

"Seriously. A girl has to have her secrets, after all. I can't tell you everything on the first date, can I? You'd decide I was boring and not ask me out again." She looked away and shrugged.

Kris reached over and took her hand, stroking it gently with her thumb. Although Haven was acting like she was kidding, Kris sensed a genuine vulnerability beneath her lighthearted surface. "I'm happy to spend a hell of a lot of time getting to know you. No worries there."

Haven's smile made Kris's stomach flip, and she'd never been so glad she'd asked a woman on a date.

❖

Kris kept replaying their kiss when the date had ended. Sultry, hot, and full of promise, it had left her weak-kneed and desperate for more, but she'd simply smiled and said good night. It felt weird, dropping off a date and then walking next door to her own place. But then, she kind of liked seeing the lights go on, and then later, off, at Haven's place. Unable to sleep thanks to visions of Haven in her lacy underwear, her thick brown hair spread out on her pillow, Kris figured she might as well get up and read for a while. She made herself a cup of green tea and glanced over at Haven's house. A faint glow from the far end of Haven's backyard caught her eye, and she frowned. Her own backyard was a mess of overgrown bushes and a falling-down shed, which she'd deal with when she had the time. She'd never really looked at Haven's backyard. She looked out the front window and noticed the convertible BMW in the driveway. Her heart sank when she remembered the hot kiss Haven had shared with the driver of that vehicle. *So much for that.*

Suddenly warm, she threw open a window and was surprised to hear faint laughter from what sounded like several women. *She has friends over at one in the morning on a Wednesday?* Her curiosity getting the better of her, she slipped on sweats and sneakers and headed next door. There were no lights on in the house, but she could hear the voices more clearly now, coming from the backyard. She flipped open the side gate and crept along the fence, a strange combination of foolishness and anticipation running through her. She came to an opening in a thicket of trees. She made her way from tree to tree until she was close enough to make out the voices.

"Good. Claire, if you could just move slightly to the left... perfect. Terry, arch your neck back a bit more, let's get some light on your collarbone." Haven's voice was authoritative but gentle.

Kris peeked around the tree and felt the blood rush from her head to regions farther south. A tiny little cabin-like structure was all lit up. In front of it, a naked woman lay sprawled on a picnic bench while another stood between her spread legs, her face pushed against the woman's center. *The women from the BMW.* And standing just far enough away were Haven and several other people who seemed to comprise a production crew, complete with cameras and sound.

Haven alternated between watching a screen in front of her and the women on the bench. Kris's attention, however, was riveted on the woman writhing on the picnic bench. She felt the slickness on her own thighs as her body responded automatically to the sounds of the woman's pleasure. Haven's occasional instructions were quiet but firm, and definitely added to Kris's growing need. The woman thrashed as she came, and when she settled into a satiated pose, Haven called, "Cut. Great job, everyone. Let's move inside and get the scene between Andi and Dana in front of the fire."

The crew started moving their gear and the women headed inside. Kris was trying to figure out how to get near a window, and was ignoring the Peeping Tom warning pounding in her head, when she stepped back and broke a branch under her foot. She froze and watched as Haven spun around to search the dark trees around her.

"Go on in. I'll be right there," she said to her camerawoman.

Shit shit shit. Kris wondered if she could make it back to the gate without being seen, but without the tree cover, there was no way. *Think, jackass.* Suddenly, Haven stood in front of her with her hands on her hips. *Too late. Shit.*

"Did you come to offer me leftovers?" Haven's tone was light, but her eyes were serious.

"I heard voices and wanted to make sure everything was okay." *Well, that was lame.*

"And is it? Okay?" Haven's expression was searching.

"Are you asking me if I'm okay with you being a...a... pornographer?"

Haven tilted her head. "Yes. That's what I'm asking you. All women, all consensual, all lesbians."

"I think you're actually every erotic dream I've ever had, come true."

Haven's shoulders visibly relaxed and she grinned. "While I like the sound of that and want to hear more, I have people waiting on me. Can we talk more tomorrow?"

Kris leaned forward and kissed her lightly, drawing it out but hoping she put more than just lust into it. "I'm home all day. Just shout."

Haven walked backward toward the cabin. "I'm not a morning person, so I'll see you after lunch."

She disappeared inside the house, and Kris made her way back to her place. *The girl next door films lesbian porn in her backyard. Wait until I tell Reed.*

❖

She let Haven in late the next day and quickly made her a cup of coffee, she looked so tired. "Long night?"

"Shooting at night makes for some great scenes, but it's not easy on the body clock."

"I can imagine."

The silence was heavy and awkward, and Haven simply looked at her, clearly waiting for her to start.

"So...porn, huh? What made you go into that?"

Haven shrugged. "I got a master's degree in human sexuality. At the same time, I noticed a gap in the market. Everyone complained about lesbian porn containing only super-femme women with long nails. So I decided to change that and make movies for women that reflected more of who they are and what they like." She sipped her coffee, looking contemplative. "And I like sex."

Kris's clit twitched in response. "Those sound like damn good reasons."

"I'm not ashamed of what I do. But I've found that when you tell people, they seem to instantly assume you're up for grabs, and they treat you with less respect." Haven set her cup down and took a deep breath before looking at Kris seriously. "So I guess I need to know where you stand."

Kris thought about it for a moment. "I was hoping you were up for grabs before I knew what you did for a living." She smiled to show she was joking and was glad Haven laughed. "Seriously, though. I think it's cool you're doing something you love for reasons you believe in. I like you, a lot. I think you're sweet, funny, sexy and I want to know a lot more about you. And frankly, I'm really glad to know you like sex. I'm a big fan, too."

Haven moved around the counter to stand within inches of Kris. "Yeah? Well, keep up the compliments and maybe we'll see who likes it more."

She gave Kris a lingering kiss that made her entire body feel like it could burst into needy flames. "I mean it, though."

Haven leaned back and gave her a soft smile. "I believe you." She moved away and headed toward the front door. "I'm away for a shoot for a couple of days. Dinner when I get back?"

"I'd like that."

Haven shot her a quick smile before the screen door slammed closed behind her. Kris blew out a breath and headed upstairs for some quality time with her vibrator.

She showed up at Haven's door three days later with a bottle of wine and a case of nerves. Over the previous three days they'd sent more than twenty texts. Though there'd been plenty of innuendo, there'd also been a lot of texts that were simply getting to know one another. Fun, casual conversation that made Kris ache for Haven to come home again. She missed her presence, missed knowing she was right next door. Not to mention, Reed was desperate for an introduction to Haven's employees and couldn't stop talking about her. When the text came asking if Kris wanted to have dinner at Haven's, she'd jumped at the chance. Now the butterflies in her stomach seemed like they were on speed.

Haven answered the door, and Kris nearly dropped the bottle of wine. A tight white tank top hugged her perfect breasts, and low-slung jeans showed the top of black lace panties when she led the way into the kitchen.

"Good trip?" Kris had to do something to distract herself.

"Mostly. Two of the models didn't speak English, so it turned into a kind of farce at times, but I think we got what we needed." She handed Kris a glass of wine and took the other bottle from her to put it in the fridge.

"I suppose sex is mostly about body language anyway, right?"

Haven set her drink down and moved slowly toward Kris, her head tilted and the look in her eyes ravenous. "Why don't you tell me?"

Kris set her own glass down and welcomed the feel of Haven's waist under her hands. She met Haven's mouth with her own, and desire swamped her. Haven moaned softly against her mouth.

"I missed you," Kris murmured.

"Take me to bed," she said, biting Kris's lower lip.

"Are you sure? I wouldn't want you to think—"

"I think I've got you pretty well figured out, Romeo. I'm not worried. Now fuck me into an orgasmic coma."

Kris didn't need to be asked twice. She scooped Haven into her arms and carried her into the bedroom. She threw her onto the king-sized bed and quickly climbed on top of her. Clothes flew through the air as they pulled them off one another, until Kris stopped for a second to take in the beauty of Haven's softly rounded curves, full breasts, and the dark patch between her legs that already looked wet. She carefully settled on top of her and whispered in her ear, "Tell me what you want, baby. How do you like to be fucked?" She ran her fingertips down Haven's sides and liked the way she shivered at her touch.

"I want your mouth on me. Slow and steady, and then suck me in."

Kris did exactly as requested after settling between Haven's legs. She loved the way she moved, how sensually she reacted, the way her thighs tensed and relaxed. And, finally, the way she cried out and arched when she came. Kris didn't think she'd ever seen anyone so beautiful. She entered her slowly, first with one finger, and then another, and when Haven moaned, she fucked her deeper and faster, until, her hands balled in the sheets, she came again, coating Kris's hand.

She pulled out and moved to lie beside Haven, who curled up against her. *She's a perfect fit.* Kris wrapped her arms around her and they lay silently for some time. Finally, Haven looked up at her. "That's way better than porn, if you were wondering."

Kris smiled and kissed the top of Haven's head. "I wasn't, but thanks for letting me know." She lightly caressed Haven's back, tracing the rose tattoo on her shoulder.

"So, does that mean I'm the kind of girl you would take home to mom?"

While her tone was light, Kris could sense the vulnerability in the question. "Are you kidding? My mom would be so ecstatic we'd never hear the end of it."

"And what about my job?"

Kris tilted Haven's chin up so she could look at her properly. "We'll tell her exactly what you do. You're an amazing woman, and I'll hang around until you know just how amazing you are."

Haven snuggled closer with a contented sigh, and Kris closed her eyes. *My own safe haven.*

GOLD

Giselle Renarde

Y ou look at me and say, "That butch could never be a gold digger."
Shows what you know.

If they handed out awards, I'd be goddamn Gold Digger of the Year. Of the decade! I've been at it a good long time.

Picture a gold digger right now. She's leggy and blonde, right? Tall and slim. Long hair, meticulously coiffed. Nah, man. That's my target demographic. These ladies of the house, lounging by their pools between collagen injections—they're my prey. They're sitting ducks.

And maybe they're gold diggers in their own right. Sure, okay, you got me there. Their much older husbands paid for these mansions they live in, paid for me to be here cutting the grass and weeding the gardens, planting new life in the springtime and tearing it out in the fall. Winter, I take it easy, watch my huge-ass TV—a gift from Lady Muck the Third.

Not all gold diggers are in it for the jewellery. No woman in her right mind would buy me diamonds. Do I look like I'm gonna wear a goddamn tennis bracelet? I got a nice watch, one time. That was a good call. Suited me to a T.

I still sold it, though. Damn thing paid my rent for the next eight months.

Looking back, I should have kept that watch as an investment, like how people buy art or coins. Money's easy to come by when you sleep with the right women. In my case, the right women are the wrong women: married to dudes who are loaded, always away on business, entertaining mistresses on the road.

These women I work for, the poolside loungers, they'd deny it to your face if you asked them straight out: "Hey, you think your husband's screwing another chick?"

"Goodness, no!" they'd say, and they'd laugh the way only rich women can. "Haw-haw-haw, dear me, no. My Wellesley would never stray. He *loves* me, you see."

Yeah, sure he does. Just like he loved his first wife when he started seeing you on the side.

Second wives always act oblivious, but they know the score.

That's why they fall into my trap so easy.

Easy isn't even the word, man. They're putting out vibes the second me and Marco and Petey and Pip set foot on the property. Course, the vibes aren't meant for me. Rich ladies got their eyes on strapping young men. Too bad for them Marco and Petey only have eyes for each other.

Still, the rich ladies are shameless flirts, bringing out lemonade, swinging their hips, wearing nothing but black bathing suits cut high on the hips and low on the chest. Leaning over just right and raising their eyes and saying, "Is there anything else I can get you?"

And by the time she says those words, I'm the only one left. The guys have taken their drinks and gone off together. Pip's sitting across the yard nursing that reusable water bottle she brought from home.

So now it's just me and Lady Muck. She put it out there for the guys, but I'm the one who looks her up and down with my patented stare. I'm the one saying, "I bet it gets lonely in this big ol' house at night."

She looks at me like she's seeing me for the first time: my strong calves cut to shreds by the weed whacker, the muscular gold of my arms, short hair so sun-bleached it's almost white. She's a little afraid, but she likes the taste of fear. Makes her feel alive, or at least a little less bored.

You think looks like these can't make bank? Think again. A pretty girl would never get a cent out of these poolside women. Take

Pip over there, with her skinny limbs and that face like a doll, like it would break if you looked at it too hard, and that smooth brown skin glistening in the sun as she pulls grass clippings out of her perfect curls. What would Lady Muck's rich husband do if he found out his wife was getting down with a girl like Pip?

That's right: He'd pull up a chair. "Go at it, ladies. I'll get the popcorn."

But with me? No way. I'm a dirty secret, in every sense. What husband wants his collagen-injected wife screwing around with a hulking hunk of muscle-mama? What wife wants her high society friends finding out she's been slumming with a gardener like me? Her knees buckle when I step inside her garden, but she doesn't want the world to know.

It plays to my advantage. If I make the slightest suggestion I might tell anyone we've been going at it like rabbits, she'll pay me handsomely to keep my trap shut.

Then on to the next.

On to the next...

I'm sitting with my back against the Millingtons' fence, surveying my surroundings, when Pip lowers herself beside me. She doesn't want to get her khaki shorts dirty, so she hugs her knobbly knees, keeping her feet on the ground and her butt raised off it. She opens her bag in the shade of the oldest tree on their property and says, "Finally lunchtime. This morning went by sooo slow."

"The Millingtons have a daughter who just got home from college."

I'm really just talking to myself, but Pip says, "Oh, yeah?"

I point out the plain-looking girl reading a book in the upstairs window seat. "It'd be good to get my hands on some young blood for once. She's not exactly a looker, but a trust fund could be just what the doctor ordered. I could retire from all this, live in the lap of luxury."

"Is the Millington girl a lesbian?" Pip asks.

I give her a look like "as if that matters" while she takes two sacks of cut vegetables from her lunch bag. It's mostly carrot sticks today. Better when she brings me snap peas and red peppers, but I'm sure she's on a budget.

Pip hands me a chicken wrap, and I can only hope she left out the hummus today. Before I can ask, she sighs and says, "Don't you ever want a relationship that's based on love instead of money?"

"Sure," I tell her. Take a bite of the wrap. No hummus today. Pipsqueak's learning. "After I snag the Millington brat, that's when I'll worry about love. I want to be set for life before I start thinking about all that."

Pip asks, "Are you saying you would marry someone you didn't love?"

"If she's got Millington money, you bet. Wouldn't you?"

"Not if I didn't love her. I'd rather live in a shack with someone I love than live in a mansion with someone I hate."

I gnaw at the wrap Pip made me, gazing at the Millington girl all the while. "I doubt I'd hate her. She looks like an okay kid. And if she's anything like her mom in the sack…"

"Eww!" Pip slams her fist into my side so hard it hurts, but I don't react. Don't want to give her the satisfaction. Still, she says, "I can't believe you slept with Old Lady Millington. She's a million years old!"

"She's barely sixty. And with all the work she's had done, she doesn't feel a day over forty."

"Shut up!" Pip squeaks—hence the nickname, by the way.

Once the girl gets riled up, I can't help myself. "Old Lady Millington got her pussy tightened, you know."

"Gross!" Pip stands and kicks dirt at me. "I don't want to hear about this."

"What's the surgery called, where they make you a virgin all over again?" I can't help myself. "You think the daughter's still a virgin? I bet she is. Look at those glasses."

Pip launches her foot at my ass, and gets me good with her steel-toed boot. It's a shocker. Enough for me to hop up and walk away, saying, "Jesus, get a grip!"

I'm heading for Marco and Petey when Pip shouts, "*You* get a grip, Devon."

She's never raised her voice to me before. I'm halfway across the yard, but I turn. I can't stop myself.

Gesturing to the Millington girl in the window, she says, "You think a girl like that would ever marry someone like you?"

I feel like I've been slapped in the face, and even though I've been called much worse, I can't find it in me to retaliate. I just cling to the wrap she made for me, and the carrot sticks in a baggie.

"Bored housewives are one thing," Pip says. "You're not part of their real lives. You're just a bit on the side, the human equivalent of day drinking and a mild addiction to painkillers. You marry a girl and *boom*, you're real. You're there at dinner parties and society dos. I don't care how good you are in bed—that Millington girl wouldn't take you to a charity ball if you were the last dyke on earth."

Every word makes me madder than hell, but I can't lash out at the little doll. What's worse is…she's *right*. That's what hurts the most. Not the words. Words are just words. It's the *truth* of the matter. That's what really gets me.

Pip's right. This long-term plan of mine will never work out. No blue blood in the world wants to be seen with a crass and calloused landscaper.

I've always prided myself on being everyone's dirty secret. I can't change gears now.

Pip doesn't speak to me for the rest of the day. I don't even look at her. I can't. But I can't stop thinking about her, either. First I'm stuck on what she said. Later, after I get home, I'm thinking about… about *her*. Which is something I've never done before. Never gave the girl a second thought.

Who *is* she? Why's she doing this work? Pretty girls usually opt for indoor vocations, and she's scrawny for a landscaper.

Next morning she doesn't show up for work. Can't help thinking it's because of me. I call her cell but she doesn't answer, doesn't call me back. I don't leave a message.

At the end of the day I call Vik, who does the scheduling for our company. I ask him if Pip switched pods. He says, "Pip?"

"Pipsqueak," I tell him, then remember that's just my nickname for her. "The girl. What's her name? Laetitia?"

"Lorinda?" Vik asks flatly.

"Yeah, her. Did she switch to a different pod?"

"No."

I'm waiting for more information, but none is forthcoming. So I pull a pen from the glove compartment and say, "Give me her address."

"Email address?"

"Street address."

He does, reluctantly, and I write it on my arm. I'm about to get out the map when I realize I don't have to. She lives right down the road. How is that possible? The houses in this neighbourhood cost an arm and a leg. Unless she's a live-in—a nanny, maid, personal support worker, house-sitter, who knows?

It's a two-minute drive. The house is spectacular. Manicured lawn and all. I park on the street and walk up to the door, feeling nervous as hell. Itchy too, and not just from the sun and the grass clippings stuck to my skin.

Maybe I should go. What am I even doing here? If she's staff, she's probably not allowed to have visitors. I don't want to get her in deep shit just by showing up.

Too late. The door opens and there's a black man in a suit on the other side. He's got a soft-topped leather briefcase tucked under his arm and he's facing away from me, calling up the stairs, "I'm heading out to that investors' group. Back by eleven!"

Pip's voice calls back, "Okay!"

My heart pounds against my ribcage.

The suave older man turns and spots me and jumps. He says, "Thanks, we already have a service. If you'll excuse me, I'm just heading out."

"No, I'm not selling…I'm here for Pip."

He cocks his brow.

Dammit, not Pip. What's her name? Not Laetitia…

"Oh!" He laughs like he's in on a joke I don't get. Then he says, "You must be Devon."

Not sure how he knows that, but I say, "Yeah."

He sticks his head inside and calls, "Honey, it's your friend from work." Then he says, "Head on inside. Lorinda will be right down."

As he makes his way to the luxury vehicle in the driveway, he glances back at my dirty boots.

I say, "I'll take them off."

He gives me a gracious smile as I enter his house. I haven't even closed the door when Pip appears at the top of the grand staircase like a goddamn vision. She's wearing this designer suit, tailored, fine fabric.

That's when it hits me: I'm not the only gold digger in our pod. Look at this girl playing house, queen of the castle! She's got her hooks in a good one. That old guy wasn't bad-looking. Nice dresser, too. God only knows why she's been toiling in the sun with me all summer.

Late-afternoon sunlight cascades across her shoulders, coming in through the rose window above the staircase. She looks like an angel with these wings of light, super-human. She's gorgeous.

"You weren't at work today."

She says, "I told you last week."

"Told me what?"

I'm standing on the jute mat. Haven't taken my boots off yet. Don't know whether it's worth it. She might just kick me out.

"I had that interview today, for the internship."

"Internship?"

"At the art gallery. I *told* you."

It hits me that I haven't listened to a word she's said all summer. Her voice is like the twittering birds in the trees. We plant shrubs, and her voice blends in with the chipmunks nattering to one another across the yard.

"How did you find my house?"

"Vik gave me the address."

She sucks her teeth, then says, "You might as well come in now that you're here."

I squat down to take off my boots.

Pip says, "Oh, don't worry about that."

"I told your husband I'd take them off."

She throws her head back and laughs. "You mean my *dad*?"

"Oh. Your dad?"

"You think I'm married?" she says. "To a *man*?"

"I…don't know…"

My boots slide off. My socks are greyish green underneath.

"You want something to drink?" she asks.

"Okay. Water."

"Just water?" She starts down the stairs, floating like an angel. "I was about to order dinner. You're welcome to stay, if you don't have plans. My treat."

"Pfft, I guess so!" That was rude. So is this: "I don't get it. Why do you work if you're rich? Is it like…some kind of social experiment?"

She glares at me but smirks as she leads me into the gourmet kitchen. "I pay rent to my parents. They insist. They didn't want me growing into one of those snooty trust fund kids that take money for granted."

I sit on one of the stools by the granite counter and ask, "What do your parents do?"

"They're research scientists, but they both worked their way through college. They didn't have everything handed to them on a silver platter." She takes a bottle of water from the fridge and passes it to me, then opens a drawer and takes out a stack of menus. "What do you feel like? I'm in the mood for Thai."

I feel like I've walked into another dimension. "Wait, you had a job interview?"

She nods as she flips through delivery menus. "For an internship. My parents warned me I'd have trouble finding work with a master's in art history."

"They wanted you to be a scientist too?"

"Or an engineer." She shrugs.

"So why the job in landscaping?"

Another shrug. "It's fun. You get to work outside, work with your hands, see other people's houses—or at least their yards. Meet some interesting people."

She bites her lip as she stares at the Thai menu.

"But if you get the job, the internship, then you're leaving us?"

"It doesn't start until September. Now tell me what you want. Should I order for you?"

I'm bewildered. This house is overwhelming. And seeing Pip all gussied up... I mean, it suits her better than khaki shorts and T-shirts with the sleeves rolled up, but still. It's an adjustment.

And in the back of my mind, I'm seeing dollar signs. Ka-ching! Ka-ching! Ka-ching! Like three bright red cherries on a slot machine.

"I should go." I twist the cap on my water bottle and leave it on the counter. "I'm not dressed for dinner."

Pip laughs. "What are you talking about? We eat meals together every day."

"Yeah, lunch," I say. "Dinner's different."

"It's just delivery. We'll eat over there, in the breakfast nook."

"Padded bench—I'll stain the fabric with my work sweat. You'll never get the stink out."

"Take a shower if it makes you feel better." Pip grabs me by the wrist, and for the first time I feel her strength. I never knew she had it in her. "Devon. Stay. Please?"

I can smell the day's work on me. I can smell the flowery sweetness of Pip's perfume.

This isn't right...but I can't leave her.

She's beaming like you wouldn't believe while she gets me fresh towels and shows me into the guest suite. Her clothes wouldn't have fit me when I was twelve, but she finds a pair of her mother's track pants and one of her father's T-shirts for me to put on when I'm squeaky clean.

I spend longer in the shower than I should, trying to figure out this struggle that's going on inside me. Part of me wants to be here, stay here, eat what the rich people eat. Another part of me is anguished by the thought. Why? I don't know.

All summer I've been oblivious. Now I see it. I see the sparkle in Pip's eyes. She's into me. The lunches, the following me around like a puppy...it all makes sense now. And then I see this house!

The girl's loaded, or at least her parents are. I've won the lottery with this one.

So why do I feel so...anguished?

Her parents' clothes are clean and fresh and smell good enough to eat. I towel-dry my hair and make my way downstairs as Pip pays the delivery driver.

"Here, I'll take those," I cut in, taking the bags of food from her and carrying them to the kitchen. "Jeez, how much did you order?"

"I like leftovers," she tells me. She's already set the table in the breakfast nook. It looks out over a beautiful backyard.

"You've got a pool?"

"Yeah, we don't really use it. Oh, I should have offered you a swim instead of a shower! I didn't even think."

"I don't have a bathing suit anyway."

"Well...that's okay." She sits across from me chewing her bottom lip. Beautiful mouse. She's something special, too good for the likes of me.

Suddenly I know why I can't get settled, why I'm irritable and uncomfortable. "You were talking about *you*!"

She meets my gaze, but she doesn't get it. How do I explain?

"Yesterday," I say. "When you said about the Millington daughter, when you said girls like that don't go for dykes like me, not for the long haul. I can be someone's dirty secret, but not someone you bring home to mumsie. You weren't talking about the Millington girl at all. You were talking about *you*."

Now she gets what I'm saying. I watch her expression shift from blissful to pissed. She lifts plastic take-out containers out of paper bags and slams them on the table. "Is that really what you think of me?"

I'm in trouble, but I'm not sure why.

"You think I'm one of *them*? Me and the Millington girl, two peas in a pod? Oh, I got extra snap peas, by the way, because I know they're your favourite."

"Thanks..."

She growls. "I can't believe you would put me in the same category with them. On the same planet, even!"

"With the Millingtons?"

"Yes, with the Millingtons!"

"Well, you *do* live right down the street from them."

"I may live in a big house, but I am *not* a silver spoon trust fund brat. In case you haven't noticed, I work for a living. I work just as hard as you."

"Yeah, but..."

"But what?"

"Well, I mean, you really don't *have to*."

Her mouth opens, but no sound comes out.

"Like, really?" I ask. "What's the worst that would happen if you didn't pay your rent? Your parents aren't going to throw you out on your ass. I mean, they're just *not*."

Pip purses her lips, then sits down heavily on the bench. For a tiny girl, she makes a big bang.

She starts opening dishes and angrily putting serving utensils in each one. "Go ahead," she says coolly. "Serve yourself."

"I'm sorry," I say, because sorry is always the answer.

"For what?"

"For..."

"I work hard, Devon!" Her eyes brim with tears, but she blinks them away. "Every day I'm trying to prove myself to you, get you to notice me, but it's like I don't even exist. All you see are these society ladies who haven't done a day's work in their lives! What's so great about them?"

"Their money!" I say. "Their *money*. Not them. They're horrible. Do you know how they treat me? How condescending they are?"

"Yes!" Pip says, half laughing. "I'm right there beside you. I get it too. I get it ten times worse!"

I hadn't noticed, but I wasn't about to argue that point.

She sits quietly and bows her head, and I'm not sure whether she's saying grace or collecting her thoughts. "Let's just eat, okay?"

"Okay." I watch her across the table. "I'm sorry, Pip."

"What for this time?"

I wait for her to meet my gaze before saying, "I'm sorry for not noticing. I'm sorry for not seeing you."

She flicks her wrist like it's nothing, but I see that smirk growing across her lips. "Maybe I shouldn't have been so subtle."

"I don't think you actually were. Making me lunch every day? I should have clued in."

"It's been my pleasure," she says, looking deep into my eyes. "It's been my absolute pleasure, Devon."

Dammit, I'm grinning like a fool. I just can't help myself. "Will you be at work tomorrow?"

"No," she says, and before I can ask why she reminds me, "Tomorrow's Saturday. I'll be in on Monday, fresh as a daisy, ready to work."

I don't think I can wait that long to see her again. Two whole days? I'll have to ask her out tomorrow night. Not sure what rich girls do with their weekends, but we'll figure something out.

When Pip looks down at my plate, she rolls her eyes. I haven't put anything on it. She asks, "Do I have to do everything around here?"

She's smiling as she leans across to load me up with Pad Thai. "Tell me the truth, Devon. If you had to choose between love and money, what would you pick?"

"Both," I tell her. "Why choose when you don't have to?"

Pip bites her lip as she dishes out some rice. When she gets to the eggplant, she stops. "Oh. They always put a lot of garlic in this dish. Maybe give it a miss?"

"Why?" I ask. "I'm not allergic."

"I know. Only...I was thinking..." She looks so embarrassed, so shy and insecure. "I was thinking you might want to kiss me later. Kissing and garlic don't mix."

She doesn't even look at me, but she seems to be in actual physical pain as she waits for an answer.

On the inside, I'm rolling my eyes, thinking: Is this for real? This posh girl wants me, and I want her back. Is Pip the magic ingredient my life's been missing?

"Yeah, you're right," I tell her. "No garlic for me."

LOVE UNLEASHED

Karis Walsh

Lydia St. George hurried downstairs to the ground floor of her 1930s Craftsman-style home, pulling her blond hair together and securing it in a haphazard bun with a big clip. She grabbed her camera kit and slowed to a sedate walk as she came out onto the porch. She made it to the sidewalk at the exact moment four large dogs and two tiny ones passed by the tall shrubs lining her yard.

Perfect timing.

She laughed and wove through the web of leashes connecting the yapping animals to her neighbor four houses down. Lydia didn't even know her name—having christened her D.W. for Dog Walker in her mind—but she knew her schedule to the second. She often managed to cross paths with D.W. on her way to work, although her job as a freelance photographer didn't require her to be at the office at a precise time. She made her own schedule for the most part, and she liked it to coincide with D.W.'s.

"How's the reno going?" she asked. She always kept their conversations limited to small talk, about their houses or the weather, preferring not to get more involved than that with anyone right now. Her effort to keep a little distance between them—keeping D.W. in the realm of fantasy and not reality—was helped by D.W.'s inability to stop and chat with her six charges pulling frantically on their way to the park, or the nearest fire hydrant, or wherever they went on these walks.

"The kitchen is almost finished," D.W. said, standing next to

Lydia with her arms spread wide, pulled in different directions by the dogs. Her brown hair glimmered with reddish highlights in the rare Washington sunlight, and her cheeks were pink from the stiff breeze coming off Puget Sound and swirling around Seattle's Queen Anne Hill neighborhood. Eyes as green as cool jade were quick to show expression, whether it was humor as her dogs entangled her feet or joy when she talked about her house, unlike Lydia, who had often been told she was a closed book. "I'm painting it a soft rust color, and the cabinets will be deep yellow with brushed gold handles."

"Sounds lovely," said Lydia, more to prolong their talk than because she was convinced it was a true statement. When D.W. talked about the paint she used in the various rooms she had redecorated, she used words like *soft* and *pale*, but the result still sounded like a riot of color to Lydia. She'd renovated her own house three years ago, when she still worked in finance and had money to spend, but her palette choices had been contemporary and neutral. The contrast was reflected in their clothes as well. Although Lydia didn't have to conform to a certain dress code in her career, she stuck with the business casual clothes in which she felt most comfortable, like her pressed dark denim jeans and crisp white button-down shirt and brown corduroy blazer. D.W. was enveloped in a puffy lime green ski jacket, with faded, frayed jeans and bright red sneakers.

"I like the way the house is coming along," D.W. said with one of her killer smiles. "It'll keep me broke but happy."

Lydia smiled in return, mesmerized by the curve of D.W.'s lips, until she realized she had been silent for too long. She held up her camera bag. "Well, I'd better get to work. Have a good walk."

D.W. let the dogs pull her down the street a few yards before she called over her shoulder. "You should come see it sometime." She had turned her face forward again before Lydia could read her expression.

Go into D.W.'s house? Where they'd be alone, and talk would become more personal? In Lydia's dreams. Well, quite often in her dreams, in fact, but not in real life. She got in her car and sat for a while before starting the engine. This was the first time either one of them had made an overture reaching beyond the confines of their patch of sidewalk. Did it mean anything more than a polite gesture? She drove south to Belltown. Spending time with D.W. was a brush with beauty. Lydia felt electrified by her, energized for her day. She was convinced most of the magic was in the myth, however. They were as different as their decorating choices would suggest, but their costly, run-down houses, like the rain falling on them most autumn days, was something they had in common. Lydia knew D.W. had inherited hers from her grandparents. Otherwise how would she be able to afford a million-dollar neighborhood on a dog walker's budget? Lydia couldn't imagine she made much more than the average teenage babysitter, but she never asked about anything as personal as money. She herself was barely able to afford the home she had once bought so easily. Fueled by stories in the media about high-powered executives who gave up their fancy jobs to pursue some passion like cooking in the French countryside or raising alpacas or growing organic herbs. Everyone in those stories—in front of the camera at least—seemed thrilled by their decision. None of them said how much it sucked to dip into a dwindling savings account every month when they paid the mortgage. Lydia loved her new work, but she missed her old paycheck more than she cared to admit to anyone but herself.

Broke but happy, like D.W. had said. The former all the time, the latter most of it.

Lydia parked in the garage and took an elevator to the Emerald City Photographs offices. She was one of several freelance photographers the company used. Even though most of the others claimed to want to move into the fine art side of photography someday, when they'd be featured in galleries and sell prints for thousands of dollars, competition for the more commercial shoots and commissions was fierce. Lydia had been at the top of her field one day and the bottom of this new one the next. She was still clawing her way up. Unlike the others, she had no interest in the artsier side of her medium. She loved taking pictures of everyday life on the city streets and finding just the right angle to show off a mountain or lake or ferryboat. Some people might say the word *commercial* with a sneer, but she was proud of what she did. She saw the beauty in the world around her, and she had a gift for capturing it at the exact right moment.

No matter how good she was, though, her photos needed to be seen before they'd be bought. And in order to be seen, they had to make it past her boss. He had his favorites among the freelancers, and she hadn't become one of them yet. She was determined to do so. Mainly because her bank account was rapidly losing its padding.

"Hi, Mr. Jenkins," she said, popping her head in his office. "Have any jobs for me today?"

"Lydia, come in. I was hoping you'd be here today. I have something better than a job in here."

She went inside the office, skeptical about what could be better than more work and more money. Jenkins was sitting on the floor behind his sofa, and she could just see the top of his balding head and his metal glasses over the back of it.

"A box of puppies," she said. How appropriate for the office, she added mentally. She walked over and sat on the couch. She supposed she should comment on their looks, like she would if a new mother showed pictures of her kid. "Um, they're cute."

"Aren't they? Do you want one?"

Yep. Should've seen that coming. Lydia frantically searched for a reason to say no. She didn't have a landlord to forbid pets, and her yard was fenced and big enough for one of these little things. Allergies? A long-held fear of dogs after being attacked when she was five? She had a couple of small scars from skateboarding accidents that might do as proof.

"You were the first person I thought of when the wife said I had to give them away. You take such fantastic pictures of dogs, I knew you had to be an animal lover."

"Oh, well…who isn't?" Lydia watched the box teeter back and forth as the puppies cascaded over one another, all wagging tails and grinning faces.

Jenkins continued. "And if you take one, we can have family reunions. I'm sure my Sophia would love to have her baby visit as often as possible."

Aha. Lydia had been looking at this from the wrong angle. If she took one of the puppies—and how hard could it be to take care of one?—she'd have an in with the boss. An invitation to his house, a chance to chat about her ideas for photo shoots. What better way to break into the old boy's network than by adopting one of the old boy's dogs?

"Sure, I'd love to have one." Lydia tried to decide how to choose from the mass of squirming animals. One small white dog with brown ears sat squished in the corner as if disdainful of all the play and fuss around him. He stared at her and she could see his small bottom teeth. She pointed at him. "That one."

"Excellent choice. He'll never be a show dog with his underbite, but he's smart as can be. He'll be a great companion."

Jenkins scooped up the puppy and put him in her arms. "Have you had a Jack Russell before?"

"No." Nor any other breed.

"They have strong personalities. You'll love them. Just keep anything you don't want chewed to bits out of his reach." Jenkins laughed. "Sophia tore up all the linoleum out of our laundry room last weekend."

Lydia managed a weak smile, but it didn't last long. The puppy gave a low growl, and she sighed. "I suppose I should get him home," she said. She had taken one of the dogs as a way to improve her earning potential with the company to keep paying for her house. Now the same dog was about to destroy the rooms she'd carefully decorated. Not exactly an O. Henry story, but close enough.

❖

The next morning, Lydia was out the door at her usual time—at D.W.'s usual time—but with the puppy in tow, wearing the new harness and leash she'd bought at the pet store yesterday. She had also bought feed bowls, bags of food, and any toy that looked like it might deter him from chewing on her furniture. He had spent the night next to her on her pillow instead of in his new dog bed, but he still regarded her with a skeptical look, as if he wasn't convinced she had the proper credentials for dog ownership. She was certain she didn't.

"Mind if we join you?" she asked, coming out from the shrub and into the midst of chaos as six dogs converged on her puppy with eager sniffs and tail wags.

"Of course," D.W. said, reining in her charges and dropping to one knee to greet the newcomer. "Did you just get him? What a sweet puppy! Who's a cutie pie? What's your name, little guy?"

Lydia hadn't mastered the art of baby talk, but D.W. had it down. One word from her, and the dog was smiling with his full set of lower teeth showing. His expression when he looked at Lydia was closer to a disdainful sneer, especially when she had spent fifteen minutes trying to untangle his harness and fit him into it. Who could possibly resist her? Lydia was ready to roll on her back for a tummy rub, too.

"His name is Jack," Lydia said. She didn't want to admit she'd been thinking of him as the Jack Russell in a generic sort of way, although he was obviously too much of a character to be generic.

"Jack the Jack Russell," D.W. said, standing up again. "Should be easy to remember. I'm Alex, by the way."

"Lydia." They shook hands, and Lydia didn't want to let go. She thought she had been electrified by her brief morning chats with Alex, but they were mere sparks compared to her touch. She sighed as they started walking in the center of the pack of dogs. She had wanted to keep D.W. as her fantasy, talking to her enough to keep her voice and looks fresh in her mind, but she needed some help with her new puppy. Now she knew her real name, and soon they'd have to talk about something deeper than renovation projects or the likelihood of sun breaks over the weekend. Her image of Alex would change, and she'd wake up from the pleasant dreams she'd had about D.W., the virtual stranger.

Although she definitely preferred the name Alex to D.W.

She kept their conversation neutral at first, asking question after question about puppy care and training. She wouldn't remember half of what she was hearing, but she hoped she'd retain enough to get through the days ahead. Jack strutted along in front of her, unintimidated by the big dogs on either side of him.

She was planning to keep to impersonal topics, but her curiosity won out. "What do you do?" she asked as they went through a gate and into a dog park. "I mean, besides dog walking. Not that you'd need to do something else, because I'm sure it's a rewarding career."

Alex laughed. "I only do this part-time, mostly to help out some of our neighbors. Two of the dogs are mine, and as long as I'm walking them I might as well take the others. I write magazine articles for a living."

"Really? What kind?" Lydia wondered if Alex had ever used her photos in an article. The thought gave her a surprising sort of thrill. She always liked seeing her pictures in an ad or magazine, but having them illustrate words Alex had written was somehow intimate and exciting.

"Mostly travel, gardening, and home décor. I also do a column answering questions from dog owners."

"Do you have a hotline? I'll be calling it at all hours."

"I'll give you my private number. You can use it any time." Alex gave her a wink and knelt down to unsnap the leashes from her dogs' collars. Lydia felt her stomach twist at the suggestive tone in Alex's voice. Maybe she hadn't been the only one who daydreamed about those short meetings in front of her house.

She let Jack off his leash, and he trotted after his new friends. Alex tossed a ball, and the whole swarm of dogs chased it. Lydia set her bag on a nearby bench and took out her camera, her eyes never leaving Alex and the dogs. She started snapping shots. She started with the dogs, capturing them as they played and ran, but soon she was following Alex and shooting her from different angles.

When they had talked about their houses or the weather, Lydia had focused on their disparate looks. She was urban, Alex appeared earthier. She was neutrals and clean, clear lines, while Alex was a rainbow of colors meshed together. Somehow, though, looking at her through the lens of the camera gave Lydia a whole new perspective, letting her see beyond the surface to the people they were. She took a picture of Alex's profile and imagined her sitting in front of her computer writing articles to inform people, to share her passions with readers. Like Lydia did with her photos. She took another of Alex from behind, her arm in mid-throw and her weight on her toes. She had been worried about learning Alex's personal story because she had thought it might spoil her fantasy, but she had been wrong. Hearing how she helped her neighbors, loved her old house, and cared enough to answer every question Lydia asked about her dog only made her more beautiful than she had been before—something Lydia hadn't thought possible.

The walk back to their street was slower after the dogs had spent their energy playing in the park. Lydia carried Jack for the last quarter mile.

"Do you want to come see my kitchen?" Alex asked when they reached her house.

"Absolutely." Lydia didn't even hesitate. She had kept Alex at a distance for too long, and for the wrong reasons. An unexpected puppy had finally forced her to get over her doubt and allow the attraction she had been feeling all along to shift to a deeper level.

She followed Alex through the hallway and into her kitchen. Warm rusts, golds, and mauves blended subtly through the room, from the walls to the cabinets to the enamel cookware on the stove. The color of sunsets, quiet dinners eaten together, nights spent holding hands and sitting close. Lydia had created a certain modern look with her décor. Alex had made a home, a place to be shared.

"It's perfect," she said.

"Now it is." Alex walked over to her and lifted her hand, twisting a strand of Lydia's hair around her finger. Lydia felt a trembling, but she wasn't sure if it was her or Alex. Or both, together.

"I have a confession," Alex continued. "I pictured you in here when I was designing it. The gold in your hair, the bronze in your eyes. You're the finishing touch I was hoping for."

Lydia opened her mouth to speak, but she couldn't find words. In her mind, she saw the two of them in a photo, looking at each other and really seeing each other for the first time. Standing close, leaning forward.

She let go of the mental image as soon as Alex's lips touched hers, and she focused instead on the sensations rippling through her. A soft explosion of tongues and warmth and pent-up passion rocked her, and she slid her hands under Alex's jacket and around her waist, pulling them closer. She dimly felt Jack near her ankle, chewing on her jeans, but pressure from Alex's hips against hers drove all her cares away. He could shred the damned things if he wanted—because of him she was here, in Alex's arms, so he had free rein to chew on anything, anytime.

Alex pulled away and smiled at her with a look of wonder in her expressive, lovely eyes. "I've wanted to be with you for so long. I can't believe you're finally here."

Lydia kissed her gently on the mouth. "I thought you were only a dream," she said. "I didn't realize until now, you're my dream come true."

BAT GIRL

Laney Webber

Rae passed me the hose and went inside the greenhouse to wait on two women who were balancing about a dozen small potted red geraniums between them. It was my second summer at MacAuliffe's Nursery. I worked weekends with Rae, who told me Jerry MacAuliffe hired her "right out of high school, back at the beginning of time." She laughed when she said it, and the lines around her eyes and mouth punctuated her laughter. Rae has a great laugh.

My first day at the greenhouse, she wiped her hand on a rag hanging from the belt loop of her cargo jeans and held it out to me. She told me her name was Rae, she was gay, she loved being gay and didn't want me to walk around wondering if she was gay. Then she asked me if I was gay.

I told her I identified as lesbian.

"Good to know." Then she showed me around.

My first summer, she taught me how to pinch back petunias and deadhead the dozens of ivy geraniums hanging in the greenhouse. We took turns waiting on customers and taking care of the plants. She told me about her marketing job, the diner she used to own in Florida, and moving back to Massachusetts after she caught her ex cheating on her.

I told her about growing up the youngest of six kids, how I used to pretend to be a librarian long before I ever was one and how

I needed to be around living things after my mother died three years ago.

We found that we both loved Scrabble, root beer, and old pickup trucks.

Today we were taking down some tired-looking fuchsias and moving them to a shadier location. It was hot, and the forecast called for at least two more days in the mid-nineties.

"Can you carry four at a time?"

Rae had two in each hand, and a line of sweat ran down her neck onto the wet blue bandana she used to try to keep cool.

"They're pretty heavy. One at a time for me," I called over to her.

"So how's that new girl you've been seeing? Darcy? Marcy? There are so many I just can't keep them straight." Rae laughed as she passed by me on another trip to the greenhouse.

"It *was* Darcy, but not anymore. Things weren't working out." I reached up and hooked the planters on the rack in the shady barn behind the greenhouse. I wiped my sweaty forehead with the back of my forearm.

"You go through them like water, don't you, kiddo? You okay?"

We walked back to the greenhouse together.

"Yeah, I'm okay. I just get tired sometimes, putting myself out there. Damn, it's freakin' hot."

"How about after we lug the rest of these suckers out back I go down the street to the Creamery and get us a couple of root beer floats?"

"Oh, that sounds like heaven." I let out a small groan and licked my lips.

Rae looked at me for a second like she was going to say something.

"What?" I said.

"Nothing."

"No, really, what?"

"If you must know, you're a bit of a sight. You've got dirt all up and down your arms and on your face. Let's get the rest of these done, then you wash up and keep a lookout for customers and I'll go to the Creamery."

"Got it, boss!" I joked.

"Not boss." Rae went past me with four more fuchsias.

Three more hot and heavy trips with the fuchsias and we were done. The heat kept the customers away, and we were able to sit and relax for a while with our root beer floats.

Last summer I asked Rae if she was seeing anyone, and she looked away for a minute, then told me that her heart "was pretty particular," and I got the impression she didn't like to talk about her personal life.

A hint of a sea breeze brushed over us during the afternoon, and we tended to small jobs around the greenhouse. I watched Rae fix a broken latch on the door while I watered the flats of yellow and orange marigolds out front for the third time that day. I liked to watch her hands when she worked. They were strong, capable hands. She looked over and smiled.

"I think that's it for today."

Rae said this at the end of each Saturday and Sunday. It was my signal to bring in the flag and go hook the chain across the driveway and flip the sign to "Closed." She took care of the money and locked up the greenhouse and the barn.

"See you tomorrow, Jess."

"Iced coffee?" I asked.

"Oh yeah."

The driveway chain was my baby, so I unhooked it to let us drive our cars out, then hooked it back up. Rae stuck her hand out her window and gave me a thumbs-up as she took a right at the end of the street.

A wall of heat hit me in the face as I climbed the third and final flight of stairs to my apartment. I fell in love with this little studio apartment in one of the historic sea captains' houses that line Newburyport's High Street. But I didn't know that during a heat wave, the building turned into a four-thousand-square-foot pizza oven.

I took a cool shower, ate some pasta salad, and read my new Ellen Hart mystery novel while the air conditioner cooled down my tiny space. My eyeballs started twirling after page thirty, and I turned off the light and went to sleep.

I woke to a ruffle of air across my face and the sound of something banging into the blinds above the air conditioner. I turned on the light, picked up my alarm clock as my weapon of choice, and crept over to the window. A triangular-shaped handkerchief-looking thing was draped over the top of the curtain rod. Otherwise, everything looked normal. I climbed on my desk chair and peered under the valance. The handkerchief chirped. I rocked back on the chair.

"It's a freakin' bat! No! No! No!" I jumped off the chair and staggered backward. My heart was jumping around in my chest. Bats and I do not get along. I had a bad bat experience when I was seven, and when I was fourteen a bat clonked me in the head while I was walking through a field. My best friend at the time said I must have had mosquitoes near my hair. *Right.*

There was no one there but me. *Time to be brave, Jess.* The bat was trying to get a better hold on the curtain rod. My head felt woozy and my heart banged in my chest. I backed up four steps into the kitchen area and grabbed an oven mitt. If I thought about it, I would chicken out.

I unlocked and opened my apartment door and the fire escape door in the hallway that led to a rotten deck and stairway. I wanted no impediments in my way when I had the bat. The desk chair didn't seem sturdy enough, so I walked three steps into the living room area and pushed the big orange recliner over to the desk, climbed on it, reached out and grabbed the bat with one hand, and wound the curtain round and round my hand. I took the entire assembly off the window—curtains, bat, and all—and ran like hell out the back door. The bat was chirping blue murder. I dropped my bat package on the deck, spun around, and closed and locked the door.

I shut my apartment door and slid down the inside of the door until my ass hit the floor. My tank top and shorts were soaked with sweat. I stayed there until my heart rate returned to normal, then took a cool shower and went back to bed. Then I got up and walked around listening for chirping sounds. I opened *The Lost Women of Lost Lake* and started reading again. I tried to list all the things I know about bats, but it didn't help. That's the thing with irrational fears. They're irrational.

I turned off the light. I heard something. I turned the light back on. Nothing. I turned off the light again. I thought I saw a shadow. I turned the light on again. Another bat!

"Shit! Shit, shit, shit!"

This one was flying around the apartment. I jumped out of bed, crouched low, grabbed my phone, and went out in the hall. My eyes never left the bat. I didn't want it to hide in there somewhere. It stopped flying and was resting on the other curtain rod. I couldn't do it again. My hands were shaking as I scrolled through my phone. Rae told me once if I couldn't sleep to check and see if she was on Facebook and she'd play a game of Scrabble with me. I sent her a text.

Hey, are you up?

I kept my eyes on the bat. My phone vibrated a few seconds later.

Yup, you ok?

Got a bat flying around my apt. Hate bats

Be right over. Street number?

106 High St Apt 6 up on 3rd flr

Hang tight kiddo, be there in 15

I'm sure it was only fifteen minutes, but it seemed like an hour had passed when I heard Rae climbing the steps. The bat was swooping around the apartment again.

"Where's the bugger?" Rae whispered.

I heard her take the last step and let out a big sigh.

"That's some haul."

"Thanks for coming. I don't want to lose him, her, whatever. It's on the curtain rod at the far end of the room," I said.

Rae stepped into the apartment. She was wearing a big floppy straw hat and a pair of bright yellow rubber boots. She put a tennis racket and a cardboard box on the kitchen table, pulled a pair of leather gardening gloves from the box, and put them on. My eyes seesawed between Rae and the bat. I put a hand over my mouth to hold in the laughter climbing up my throat.

"You look adorable." Her outfit distracted me from my fear for a minute.

"Stop it. You stay out in the hall, and I'll catch the bugger. The boots? Are you laughing at the boots? I have a thing about my feet. Don't ask. Does that door in the hall lead outside? I don't want to bring it down all those stairs."

"Roger that." I saluted Rae and smiled. "I'll open the door and stay in the hall." I felt so much better now that she was here.

Rae looked me up and down and smiled back. "You look pretty adorable yourself, kid. Here goes nothing."

I backed farther into the hallway and felt my face grow warm. It was at that moment that I realized I was standing in the hall in a tank top and underpants. My face grew hot.

Rae pointed to the orange recliner.

I nodded.

She slid the chair toward the window, and the bat took off flying again. It swooped around Rae's head. She stood very still in the middle of the room. I, on the other hand, was bobbing and weaving like a prize fighter out in the hallway.

The bat clung to the handle of a kitchen cabinet. Rae picked up the tennis racket and the box and took two steps, brought the box up with one hand, and shimmied the bat into the box with the tennis racket. She kept the racket on top of the box as she moved toward the door. I held the door open for her, ready for her quick retreat from my apartment, and slammed it behind her. I sank to the floor next to the door, forgetting that Rae was still out on the rotten back deck.

"Crap!" I stood up and opened the door. "I'm so sorry, Rae."

Rae stepped into the hallway and deposited the bat-catching paraphernalia in the corner, along with her floppy hat and gloves. She stepped out of her yellow boots.

"Got a root beer by any chance? I'm a little sweaty."

I put my hand on her arm.

"Yes, I do. And ice too. Thank you so much. I don't know what I would've done."

"Can I wash up a bit?" She held up her hands.

"Sure thing." I pointed to the bathroom and got a mug out of the cabinet.

"How are you doing?" she asked over the sound of running water.

"Better. So much better. A little afraid to turn out the lights again, to be honest."

Rae walked out of the bathroom and stood in front of me. She reached forward and tucked a piece of hair behind my ear.

"Rae, I don't know how I can go to work tomorrow and not think about you in your outfit." I hoped my words would distract me from the tingling sensation that went from my ear where she touched me and into the rest of my body. *It's Rae*, I reminded myself. *It's probably just a reaction to fearing the bat.*

"Well, I don't think I want to get the picture of you in this outfit out of my mind."

Rae's eyes traveled over my body.

"You don't?" I whispered. I could feel my body respond to her gaze.

She shook her head slowly, and stepped closer.

"I don't, Jess."

Her lips were inches from mine. In one motion she wrapped one arm around my waist and cupped the side of my face, drawing my lips to hers. She kissed me like she knew everything about me, and my knees buckled. She pulled me closer, and I wrapped my arms around her neck.

She kissed the corner of my mouth, waiting for my answer.

I pressed the full length of my body against her and found her mouth with mine. Her lips were perfect. My tongue parted them and she let me into her mouth. I backed up against the edge of the bed, and her body never left mine.

She brought her hands up to either side of my face, and our kisses slowed.

"I told you my heart was particular."

"Yes, and…"

"Jess, I fell for you the first day I met you. When you sat next to those petunias and asked me if I thought it hurt them to be pinched back—my heart was yours."

"And I thought that you weren't interested in me at all." I reached up and touched Rae's temple. "You're so beautiful," I whispered.

She ran her hand down just below the small of my back. I arched in response.

"I'm still a little leery about sleeping here tonight." I kissed her earlobe, then drew it into my mouth.

"I wasn't planning on letting you sleep." Rae's voice was raspy.

I took her hand and sat on the bed. "Come here."

"I'll come when you're good and ready." Rae's laugh was soft. I love her laugh.

The Aisle of Lesbos

Allison Wonderland

I know the folks who run this food pantry like the volunteers to say *Excuse me* when shoppers bump into them—especially if they get rear-ended—but I'm in the market for a more creative apology."

"Um…I like the way you make ends meet?"

To show her appreciation, Yvette steps forward and hugs me.

To show mine, I reciprocate, wrapping my arms around her like a label on a soup can.

But as quickly as I'm overjoyed, I'm overtaken by a feeling of anger. "How long has it been?" I demand, because I'm aware of how long it's been: six months. Before Yvette can correct me, I continue, "One day you're standing beside me in the fruit-and-breakfast aisle commiserating about the total absence of female cereal mascots. The next I'm standing alone shelving crushed pineapple—emphasis on crushed."

"I got canned," Yvette informs me, and there's no hint of mirth or worth in her voice. "Some volunteers are former clients paying it forward. But future clients paying it backward?" Her eyes dart toward her shopping cart. "That's not cutting edge. That's chopping block." After a moment, she meets my eyes. "Well? Aren't you shocked by my demotion?"

"Actually, I'm more shocked by your devotion—or lack thereof." I pluck a box of macaroni and cheese off the utility cart and give it a sinister shake, causing its contents to rattle roughly. But there's a shopper coming down the aisle, so I abstain from decking Yvette and instead place the box onto the shelf where it belongs.

"We're running a food pantry here, not a gauntlet," Yvette sasses me when the client passes us. "Besides, you've never mac'ed on me before." Her eyes narrow until they resemble slits in a piecrust.

I copy the compression. I'd ask what she means, but—

"Don't worry. That's just another one of my cheesy jokes," Yvette assures me, and her elbow-noodle smile, which normally causes an identical curve to form on my face, only makes me angrier.

"Worry? Why would I worry," I wonder, yanking another box of processed pasta off the utility cart, "that you're hundreds of days late and thousands of dollars short?"

"Thanks for making a federal charity case out of it," Yvette huffs. She slouches against the ketchup-red handle of her shopping cart, which causes her shirt to pucker and her hair to hunch against her rounded shoulders.

I've missed her hair. It has the tint and glint of black olives and is so perfectly curly it makes rotini look like spaghetti. It's not that I've ever wanted to noodle with it or anything. It's just a welcome contrast to my own convoluted curls, which always obscure the letters on my name badge when I wear my hair down, creating a weird *Wheel of Fortune* puzzle that is hopelessly unsolvable.

Well, almost hopelessly unsolvable.

Hearing every word I haven't said, Yvette looks up from her cart.

In unison we grin, thinking back to that day a year and a half ago when she came in for volunteer orientation. As the manager guided her through the aisles of sparsely stocked shelves the color of scratching posts, I watched Yvette from what was my post that afternoon: the fridges and freezers along the rear wall. She froze when she reached me and trained her eyes on my chest. I knew right away what she was looking at—since there's nothing to see in that area except my name tag.

"Volunteer Greer," Yvette read, and something about the way she said it made me feel like one of the Garbage Pail Kids.

But not in a bad way.

On her first day the following week, I forgot my badge at home and she forgot my name. "Yo, Gert!" she greeted me.

"Blueberry or plain?" I queried, and cracked a smile.

Yvette cracked up. "Neither. It gives me culture shock." She fastened her badge to her blouse. "Garson, right?"

"Greer."

"Like I said—Garson. That's your namesake, isn't it?"

"Yes!" I bellowed, then quickly mellowed. "Sorry. It's just that no one under the age of eighty-five has ever made the connection before."

"I wasn't even made until eighty-five," she shared. "You?"

"Eighty-two."

"Close enough. Oh my goodness, I love *When Ladies Meet*," she enthused, and I must have looked confused, wondering whether I'd misheard or misread what she'd said. She could just as easily have declared *I love when ladies meet* and I'd be none the wiser, since lowercase letters are undetectable by the human ear.

But Yvette put me wise. "Have you seen that movie with her and Joan Crawford?"

"No, but I've seen it with at least two dozen members of the senior center."

Yvette chuckled. It sounded pithy and posh, just like Joan's.

"That's where I work," I added, worried she'd think I had some sort of old fogey fetish.

But to my delight, Yvette was equally elderly oriented: She worked in a nursing home.

"*Let Us Be Gay*," I exclaimed, and from her expression I could tell she thought I was flakier than instant mashed potatoes.

"That's another old movie I like," I clarified, wishing I were in black and white so she couldn't see me turn red. "It's not very well-known. Norma Shearer is in it. Maybe you've seen her in *The Women*?"

"Gotta love *The Women*," she said.

Gotta love the women, I heard.

"Greer!" I hear, and veer back to the present. But it isn't Yvette who's trying to get my attention. It's Richard, another volunteer, specifically the one who replaced Yvette. "Line's backing up," he calls from the front of the pantry, where a long table is set up for bagging clients' groceries.

"You'd better go help those folks put food on the table," Yvette suggests.

"Just call me the Bag Lady. No, don't, actually. That was…"

"Insensitive?" Yvette supplies, rolling her eyes. Her shopping cart goes next, down the aisle, taking her with it.

I head up front, the utility cart thoughtfully screeching in protest because it knows that I can't. When I reach the table I begin sorting the clients' selections. I have to ensure they've taken only as much as they're allotted: two beverages, two breakfast items, eggs or butter but not both, etcetera. Whenever I can get away with it, though, I let shoppers take a little extra, if they need it. I'm Volunteer Greer, after all, not Two-Can Sam.

Yvette was the same way.

When it's her turn to check out, whatever's in her cart, I'll let her take everything.

But I won't let her take off.

So when the line thins out enough to require only one volunteer for the job, I ask Richard to take over the task of shelving the dry goods. Now if Yvette wants to leave, she'll have to get past me first.

From the front, I can see her from the back. She's in the soup aisle—where else would she be, considering that she's in the soup? I wish she'd said something. I mean, I knew she wasn't well-off, but I didn't know she was borderline on-the-breadline. What, did she think I wouldn't care? Or worse—that I would?

When Yvette approaches a few minutes later, she has this leaden look about her: a cross between chunky peanut butter and pears in heavy syrup. Or, in classic movie-speak, Apple Annie and Stella Dallas. I wish I could lighten her mood.

And her load.

"You know I didn't come here to see you," she says, setting a box of saltines onto the table.

"I know," I reply. *But how come you came when you knew I'd be here?* I almost add, but I can tell from her averted eyes that she's anticipated this logical add-on and wishes I wouldn't mention it.

Yvette looks up, and when she sees a smile instead of a smirk, I see her relax a little—smoother peanut butter, lighter syrup.

She hands me a plain canvas bag, then a large blue one, the kind that's constructed from recycled plastic. Front and center are parallel equality bars—yellow, like pineapple tidbits.

This time, only a smirk will work.

"See? The bag says it all: We're equals. So if you're embarrassed because you think there are overwhelming class differences between us now, don't be. I'm not. I know you have class and I don't."

Yvette responds with a blunt half-laugh, the kind people use when they want to acknowledge you but not encourage you.

"How's your mom?" I ask, bagging a canister of quick oats with all the speed of a movie on pause.

"Well, as much as I'd like to restrict the letters MS to feminist magazines, I don't think I'll ever be that empowered." She lowers her eyes, picks at the label on a can of alphabet soup. "My boss sure didn't mind when I worked overtime at the nursing home, but when I started doing a lot more nursing *at* home? I shouldn't be *there*. And I definitely shouldn't be there for her in her hours of need. So he cut mine—down to zero."

Her shrug is casual.

As in *casualty*.

"I guess 'It gets better' are words to live by, but they're not exactly words to live *on*. Unless you can, you know, eat your words."

A smile jiggles her lips. "It's a good thing we're not both suffering from 'food insecurity,' because I have no words for you, Greer."

"You will when ladies meet again," I assure her, setting the packed sack of parity into her shopping cart.

Yvette studies the equality sign, which, thanks to the selfless contortionist act the bag performed to protect the provisions, is now an approximation thereof. "How do you know?" she asks eventually.

"Because," I answer immediately, "*aisle* be seeing you."

Yvette looks at me. I look back. Her eyes are the color of a treasure chest, and the gold in them reminds me of the wrapper on a Twix bar.

Or an almond Kiss.

After a moment, she returns, "*Aisle* be back."

❖

"I text and ask if you want to get together and watch Barbara Stanwyck in *To Please a Lady* and you text back: *Can't, sorry, I'm going through some stuff right now.* Then I never see or hear from you again, so apparently, you prefer to displease a lady."

Yvette tilts her head back, face pinched like a paper airplane. We're sitting in front of my TV and she's resting on my lap, elbows propped atop my knees, the way Lucy leans on Schroeder's piano in the Peanuts comic strip.

"I wish I were at the food pantry right now," Yvette grouses. "Then I could shop till you drop the subject." Her curls swish against my thighs and she sighs.

Bette Davis eyes us from the screen.

Please, I've prayed to no designated deity ever since Yvette stopped coming to the pantry, *let us be gay again.* But "I don't know why I thought we could just pick up where we left off," I resume rambling. "They don't call it recon-silly-ation for nothing." I didn't realize it at the time of our reunion, I guess because I was too delighted to feel slighted, but in the two weeks since, I've found that I need closure before I can be open to repairing our friendship.

"Come on, Greer—you may love when ladies meet like I do, but I doubt you love when ladies don't make ends meet. Like I do. Or don't do."

"Volunteerism is not a form of discrimination," I reply, plucking a pretzel from the bowl beside us. "You actually thought I wouldn't want to associate with you just because you got...pauperized? I don't buy it."

"Why not?" Yvette snaps. "You can afford it."

Suddenly, she sits up, then gets up.

For an instant, I'm tempted to channel Joan Crawford's hardened harlot in *Rain* and let her leave, because I'm tired of being on her well-to-do list.

But when I see the tears jerk at her eyes, I stand and grab her hand, thrusting my perspiring palm against hers.

Yvette doesn't look at me, instead presenting her profile as a compromise. I see her throat ripple as she swallows hard, and I wonder if her mouth feels as dry as graham crackers the way mine does.

Behind us, Bette utters her character's coquettishly convenient excuse to eschew intimacy in *Cabin in the Cotton*: "I'd like to kiss you, but—"

"I fell on hard times," Yvette interrupts her. "Then I fell for you. Well, not in that order, but you get the picture."

And what a queer picture it is. "Wait a minute," I implore, reaching toward the floor and fumbling for the remote. Eager to trade in the familiar black and white for a modern Technicolor rainbow, I press pause. "Yvette, are you giving me closure *and* an opening?"

Gradually, she comes into soft, sharp focus.

I watch as the fear in her eyes shades into relief, then upgrades to affection.

I wish I had better…not gaydar, but…affection detection? Yes, because I can tell it's been there a while—maybe as long as mine.

I feel my lips twisting like a wire coat hanger as I swing like Mommie Dearest's ax between *It's about time* and *It's too soon*.

A lengthy and lovely silence follows—the kind that lets us look at each other, lets us listen to each other's heartbeats, lets us be gay together.

Yvette's thumb twitches, and when I look down at our allied hands, I realize I've been holding hers so hard, it's gone ghostly. I let go, watch, wait until the color comes back. She looks much prettier in apple butter brown than potato soup white.

She'd look even prettier in a close-up shot.

So when the silence quiets down, I query, "Hey, Yvette, where do Bette Davis fans go when they get scared?"

"Hmmm…*The Petrified Forest*?" Yvette ventures.

"No, they go straight—" I stop, snicker, start over: "They go gaily into my arms."

For a moment, she simply stands there, like an actress frozen in a publicity still. But then the image leaps to life as the cerise crease of Yvette's lips stretches into a smile, and her smile zooms in on mine.

From the film canister curve of her hips to her lips' sweet surprise—tangier than Lemonheads and juicier than Starburst— Yvette's kisses are worth their weight in Harlow gold.

And worth the wait.

Her hair smells of summer rain and autumn leaves, and I plunge my hands into the rich curls.

Meanwhile, my insides have begun melting like scorched celluloid and my thoughts now reflect those of a fallen woman as opposed to those of a little girl lost.

As the kiss fades out and proud, a wealth of colors flickers behind my eyelids: jungle red, Oscar gold, marquee orange.

"So," I say, when we separate, "if I said 'Desire me,' you'd know I wasn't talking about that Greer Garson movie, right?"

Yvette answers with a smug mug that gives her more face value than any of those ballsy big-screen broads. "Listen, Greer, I know I'm down and out, but are you down for going out with me?" She tops off the invitation with a kiss to the top of my hand. "See, now that's how you live from hand to mouth," she reveals, fingers fondling the skin where her lipstick made me a marked woman.

When taken together, our laughter sounds a lot like a humoresque.

Better that than a torch song.

Best to accept her invitation. "Yvette, I am absolutely down for going out with you. I've always wanted to pursue a relationship with a chum who makes the bum in *My Man Godfrey* look like a gazillionaire."

Yvette regards me as though I'm a few frames shorts of a film reel. I much prefer her gaze when it's Mildred Piercing.

"Sorry. Was that in poor taste?"

"Yes," she answers, draping her arms around me like a stole. "Fortunately, I can't say the same for your kisses."

❖

"The purpose of a man may be to love a woman, but the purpose of a woman is to love a mandarin orange." So saying, I cast a couple of cans into Yvette's cart. "Hey, can we watch *The Women* again tonight? I always get so much inspiration from that scene where Paulette Goddard says to Norma Shearer, 'You should have licked that girl where she licked you.'"

"Who's the needy one now?" Yvette challenges, but her face is already redder than the handle of her shopping cart. "Bette Davis vows never to be below the title; you promise always to go below the belt."

"Yet I still get top billing in your life," I counter, and follow her to the one at the front of the pantry.

"Underprivileged girl under privileged girl," Yvette quips, removing a cup of whipped yogurt from her cart. "We're equals, Greer, remember? I shouldn't be beneath you."

"Oh, make like Norma's noggin in *Marie Antoinette* and knock it off, would you? Besides, that's *your* position, Yvette. Mine is that being with you is a privilege."

"Right," she returns, and at first I think she's correcting me. But one look at the abundance of pride in her eyes tells me she's actually in total agreement. A ripple of desire, reminiscent of the thirties 'do dubbed *finger waves*, undulates under my skin. Who knew concurring could be so alluring?

But then, nobody ever could resist the allure of the girl next door, could they?

I extend my hand for her next item. But this time, Yvette's not giving—she's taking.

I treasure the warm look in her eyes as she replies, "I see your hand out and I accept."

So here we are, on the cusp of the credits, a couple of film lovers who are starting where others would end and forsaking all others for a pocketful of miracles.

And maybe one day, if I'm not getting *too* far ahead of myself, a catered affair of the vow-exchanging variety.

Bette Davis promised us all this, and heaven too.

And you'd better believe *aisle* be Bette—well, ready—for anything.

KISS CAM

Lisa Moreau

I'm not stupid. Suze isn't walking into Staples Center with a huge smile on her face because of me. The smile is for the courtside seat tickets clutched in my sweaty palm. Suze loves the Sparks, LA's women's professional basketball team. Me, I couldn't care less about sports or a stadium filled with 90 percent lesbians. I only have eyes for Suze. That should be a love song, if it isn't already. So when the LGBT Center had a Sparks raffle, I dished out five hundred big ones. It was for a good cause, and I do mean more than trying to get my ex back. Did I forget to mention Suze is my ex? We, or rather she, broke up six months ago, but we stayed friends. At the time, she said she needed "space," which doesn't make a whole lotta sense considering we've seen each other every day and nothing's changed except that we're not having sex. So the way I figure it, all we need to do is kiss and make up, and we'll be back to where we were six months ago. And that's where my friend, Miko, who runs the Staples Center Kiss Cam, comes in. They point the camera at two unsuspecting spectators and flash the video on a humongous screen with everyone whooping and hollering for them to kiss. Some are embarrassed, while others really go for it, but essentially everyone kisses the person they're paired with since the audience is so relentless. See, what Suze doesn't know is, Miko will point the camera at us, which will result in a lip-lock that'll set us both on fire. Yeah, I thought it was a genius idea, too.

"Wow, courtside seats. How much did you say you paid for the raffle ticket, babe?" We still call each other babe. See what I mean? We're practically a couple, aside from the physical stuff. Suze sits in a folding chair with me beside her. Seems like they'd have something nicer than flimsy outdoor Ikea furniture on courtside. Guess I was picturing something like first class with waiters bringing us cool towels and chocolate sundaes. But I'm too excited to complain.

"Five hundred dollars." I puff out my chest when Suze's eyes get big. "It was for a good cause." I furrow my brow, hoping she doesn't ask what that is, 'cause for the life of me I can't remember at the moment. But she doesn't. She's too busy gawking at her favorite player, Linda, or Leslie, or something, one of the tall gals over there bouncing the ball.

I rest my arm on the back of Suze's chair, almost touching her muscular shoulders but not quite, and lean in. "Do you want something from the concession stand before the game starts?"

She turns and almost swipes my nose with hers we're so close. "A Sprite would be nice."

"You sure you don't want something with caffeine?" I wince the moment it's out of my mouth. Why would I want her to partake in a stimulant unless it's to stay awake all night having torrid sex? But her mind doesn't go there.

"I like Sprite. Thanks, babe." She squeezes my knee and shoots me a wink. Man, I'm ready for that Kiss Cam, like right now.

Standing in the ultra-long line waiting to get the Sprite, I wonder why Suze broke up with me. It's not like I hadn't already thought about that every single day for the past six months, but I still don't get it. Honestly, she did say more than needing "space." There was something about passion, or lack thereof. Admittedly, the sex was…just okay. If I were an Olympic judge I'd have to give us a 5.0, which isn't bad but wouldn't win any medals. I read in *Cosmo* once that the most important organ in sexual arousal is the brain, and considering I've never had an erotic thought in my life, I'm probably the one that's keeping us from winning the gold. If I couldn't turn Suze on when we were together, what makes me think I can do it now?

I get back to our seats, feeling a little down, and hand Suze the Sprite. The game has already started and some chick is now sitting next to me—too close for my taste—so I scoot my folding chair closer to Suze, which doesn't help much since we're packed in like sardines. I give the girl a raised eyebrow look, hoping she gets my telepathic message to move over. She doesn't. Instead, she's trying to rip open a package with her teeth, gnawing and growling like a dog with a bone. It's pretty funny to watch, 'cause she doesn't look like the type who'd use her teeth for anything other than politely chewing with her mouth closed. She's the complete opposite of Suze. On one side of me is an androgynous, sporty girl (that would be Suze), and on the other is someone who looks like she just stepped out of a Jane Austen novel.

I keep watching, since she's way more interesting than the game, and gasp a little when she finally rips open the package and pulls out a gargantuan pickle. This thing is *huge*. You know, the kind that's been sitting in a vessel on the counter of a restaurant for twenty years because no one in their right mind would ever try to eat anything that big. Immediately, I hold my nose because the stench is horrendous. Pickle girl is going to totally ruin it for me. Thanks to her, the place smells like a hamburger joint. Not exactly the romantic setting I'm going for.

So I'm expecting to see her take a teeny-weeny bite out of the green monster—barely making a dent in the thing—but instead, she holds it with both hands, shoves the tip into her mouth, and bites down hard, pickle juice oozing down her arm. After chomping and swallowing, she slips the pickle between her lips, lightly scraping it against her teeth before taking another big bite. As much as I want to tear my eyes away, I just can't. It's like watching a train wreck. You don't wanna look, but you just have to. And then she does something really weird. She stops chewing, turns her head, and jabs the pickle in my face, like she's asking if I want a bite. Before I can give her one of my you-must-be-insane looks, I get distracted by her eyes. They're sorta light gray, but with a greenish gold tint. If the color was in a paint store, it'd probably have an exotic name like Secret Rendezvous or Mysterious Tweed or something. Suddenly, her eyes go soft, eyebrows slightly draw together, and she blinks several times with freakishly long eyelashes. This sorta worried look flashes across her face when I don't respond, which makes me feel kinda bad, so I scrunch my nose and shake my head. She shrugs, turns around, and takes another chomp on the thing. This girl is so captivated by that pickle, I don't even think she came here for the Sparks.

Finally, I peel my gaze away and get my head back in the game—the Kiss Cam game, not the basketball one. Excitement ripples down my spine when I look at the scoreboard. It's almost second quarter, and that's when they do it. I rub my hands together and pucker my lips. Things are looking up, especially since pickle girl decides she's had enough and stuffs the half-eaten monster back into the bag, which helps to eliminate the nauseating scent. She slumps and pats her stomach, looking like she might barf. I watch her out of my peripheral vision in case I need to take cover from pickle vomit when suddenly she sits up, grabs a bag under her chair, and pulls out some wet wipes. I hadn't noticed until now how lovely her hands are. It strikes me as odd that "lovely" comes to mind since it's not my typical repartee when describing someone, but that's what they are, with smooth, pale skin and long, delicate fingers. If she's a lesbian, I bet those long fingers come in handy. My mouth goes dry and my jaw drops a bit when I can't help but imagine those fingers thrusting deep into wet folds, stroking in and out slowly. I cross my legs and squeeze my thighs together hard.

She takes one of the wet wipes, with those long fingers, and glides it across her mouth several times. Then she slightly parts full lips, which are moist and a little red from the towel contact. Instinctively, I lick my lips and wonder if she's a sensual kisser. She certainly has the perfect mouth for it. In fact, she might have the sexiest mouth I've ever seen. I take a quick glance at Suze for comparison. Don't get me wrong, I love kissing Suze, but her lips are a bit on the thin side. I look back at pickle girl's mouth just as she's slowly running her tongue over her top lip. I groan, maybe a little too loud, since she looks directly at me with a slight grin on her face. She reaches over, places one finger underneath my chin, and pushes upward, which causes my gaping mouth to close. I blink fast three times in a row and swallow hard.

My heart lurches when the second quarter buzzer sounds, the Kiss Cam just moments away. I jerk toward Suze when she stands up and stretches.

"Where are you going?" I ask.

She leans down and whispers, "I gotta pee."

"No!" I realize how forceful that sounds, so I add, softly, "Wait a few minutes. It'll be too crowded right now."

When the song "Kiss Me" blares over the loud speakers, my stomach clinches with anticipation, excitement.

"Oh, I love when they do this." Suze sits back down.

The camera pans to an elderly lesbian couple. Surprise lights up their faces right before they laugh and give each other a quick peck. Everyone says, "Aww." The next victims are a straight couple. The guy takes his cap off and holds it up as he, supposedly, kisses his girlfriend. Spectators heckle the couple with boos from the hidden kiss. Tough crowd, but I don't need to worry about that. Suze and I are about to put on a show.

My heart stops when I see myself on the gigantic TV screen. The crowd goes wild yelling, "Kiss her! Kiss her!" Just as I'm about to grab Suze, I do a double take. The picture is all wrong. I'm there, but in the place of Suze is pickle girl. I look at Suze, pickle girl, and then back at the screen. It takes a second to sink in.

Miko is a moron! She's met Suze at least a dozen times. She looks nothing like pickle girl. Well, what am I supposed to do now? I feel a tap on my shoulder and turn around to mysterious tweed eyes. Pickle girl slightly shrugs and cocks her head as if to say, "You wanna?" The crowd is getting louder, meaner. This could get ugly. I raise an eyebrow and tilt my head as though to say, "I'm supposed to kiss that girl behind me, but I guess we better just get this over with before people start throwing hot dogs at us."

My heart pounds out of my chest when I stare at pickle girl's sexy mouth. The thought of kissing her makes my head hot, woozy. She slightly parts her moist, red lips, and I moan a little at the sight of the tip of her tongue. My gaze jumps to her half-closed eyes, which are teeming with passion, like she's turned on before even touching me. As she leans closer, I feel her warm breath on my lips, one hand on my thigh and another on the back of my neck. When she's two centimeters away, she waits…and waits…for three excruciating seconds before finally claiming my mouth. Oh wow. The music, chants, spectators, everything disappears except for her soft lips. Her fingernails dig into my thigh when our tongues touch. I find it odd that she doesn't taste like pickles, but instead sweetness caresses my taste buds. The hand on the back of my neck pulls me closer, deepening our kiss. I want—no, I need—to feel her body against mine, so I wrap my arms around her waist and press my breasts against hers. God, she feels so soft, and she fits into my body perfectly, like a puzzle piece. Shivers cascade down my spine when she runs her hands through my hair as her lips move against mine. I'm keenly aware that the wetness between my legs is increasing and my insides are pounding to the beat of the muffled music. I can't remember being so turned on by a kiss before.

Suddenly, a forceful tug pulls us apart. Instantly, I miss the feel of her mouth against mine. We're both breathless, faces flushed, lips tingling, staring at each other. The music and spectator chants fade back into focus just as something yanks me around. Suze. She looks at me with a "what the fuck" expression. Instead of punching me, though, she interlaces our fingers and raises my hand to her lips. After kissing me softly she lays our clasped hands in her lap and pushes her chair closer to mine. I guess seeing me kiss another woman is all it took for Suze to want me again. Had I known that, I'd have smooched someone six months ago.

I have an insatiable desire to turn around and look at pickle girl. When Suze tears her eyes from mine, I take a peek, and what I see breaks my heart. Pickle girl's beautiful mysterious tweed eyes are filled with sadness. I want to take my thumb and wipe the worried crease from her forehead. I want to stroke her cheek and ask what she's thinking, feeling. She looks at our joined hands for several seconds before she stares straight ahead, pain etched across her face. My heart aches a little. Suze squeezes my hand and excitedly points at the TV screen. It takes a second to comprehend what I'm seeing.

Miko must have realized her mistake, because Suze and I are on the Kiss Cam and everyone is yelling for us to make out. This is it. This is what I've been waiting for. And it's even better than I'd planned because Suze looks like she can't wait for me to ravish her. So what am I waiting for? Isn't Suze everything I've ever wanted? Why do I feel like my mind is pulling me one direction, but my heart another?

My body stiffens when I feel a soft tap on my shoulder. It takes me a moment to realize what that tap means, but when I do, excitement bubbles in my solar plexus. I break out in a wide smile, jerk my head around, and kiss pickle girl in a way that makes me giddy. We break apart 'cause it's too hard to kiss when we're both smiling so much. I love the sweet look she gives me and the way her eyes sparkle with delight. She grabs the big pickle and places the tip of it to my mouth. It slips between my lips, and when I bite down, sweetness touches my tongue. As I chew slowly, never taking my eyes off her, I know without a doubt this is the best pickle I've ever had.

THE GIRL NEXT DOOR

Beth Burnett

I really hated the girl next door. She was such a stereotypical California girl, tall, and slender, and blond, and so stupidly perfect. No matter what time I'd go outside to drink my coffee on the porch, it seemed I would always see her. She'd be bouncing through her yard pulling weeds in her little sundress with a pink bandana tied artfully around her long hair or getting ready to go for a run in a perfectly coordinated jogging outfit with matching shoes. The sight of her always made me reach for an extra doughnut.

The day she moved in, my roommate Sam came bursting through my bedroom door full of excitement. "Did you see the new girl next door? She's hot."

I took off my headphones and sat up. "Yeah? What's she look like?"

"Blond, perfect. Like a swimsuit model."

I shut her down, uninterested. So not my type.

I confirmed it the first time I saw her. I couldn't believe my roommate was still interested in that cookie-cutter stereotype. I'd dated enough of them to know that they are all high-maintenance gold diggers who would stomp all over your heart as soon as you stopped trying to placate their every need. No thanks.

She was always waving at me and smiling. I'd give her a smirk and a half wave back, you know, the kind that says, "Don't come over and talk to me."

Sam was always talking about how nice she was. Apparently she loved puppies and hiking and Jane Austen. Of course she did. Sam had a history of dating wildly inappropriate, generally straight women who were looking to see how the other half lived. Sam never had trouble picking up women because she looked like James Dean would if he had been a butch lesbian instead of a dude. It was all well and good for her. When we went out to a club, the femmes would flock around her in a frenzy of barely controlled excitement.

I, on the other hand, am a little short and a little chubby, and no matter how closely cropped I ask my barber to cut my hair, my curls always look a little unruly. I tend to favor sweater vests and bowties and Sam says I look like a short, chubby Bill Nye, the Science Guy. Women tended to flock around me to pinch my cheeks and tell me how adorable I am.

Over the next couple of weeks, I found out her name was Lauren and she was a fitness instructor. Sam was entirely enthralled with her and came home every day with a new tidbit of information.

"Did you know she likes scuba diving? She told me she's into crocheting. She just started learning to play the harmonica."

Sam already had a girlfriend, so I wasn't sure why she was obsessing over Lauren, but I knew it was a matter of time before she'd bring her over for dinner and I'd have to make small talk about aerobics or how blond was too blond or some other such nonsense.

I hadn't even spoken a word to her yet and I already hated her, so I was particularly irritated when I came home to find her standing at my front door. She turned as I pulled into the driveway and ran down the porch steps to meet me. Her face was pink and blotchy as if she'd maybe been crying.

"Hi," she said before I even managed to get out of my car. "I'm so sorry to bother you, but my car won't start."

"I don't know anything about cars," I said, shortly. "Sam can probably help you when she gets home."

"You don't understand." Her eyes started to fill with tears. "I have to be somewhere. It's an emergency."

I sighed, looking at my watch. It had been a long day at school. The students were more unruly than normal, and I had been looking forward to busting through these homework assignments before losing myself in an *Orange Is the New Black* marathon.

"Please," she said again. "It's an emergency."

"Fine, come on."

I got into the front seat and started tossing all of the old coffee cups, books, and spiral notebooks from the passenger seat into the back. She smiled as she got in, holding a Reese's wrapper. I grabbed it from her hand, crumpled it, and tossed it into the back.

"Those are my favorites."

I cast a sidelong glance at her slender figure and said nothing.

Noticing my look, she smiled. "I have to run a couple of extra miles to make up for it."

I didn't answer, and other than her occasional directional requests, we rode in silence. I imagined I was taking her to the gym so she wouldn't miss some spin class. She directed me to turn onto Palm Street, and I was surprised when we pulled into the parking lot of Sunrise Manor.

"Isn't this a hospice care?"

"Yes. Come in with me if you like."

We walked in the front door to the antiseptic smell of heavy-duty cleaning supplies and cloyingly sweet air fresheners. The lobby was decorated in pale desert colors with beautiful artwork and overstuffed couches, but there was no mistaking what it was.

She led me down the hall, into a small room near the end. Bright pictures lined the walls of the room; they matched the wildly colored quilt on the bed. An old woman was in the bed, quiet. For a second, I thought she was dead, but I realized she was unconscious.

Lauren sat down next to the bed and reached for the old woman's hand. "Hi, Gran. I'm here. I've brought a friend with me today. Her name is..." She looked back at me. "Sam always refers to you as her roomie."

I smiled, sitting in the other chair. "I'm Kate. It's nice to meet you."

Lauren turned back to her grandmother, talking softly to the unconscious woman while I sat and listened, feeling more and more like an asshole with every word. She talked to the woman for about forty minutes, and in the course of that one-sided conversation, I found out that she had painted all of the pictures on the walls and had made the quilt for the old woman's bed. I learned that her parents were both dead and that this grandmother was the only family Lauren had left in the world. I learned that yet again, I had judged someone by her appearance, and I was dead wrong. As always.

When she finally stood up to leave, Lauren leaned over and kissed the older woman on the forehead. She nodded at me with tears in her eyes and we left the building.

Getting back into the car, I cleared my throat. "That's your grandmother?"

She nodded. "She's been unconscious for a couple of weeks now. I wish she would just let go. It's been a hard road for her."

"I'm sorry. I didn't know."

"How could you? It's not as if I walk up to every neighbor who hates my guts and start talking to her about my personal life."

I grimaced. "I don't hate your guts. I just…I'm an asshole."

She looked out the window. "Yeah, that's true."

We rode in silence for a while. I couldn't help notice the way the gold streaks in her hair kind of shone in the late-afternoon sun.

"Look," I started. "It's not that I'm a total asshole…"

"Just a partial one?"

"Pretty much. I'm sorry. I made a judgment call based on your looks, and it wasn't fair."

She turned to glare at me. "No. It wasn't. You assumed because I'm blond and fit that I'm some kind of shallow bitch not worthy of your great big intellect's time."

"That isn't it. I just…"

"You just made erroneous assumptions, and now you feel like a jerk."

"Yes. I do. I feel like a total jerk."

"A complete and utter jerk," she replied.

"A jerk of the highest order."

"Jerky McJerkinson."

"Vincent Van Jerk," I said.

She glanced at me, smirking. "Well, at least we know we have something in common. We both agree that you're a jerk."

"We have something else in common," I said. "We both love Jane Austen."

She laughed. "Your roommate has been talking about me."

"She's smitten."

"I imagine she is always smitten with a certain type of woman. I doubt it has anything to do with my love of Jane Austen."

"I'm an English teacher."

"I know. Sam told me."

"Sam talks too much. But what's your favorite Austen?"

"You first."

"Okay, on three..." I paused to check for a nod of agreement. "One...two...three."

"*Pride and Prejudice*," she yelled, just as I was saying, "*Northanger Abbey!*"

"Ah, of course you love *Pride and Prejudice*. Obviously a sap for romance," I said.

"I can't say I'm surprised you're a *Northanger Abbey* fan."

"I do have a rather active imagination."

We turned onto our street and I pulled into my driveway. Hesitating before getting out, I turned to look at her. "I'm sorry. I'm sorry for judging you. I've been...treated not so nicely recently."

She patted me on the hand and got out of the car. Leaning back in, she said, "We've all been treated not so nicely, Kate. All of us."

We've all been treated not so nicely. I thought about that a lot over the next few days. I've built such an incredible wall of bitterness around myself. It's easy to say that women aren't interested in me because they can't see past Sam and her muscles and dark good looks, but really, it's my own wall.

After that, I waved at Lauren whenever she waved at me, and one day, I decided to put down my doughnut and go for a jog with her. I know she slowed her pace to match mine, but it didn't matter. It was fun. We started to become friends, and I could see what Sam saw in her.

And still Sam would come home ranting about her. I learned, through Sam, that she taught the fitness classes to pay the bills for her true passion, which was teaching yoga to seniors and those with disabilities. I learned that, like me, she was a vegetarian, and that she'd rather get a bouquet of organic produce as a gift than store-bought flowers.

I started driving her to hospice on Wednesdays. I'd bring her a Reese's and she would only eat it if I promised to run with her the next morning. She became more beautiful every day, and I wondered how I ever considered her a cookie-cutter type. I loved the fact that one of her front teeth was just a little longer than the other and that she had a mole on the lobe of her left ear. I noticed the way she pulled on a lock of her hair when she was nervous or thinking hard. I found the curve of her face the most beautiful shape on the planet.

In all of the years I had been friends with Sam, I had never let a woman come between us. When I realized I was falling in love with Lauren, I didn't know what to do. So I did the only thing I could. I was honest.

It isn't as easy as it sounds to tell someone that you're falling in love with them and that you have to stop hanging out for your own sanity. I decided to give her a parting gift, so I showed up at her house one evening with a DVD of *The Jane Austen Book Club* and a paper bag filled with organic produce from the farmer's market. She opened the door and smiled when she saw me.

"This is an amazing surprise." She grinned. "Lucky for you, I have absolutely nothing going on tonight."

I followed her inside and through the front room to the kitchen.

"Come on. I'm going to make us something to eat and we can watch the movie."

"Lauren." I cleared my throat. "I needed to talk to you."

Greedily pawing through the paper bag, she looked up. "You sound so serious."

"It is serious."

She pulled up a stool and sat down. "Okay, then."

"I know you and Sam have a thing going on, and I don't want

to get in the way of that. Not that I think I could get in the way of it, of course. I mean, I wouldn't get in the way even if I could get in the way. It's just, I'm starting to have these feelings for you, and that's fine. There's nothing wrong with that. It's natural. Who wouldn't have feelings for you?"

I paused, embarrassed. Poker-faced, she remained silent, not helping me at all.

"So." I took a deep breath in. "So."

"So you want to stop being friends with me because you can't handle having feelings for me?"

"Well, it's not exactly—"

"Or you feel Sam has some right of first dibs and you're going to honor that?"

"I'm starting to feel like a jerk," I said.

"A total jerk."

"A Jerky McJerkinson." I grinned.

"Jerk Van Winkle," she said, laughing.

"Lauren, I'm sorry. I just don't want to risk falling in love with you when you're starting a relationship with my best friend."

She stood up and stepped forward, still smiling. "And who told you that Sam and I were dating?"

"Well, I just assumed, since she talks about you all the time."

"What do they say about assumptions, Kate?"

I shook my head. "They make an ass out of you and me."

"Yeah. But in this case, you're the only ass."

I sighed. "I'm sorry. Again. I'm not very good at this."

She stepped closer. "Did you ever think to ask Sam why she was always talking about me so much?"

I looked up at her blond beauty, towering over me by at least four inches. "No, of course I didn't."

She smiled, leaning forward. "She's been trying to set us up."

I gulped. "She has?"

"Yeah. From the minute she found out that I thought you were adorable."

I smiled. "I am rather adorable."

"Even though you're an ass."

"I am an ass. Assey Mc—"

"Shut up." She wrapped her arms around me.

I looked up into her eyes for just a second before closing mine and leaning into her kiss.

OCTOBER MOON

Sheri Lewis Wohl

"This is stupid." Lindy Branson stared at herself in the mirror and shuddered. Lord, she looked like...what? A reject from the Middle Ages? Or perhaps a wannabe Goth? The black velvet dress was long and low cut, making her boobs stand out way more than she was comfortable with. Her dark hair hung down her back in a single braid, and her mother had insisted she put on the sliver earrings that were simply not her style.

Her mother came around the counter and put both hands to her mouth. "Oh," she breathed. "You look beautiful."

Lindy didn't agree. In her opinion, the whole thing was crazy. "Come on, Mom, this is so not me." It wasn't, either. She was not a dress-up kind of woman, and especially not in something like this. Frankly, she felt silly. Like a little girl playing in her mother's closet.

"Don't be a spoilsport. This is important."

"To you."

"Yes," she said as she put both hands on her hips. Her gown, like Lindy's, was velvet, only it was a rich blue instead of black. Her boobs weren't falling out either. Apparently age had its perks. "It's important to me. This is tradition."

"Really?" She raised an eyebrow. It was hard to buy into the tradition argument. Lindy had left for college at the University of Washington when she was eighteen and then stayed in Seattle to build her own life and career. Never once in the years she'd lived in this house had she seen her mother dress up in something like this and go party with the ladies. In the visits back home, her mom had failed to mention she was a Wiccan.

"Really. Look, you think you know everything there is to know about me, but you'd be sorely mistaken, my dear daughter. I have a life outside of all this." She waved her hands as if to encompass the home. It was a nice house with comfortable furniture, colorful walls, and a breathtaking view of the river outside the windows. It was nice and, more important, normal.

"Dad was okay with this?" Somehow she just couldn't envision her father thinking this was fine and dandy. He'd been a professor of accounting at Gonzaga University and way too logical in everything he did to be into something like Wicca. No matter how she came at it, she couldn't see Dad buying in.

Her mother laughed and her face brightened. "Oh heavens, no. He thought I lost my mind, and when this night came around each year, he was convinced I'd gone over the edge."

Now, that sounded like Dad. "But he didn't stop you."

Blue eyes narrowed, her mother regarded her carefully. "Lindy, let me ask you something. Has anyone ever told you what you could and couldn't do?"

Fair question. "Not a chance in hell."

"Well," she smiled, "where exactly do you think you learned that from?"

Lindy laughed. "Touché. But really, Mom, black velvet and a witches party? You have to admit it's a little crazy."

"Not in the least. Magic is all around you, my dear daughter, you just have to allow yourself to be out to capturing the magic. Like I said, it's tradition. We've been holding the annual Wicca gathering for over a decade. It's time my daughter makes an appearance. I'm so happy you're here."

It wasn't like she'd had a choice in coming. Mom had made it sound like the world would come to an end if she didn't come home this weekend. She could have argued the point, but it wasn't worth it. She'd learned a long time ago that there were times to argue with Mom and times to just give in. This was one of the latter.

"I'm only doing this for you. I think it's crazy."

"Go, see for yourself, and tell me in a couple hours if you still think I've lost my mind. Now let's do something with your hair." She turned to study herself in the mirror once more. There was nothing wrong with her hair. It was long and straight because it was easy to take care of that way. The braid was tidy and simple. Perfect. Why she needed to do anything beyond putting on this silly dress she didn't know. "My hair is fine."

"No, it's not. Amber is going to be there, you know." She added that last comment softly, but that didn't lessen the shock it sent through Lindy's body. "Now sit while I undo this braid. Why you hide this beautiful hair I'll never know."

"Amber?" Even saying the name made her choke up. Slowly she lowered herself to a chair, and her mother took off the band holding the braid in place. Once her hair was loose, she began to run a brush through it. It was a little like when she was a kid and her mom would get her ready for school. Except she wasn't a little girl, and what she'd just heard made her feel as though she couldn't catch her breath. If she didn't know better, she'd think she had asthma. After fifteen years, she needed to get over it, to get over her.

Her mother continued as if the bombshell she had just dropped was no big deal. "Yes, she's on leave, and Karen told me she's coming to the party." She started piling Lindy's hair on top of her head in some kind of snazzy updo.

For a moment Lindy closed her eyes and thought of the girl who'd been her first love. Amber had been everything Lindy wasn't, tall and slender, blond and green-eyed. She'd been full of ambition and drive, and no one had been surprised when she'd secured a spot at West Point. It almost made Lindy groan out loud thinking what she must look like in that military uniform. She didn't know because they'd gone their separate ways and hadn't seen each other since that late-summer day when they both left for their own adventures.

Lindy had always secretly hoped Amber would reach out to her, but it didn't happen. A hundred times she'd wanted to pick up the phone and call her. She never did. Fear paralyzed her every time she reached for the phone, just as it almost did now. It took effort not to jump up from the chair, strip off the dress, and go hide in the bathroom.

Except that would be even more stupid than this party. She was thirty-three years old. A bona fide adult. A successful businesswoman. She did not run and hide from the ghosts of her past. Amber was, after all, a childhood friend, and that was all. Really. Squaring her shoulders, she looked up at her mother. "I don't even look like myself." It wasn't a lie. She was a blue jeans and T-shirt kind of woman. Velvet and updos were not her thing.

Her mother, apparently happy at last with her hair, planted a kiss on her cheek. "You, my sweet girl, look gorgeous, and everyone will think so. This is a celebration for all of us, but in particular for me and Karen, as both of our daughters have come to share this night with us. How can it be anything but special?"

Lindy held up her hands and laughed. Mom was hard to resist. "You win. Let's party."

She only hoped she could manage to keep her cool when she finally came face-to-face with Amber.

The short trip to the party consisted of walking out the front door and going through the opening in the shrubs that separated her mother's yard from Karen Kaplin's. The two families had been neighbors for more than thirty-five years, and now the two women, both widows, were, according to her mother, in the same coven.

She still had a hard time wrapping her head around the idea her mother was a witch. When in the hell had that happened? According to Mom, when she'd posed that exact question, it was well before they lost Dad to cancer five years ago. It figured Mom would gravitate to something like Wicca; she always did like things a bit off the beaten path.

Now, Karen joining in, that surprised her. She always thought of her as the straight arrow, the mom who was the first to raise her hand at PTA meetings and the one who always got them to soccer games on time. A Wiccan was just about the last thing in the world Lindy could imagine her being, though the thought of it made her smile.

In the old days, Lindy would have opened the door and barged in with just a yell to announce her arrival. With the passage of years and the long absence, common courtesy seemed a better course. She pressed the small lighted doorbell button. A moment later, Karen opened the door and enveloped Lindy in a big hug. "Oh my goodness, it's so wonderful to see you."

Like Lindy's mother, Karen was dressed in a lovely dark blue gown. Lindy wondered if this was what Wiccans always wore to their gatherings as she hugged her back. "I've missed you," she admitted, and it was the truth. Tears started to well in her eyes and she blinked them back.

As she stepped inside she was hit by a wave of nostalgia. The house looked much as it had when she was that teenager so eager to find independence and make her way in the world. The furniture was new, but the arrangement was not. She was smiling as she moved into the living room where women dressed similar to her were milling about holding wineglasses and chatting.

Lindy stopped in front of a wall covered by photographs, some older and some more recent, and her heart started to race. Imagination was no longer required as to what Amber would look like in uniform. One was clearly Amber's West Point graduation photo. She was more stunning than anything Lindy's imagination came up with. "Get over it," she muttered. "She's probably married to some big, buff Navy SEAL."

"What Navy SEAL?"

The way she jumped at the sound of Amber's voice right behind her was definitely not cool. Slowly she turned, and if her heart was beating fast at seeing pictures of Amber in uniform, seeing her in a well-cut gown just about put her over the top. She was as beautiful in the gown as she was hot in uniform. She was most likely drop-dead gorgeous when she had nothing on. *Don't go there.*

"Amber." Oh so smooth. It was like she'd never been around a beautiful woman before.

Amber smiled and reached out to hug her. "God, it's good to see you."

And to hold her, Lindy wanted to add. As much as she hated to be a cliché, Amber was her first love, and to hold her in her arms right now was a little slice of heaven. She had definitely not outgrown her first love. Nope, not at all. Sucked to be her.

"You look great." Pretty lame. It was not getting any better.

Amber stepped back and held her out at arm's length. "Lindy, I love the hair."

Lindy rolled her eyes. That made one of them. "Mom's handiwork."

Her smile lit up her face. "I bet you still wear it long, straight, and in a braid."

"Sucker's bet." It warmed her heart to think that Amber remembered.

Amber hugged her again. "Seriously, Lins, it's so good to see you. You don't know how much I've missed you."

Lindy stepped away and didn't know why. Maybe because it hurt a little to hear her say she missed her, because if she had, wouldn't she have tried to get in touch with her at least once?

"I've missed you too." No sense lying even if her feelings were hurt. She'd missed Amber so much she'd stayed away for fifteen years, only coming back for visits short enough to ensure there was no time to visit with neighbors, even if they lived next door. She'd made certain to keep as far away from any reminders of Amber as humanly possible. Her success had been 100 percent. Until tonight.

"Come on." Amber tilted her head toward the back door. "Let's leave the witches to their party and go have a drink out by the river."

"Isn't it a little cold?" It was, after all, the end of October, and in this part of the country, chilly outside. Besides, the riverbank was typically cluttered with fallen leaves and branches. Not exactly what she wanted to pick over in long black velvet. Nor did she want to be alone with Amber in the moonlight. Her heart could only stand so much.

"No worries, Mom put in an awesome fire pit patio thingy down near the water. One flick of the remote, and whoosh, we have fire. She had the right idea when she put in a gas fire pit. No fuss, no muss. There are chairs and everything. Come on." She held out a hand to Lindy.

Still, Lindy hesitated. Oh, she wanted to go bad enough. She just wasn't sure her heart was up to it. All this time apart, and after five minutes it was as if they'd seen each other yesterday. She was still as drawn to her as ever.

"Okay, let's do it."

Amber's face lit up, her eyes dancing. "That's the Lindy I remember. Wait here a sec."

She didn't give Lindy a chance to say anything. Instead, she raced toward the kitchen, returning two minutes later with a bottle of wine and two glasses. "Now we're ready. Let's go catch up."

As they were walking toward the river, Amber asked, "You notice there seems to be some kind of order to the dresses?"

"What?" Lindy was concentrating on not tripping on anything as they crossed the yard heading toward the promised chairs and fire pit. The moonlight was romantic and all, but it wasn't a whole lot of good when it came to negotiating the terrain in a long dress.

"The dresses. You and I got stuffed into these fancy get-ups, and if you took a look around, some of us are in black, some in green, and a couple, specifically our moms, are in blue. I wonder what it all means."

They'd reached the chairs, and as promised, they were nice and ringed the elaborate fire pit. From a patio chest, Amber fished out a remote and, with a press of a button, had fire warming the air.

"Pretty sweet," Lindy said as she lowered herself to the double seat that faced the river. She almost jumped when Amber sat next to her instead of picking one of the other chairs.

Neither of them said a word as Amber uncorked the wine, poured each of them a glass, and then set the bottle on the ground. She leaned back, took a sip, and stared up at the sky.

"Do you ever wish things had turned out differently?"

Only about a million times was what Lindy wanted to say. "Like what?" From everything Mom had told her, Amber's life was amazing. She'd been all over the world, was highly regarded and very successful. Someday she was going to be wearing stars on her uniform.

"Like you and me."

Lindy almost spat out the wine she'd just taken a sip of. "I don't understand." And she didn't, either. Yes, she'd loved Amber and probably still did. Amber had never been anything but a good friend. She'd dated guys in high school, and even though Mom never mentioned men in her life, Lindy had always assumed there were.

Amber leaned down and set her glass on the ground. Then she turned until she was facing Lindy. In the moonlight her eyes sparkled. "Have you ever heard the old saying 'You don't know what you have until it's gone'? Well, I've had to live with that one for fifteen years."

Lindy's heart felt like it was going to burst. Amber couldn't possibly be saying what she thought she was. "Amber…"

"Let me finish. I came tonight for one reason and one reason only: you. Mom told me you were going to be here, and I got on the first plane. I had to see you, Lindy. I had to know for sure."

"Know what?" Did she really come across as stupid as she sounded to her own ears?

"This." She took Lindy's face between her hands and leaned in to kiss her. It started out tentative, soft, and quickly turned into something far more passionate.

When Amber pulled away, Lindy could hardly breathe. "I've dreamed of that for years," she admitted softly.

Amber's smile was beautiful. "I'll tell you my big, dark secret. So have I."

"What?" Could it really be true?

"I think I knew long before I left for West Point and you headed off to the University of Washington."

"Why didn't you say something?" Fifteen years. Fifteen long years she'd waited to hear something like this, to hear anything that might give her hope.

"I was afraid. I wanted to go to West Point. I wanted to be the officer I've become, and in my mind that meant I had to be what the world expected me to be."

"Straight."

Amber laughed. "Oh yes, straight."

"How'd that work out for you?" She said it with a smile.

"Well, I did meet some nice guys along the way. Quite a few toads too."

"I'll just bet."

"I met some nice women along the way too."

That thought made her heart constrict. "But?"

Amber took her face in her hands again, staring into Lindy's eyes. "But no matter where I looked, I couldn't find what I was really looking for."

"And what was that?"

"You."

Tears pooled in Lindy's eyes. "Are you screwing with me?" This couldn't really be happening.

Amber shook her head. "One of my best friends was killed several months ago by a suicide bomber. She was smart and beautiful and so incredibly talented. She was the kind of woman who was going to change the world. One day she was there and the next she was gone. It was losing Gail that made me realize what I'd been doing all these years, and that was hiding from the one person I truly loved."

The tears couldn't be held back anymore. "You know I've loved you for years."

Amber nodded. "I didn't realize it until later. Until we were apart. I think I took you for granted. You were my best friend, and it took me a long time to understand that it was my best friend who held my heart. Lindy, I love you, I've always loved you, and I'm not hiding from you anymore. Can you forgive me for being so dense?"

Easy. "I can forgive you anything."

"Really?" For the first time, Amber looked uncertain.

Lindy smiled. "Really." She pulled Amber close and kissed her deeply, letting the love that had lived in her heart for all these years have free rein.

The sound of clapping made Lindy pull back. Both Lindy and Amber turned to look behind them. Their mothers stood side by side on the edge of the lawn, clapping and smiling. The moon spilled warm light down, bathing them in a buttery glow.

"It's about time," Lindy's mother said. "It's taken us years to get you two to come to your senses. We finally had to call in our sisters to weave a little magic."

"I thought you said this party was a tradition," Lindy said.

"It is," her mother answered. "Each year we come together under the October moon to help those who need a little push. We finally decided this was the year to give you a little needed push."

"You cast a spell on us."

Her mother laughed. "Not really. Let's just say it was more a case of the universe conspiring to bring you together."

Lindy smiled and turned back to gaze at Amber, who took her hands. "I don't care if they did cast a spell, I'm just happy that I finally got the girl of my dreams."

"The girl next door," Amber said, laughing. "It's so clichéd."

Lindy pulled her into her arms and whispered into her ear. "It's so perfect."

CHEMISTRY

Lea Daley

There *is* such a thing as chemistry, but that doesn't mean you can trust it. Chemistry can point the way, or lead you astray. The problem is figuring out which direction it's taking you. I wondered about that after meeting Nicola Sevier on the closing day of the Wyldwomyn Music Festival. Her last name was pronounced "severe," as in *severe crush*—appropriate because the woman exuded an almost magical charm. Her dark hair, cut in an asymmetrical style, fell across one of her smoky gray eyes. She was tall, with to-die-for biceps, and legs that I instantly imagined wrapping around my neck. As for her breasts, amply displayed courtesy of a scoop-necked T-shirt—don't get me started. I'll slide off my chair.

We liked all the same music; we shared the same political beliefs. And that last part really mattered right then. It was the summer of 2016, when longtime friendships were ripped asunder by the political feud. If Nicola had said she was voting for my second choice, she might have lost some of her allure. But no. And I especially liked that she'd shown up at Wyldwomyn, which was so little publicized that just knowing about it automatically conferred über-cool status. Of course, I was only at the festival because my best friend had stumbled across it years earlier. This was the first time that I'd attended without London.

Wyldwomyn took place in the Ozark Mountains of Missouri, and if you thought of it as a smaller-scale, lower-rent version of its Michigan sister, you wouldn't be wrong. Hosted by a gaggle of second-wave feminists on Dykeland, their collectivist farm, the festival was a three-day immersion in the past. Complete with cheap, communally cooked food; outdoor "plumbing"; and an abundant supply of mosquitoes. But the music was exceptional—that was the hook. Up-and-coming artists from all over the country performed; when one of those acts penetrated the zeitgeist, we could claim we'd discovered it.

The downside? Our hosts had an ulterior motive: to saturate us in 1970s feminist philosophy, which my generation found laughably deficient. Each summer we suffered through "consciousness-raising" sessions with total strangers. And we were herded into awkward workshops on decoding the female body that actually involved inspecting our nether regions with cheesy hand mirrors. As if we hadn't already explored our sexuality—and then some.

Worst of all were the passionate lectures on the patriarchy. With a capital "P." To the extent that I thought about those matters on my own time, the patriarchy was like a receding fog. I wouldn't want to drive through the murk, but it was a distant problem, and clearing nicely. The sun would come out soon. But for those old gals, the Patriarchy was a looming threat, as concrete as a black-clad burglar scaling the walls of our homes, looting our treasure. And it was pointless to call the police because cops were just another arm of the machine, indifferent to the multitudinous ways women were brutalized by it. "Protect and serve, my ass!" I'd heard Comfrey mutter more than once.

Mostly we queued up for Wyldwomyn's ancillary events because the concerts didn't start till afternoon. And because the founders were so quaint and earnest, almost like living exhibits of their bygone era. Each had adopted a new name. Willow. Star. Sorrel. Terra. And they'd rejected a hundred things we willingly embraced. Fashion, makeup, porn—even shaving. I doubted any of them had heard of a landing strip or a full Brazilian. Yet they were missionary in their zeal to educate us young folk.

Apparently there was a capitalist conspiracy designed to strip women of our hard-won—if unequal—wages. Corporatists were working overtime to persuade us of our innate inferiority so we'd spend big bucks on makeup, corsets, hair coloring, and spike heels. It was futile to argue that many third-wave feminists liked wearing dramatic styles, at least occasionally.

Those weren't *authentic* choices, Raine insisted. In a patriarchal society, a woman's "performance of femininity" inevitably reflected male values. If men preferred modest women, females concealed their hair, their bodies, even their faces. If men preferred women who looked like porn stars, females dressed like...well, some of *us*. Yet men were universally unencumbered by restrictive apparel, face paint, wax jobs, or objectification.

I'd heard that rant repeatedly and avoided it when I could. Still, I tried to view the archaic rituals at Wyldwomyn as part of the price of admission. If nothing else, the exercises supplied comic relief at home—assuming London wasn't present. Because she worshipped our hosts, from the tips of their little gray heads to the fraying hems of their overalls. I wasn't allowed to poke fun at them—not even in the gentlest way. On the return trip to St. Louis after our first festival, London said, "They know things we don't, Ali—important things."

When I accused her of drinking the Kool-Aid, London's response was uncharacteristically fierce. "Why *shouldn't* we be accepted in our natural state? If guys don't need makeup, why do we?"

"Because it's fun? Because I look better with it?"

"Says who? I've seen you barefaced, and you looked terrific."

"You're not exactly my target audience," I'd said flippantly.

London smacked me with her copy of *The Beauty Myth*, so I knew I'd won that round.

But each summer, she hung with the wyldwomyn whenever possible. Not surprising, I suppose—she was a throwback to some former time. London would rather phone than text, rather read a "real" book than a Kindle, preferred stolid Craftsman cottages to glossy new condos. She fit into life on Dykeland like she'd been born there, or like she was an honorary member of the tribe. She could have been a granddaughter of Linden or Raine or Solstice—

not that any of those hardcore dykes had children. And London *looked* like she belonged there, too.

She was petite, a sprite of a woman, with fine, honey-blond hair that fell sweetly about her face if she went too long between cuts. She had sky-blue eyes, an adorable button nose, and a subtle cleft in her chin. London didn't care a fig for fashion, yet she had a style all her own. A pared-down look built on faded jeans, crisp oxford shirts, and supple leather boat shoes. It didn't take much to imagine her aging in place on the farm, working the land, season after season.

In childhood, London and I were next-door neighbors; as undergrads, we were roommates. Now, while pursuing graduate degrees, we rented crappy apartments in the same low-rise complex on the outskirts of Midtown. We were constantly immersed in one another's lives—unless I was in the throes of a romance. Most of the time, though, we moved seamlessly from bingeing on *Orphan Black* in London's place, to gobbling up snacks in mine, to fleeing summer's heat on the fire escape outside our bedroom windows.

I hated that she hadn't been able to join me that summer. And her absence didn't go unnoticed among the wyldwomyn. I was peeling potatoes on my assigned shift when Terra said, "I haven't seen London Woodruff this year."

"Yeah. She had to attend some training on a major tech update at her job. It almost killed her to miss out."

"She's special, that one—really special. I hope you know that her size is just a trick of light."

I stopped working and turned toward the weathered dyke. She was studying me with a speculative look, and something in her posture suggested I didn't quite measure up. "What do you mean—'trick of light'?"

"You see London as tiny, easy to overlook. But actually, she's *enormous*."

Apparently Terra was talking some new-age nonsense about London's "spirit." While plainly conveying that mine suffered by comparison. I met her gaze with my haughtiest look. "There's a reason she's my best friend, you know."

"But is it the right reason?" Terra asked over one shoulder, as she left to fetch more potatoes.

"What the hell?" I muttered to the empty kitchen. "Of course it's the right reason." And just then, I longed to have London's reassuring presence at my side.

Still, if she'd been there, I might never have spoken to Nicola over a breakfast of stale granola and green tea, initiating a conversation that engaged us all day. At the concert that night, cool breezes seemed to blow in good fortune. A million-zillion stars winked above the backcountry fields. And maybe the moon shone down on me with special favor. Because as the last note died away, as the last spotlight dimmed, Nicola kissed me. And kissed me. And kissed me.

I'd paid extra to bunk in a cabin, but it came equipped with roommates. So Nic and I dragged her ratty tent and paper-thin sleeping bag down a hill, as far from everyone as possible. And there we did our best to pretend we were the only people alive. More than alive—soaring, effervescent, dancing among the planets. I'd never had sex like that; I'd never known there *was* sex like that. After we collapsed, I spent the few remaining hours just listening to Nicola breathe. Because those fireworks were the final hurrah. The festival was over. We'd leave in the morning.

At eight, we downed a hasty meal, then Nic kissed me good-bye, and to hell with onlookers. I found the shuttle bus for my group but didn't expect to see her again—I didn't even know where she was from. And since I'd never been the most popular dyke at any ball, my expectations weren't irrational. On the long ride home, I told myself it was enough to have shared that extraordinary interlude with her.

But Nicola texted me a few days later. I was surprised to learn that she lived in a northern suburb of St. Louis, only thirty minutes away. That night we met at a bar in Soulard, then wound up in my bed. Soon afterward, she was claiming a lot of my time. I was never sure I had her complete attention, though. I'd noticed Nic noticing other women, and sometimes when I suggested getting together, she'd say she was busy. Period.

One morning I called hoping she'd join me for a night of outdoor theater. But I got no take—and she offered no explanation. I was seriously bummed. I could go to the play alone or invite a friend. Share a bottle of wine and the picnic supper I'd planned for Nic with someone else. Try not to think about how the seductive Ms. Sevier was spending a perfect June evening. Especially when she could have been at Shakespeare in the Park with me.

After wrapping up my tasks for the day, I biked to the U library, where London worked. She was terrified modern technology would destroy that venerable institution, so I often checked out stuff just to help with statistics. When I entered, she was doing some nameless thing at a computer. But as I closed the gap between us, London looked up. Instantly her helpful librarian expression morphed into a sunny smile. "Hey, Ali!"

"Hey, yourself. How late are you working?"

"I'm just about to clock out. Why?"

I leaned across the counter, batted my lashes, and lowered my tone to vamp level. "Could I interest you in a picnic supper, *A Midsummer Night's Dream*, and me?"

"Oh, yeah! Give me five minutes to wrap up."

I watched London close down for the day, thinking about her devotion to the job. She knew everything about literature, including exactly what I should read at a given moment. A few years back, I'd dropped a Stieg Larsson novel on the checkout counter—I wanted to know what all the fuss was about.

London shook her head. "You'll be sorry."

We indulged in a playful tug-of-war before she gave up and scanned the book. Unfortunately, she was right. *The Girl with the Dragon Tattoo* was way too graphic for my taste. Crazy, I know; everyone my age has a stronger stomach and a greater appetite for violence than I do. When I returned the book, London was kind enough not to lord it over me. She did make me check out *Slaughterhouse Five*, though. A penance for failure to heed, I thought.

A week later, I took back that novel, too, smugly reporting that I didn't like it. London just smiled, renewed it without asking, and told me to try again. The second time around, I recognized the truth: The damned thing was brilliant. So brilliant I couldn't shut up about it. And London was right when she suggested I check out recordings by Rodrigo y Gabriela. I fell in love at first strum but would never have found the duo on my own. Sometimes London seemed almost telepathic—at least where I was concerned.

The night we went to Forest Park for a hit of culture, London was preoccupied. We finished our picnic supper before she asked, "Who's the latest heartthrob?"

I supposed she'd seen Nic coming and going. And of course, she couldn't have missed my departure from our usual routine. I looked around before answering. The sunset was spectacular. The audience lounging on that velvet lawn was jovial. The green show featured lively Renaissance music. And a trio of jesters combined expert juggling with witty repartee. It was hardly a night for bitching. But after two glasses of wine, all bets were off. I poured out my heart about Nic—the attraction, the uncertainty, the anguish.

London listened without interrupting, although I knew her face so well she really didn't need to speak. When I finally wound down, she asked, "Is Nicola good for you?"

Was she? I hadn't given that much thought. Nic made me laugh. She encouraged me to try things I'd never imagined. She was *certainly* good for me in bed—just thinking about that made me blush, because London was watching while I replayed Nicola's best moves. Still, there was that frustrating elusiveness, a hint of a darker side. I sipped more wine before admitting, "I'm not sure."

London drew her knees close to her chest and wrapped her arms around them, so I knew she was trying to hold something back. Finally, she said, "That's a lot of emotion to invest in someone who sounds slightly sketchy."

Thankfully, the play started so I didn't have to respond. And I took heart during Act One when Lysander told Hermia, "The course of true love never did run smooth." Exactly! Who was I to expect otherwise?

Yet London's words lingered long after I was in bed, staring at the water stain I used as a Rorschach test. Why *had* I let myself get so involved with a woman who kept a huge part of herself sequestered from me? And why couldn't I have a relationship with Nicola that was as carefree as my friendship with London?

I asked my sister that question the next day. Bette has ten years and twenty IQ points on me. And she's overly fond of exercising her right to free speech. As expected, she offered an unsparing answer: "Look at your crushes in high school—before you realized you were a lesbian. Assholes, all. Then there was that lunatic hand model in your sophomore year of college. And the Wiccan priestess, or whatever, last year. You gravitate toward sexy topped off with crazy. I don't know why you conflate romance with danger and uncertainty and a high probability of heartbreak, but that's your history."

Did I associate romance with danger? Maybe—Bette had made a good case for that. I decided to test her theory when Nicola suggested staying with me for a week. Which was stellar—until day three. As we returned from yoga class, Nic startled me by racing to my mailbox, then flipping through the contents. I raised my eyebrows at her cheekiness and promptly reclaimed my property. But she was leaning over my shoulder while I ripped open an envelope containing a quarterly check for college expenses.

"Lend me a thousand, Ali? It would really help. I'm a little short for my rent."

Though her breath was warm at my ear, it sent a chill down my spine. Maybe Nic was joking—I hoped she was joking. Shaking my head, I stashed the check in my bag. "Nicola. This is scholarship money. I couldn't make it through the semester without it."

"Don't you trust me to pay it back?" Said snidely, with a stormy, unfamiliar vibe on the side.

Hoping to defuse the tension, I mustered a self-deprecating smile. "Just consider me ridiculously neurotic, okay?"

To my horror, Nic snarled, "I consider you a lot worse than that!" She slammed her boot at one wall, where a size eight hole promptly materialized. Then she flung my door open and punched her fist through it. Stomping down the corridor, she yelled obscene insults all the way to the elevator. And just like that, the intoxicating dyke I'd been mooning over for months vanished.

I was shocked. Shaken. Proud of myself. And very, very scared. I pulled out my cell to call Dietrich, the building supervisor. "It's Ali in 3-B, Dete. I've got a problem."

He arrived practically before I'd pocketed my phone. Wiggling his fingers through that jagged hole, he growled, "Cheap damn hollow-core doors!"

"That's not all," I said, waving him inside, pointing out the damaged drywall.

"Jesus, Ali! this'll have to come out of your deposit. Did you have a drunken party? 'Cause I didn't get the invitation."

"Not even," I said. "If I pay for a better door, a *real* one, will you install it? Along with some extra locks?"

Dete looked me up and down. "Did that bastard hurt you? Do you want I should call the cops on him?"

"Not a him. And no. I just need a decent door—and to have my head examined."

"You're on your own for a shrink, but you'll have the door before I go off duty. The drywall repair's a few days of work. The mud has to set up before I paint."

"Whatever it takes, man."

Despite a new door that would have done Fort Knox proud, I lay awake that night worrying about Nicola. What if she came back? Broke a window by the fire escape and charged inside? Created a scene? Threatened me?

At midnight, I pounded out a text to London: *Are you awake? Can I sleep at your place?*

Yep & yep.

So I scrambled into clothing, then used my key to enter London's apartment. She was sitting on her futon beside a stack of pillows and linens, looking like a drowsy Peter Pan. Hair all mussed. Wearing shorts and an Indigo Girls T-shirt. Cuter than cute.

I plopped down on the other end of the futon and began filling her in. "I'm not seeing Nicola anymore. She's batshit crazy. And you'll need a new key to my place..."

Before leaving for class the next morning, London walked me to my door, one floor below hers. And she insisted on prowling around my tiny apartment to make sure nothing was amiss. At first I smiled indulgently, wondering how a half-pint like London thought she could have faced down Nic. But there was iron in her posture, anger in her eyes, and that search was beyond thorough. London even looked taller just then. What had Terra said at Wyldwomyn? "Her size is a trick of light...Actually, she's *enormous*." In a flash, I saw what Terra saw: someone who would protect and defend me to the death. What had I done to deserve such loyalty?

London's laughter broke through my trance. Gesturing at the usual disorder in my apartment—which looked much like your basic crime scene—she said, "No one's here. It must have been an inside job."

"Very funny. But thanks for everything...as always."

❖

Days passed without a word from Nicola, then week after peaceful week. Yet I missed her—how fucked up was that? Still, I suspected I'd gotten off lucky.

One desolate day, I dropped in on London at the library. The instant she spotted me, she disappeared into the stacks. On her return, she handed over a book. "You should read this—in case Nic comes back."

My eyes widened when I saw the title: *The Sociopath Next Door*. "That's harsh."

"Read before deciding..."

I shoved the hardback across the counter. "Not interested. Really—it sounds like a bridge too far."

London sighed, then stuck the book on a cart for reshelving. "Your loss."

"Oh, well...Are you up for dinner this Saturday?"

"Sure. My place? I'd like to try a new recipe."

"When have I ever turned down food? Especially if it's your cooking?"

"Bring dessert," she said.

That night, the word *sociopath* rolled relentlessly through my mind, so I jumped on Google. Where I found a bajillion articles describing that bizarre breed. Sociopaths were typically charming— but their charisma was merely a façade in service to selfish ends. They were dishonest, manipulative, calculating, unreliable, and often dangerous. They were also incapable of genuine love. Which sounded frighteningly familiar. And apparently, my hunch was correct: I'd gotten off lightly when Nic disappeared, because sociopaths were usually as hard to shake as they were vicious. Deeply depressed, I shut down my laptop. If Nicola Sevier wasn't a sociopath, I wasn't a drama major. And as an actor myself, why hadn't I realized she was a phony?

❖

Over dinner with London that Saturday, I told her what I'd learned from the Internet. She shot me an infuriating I-told-you-so look.

"You think you know me better than I know myself!"

"We've been in each other's back pockets since infancy. I know what you eat for breakfast, what you take for a headache, where you hide your chocolate when your nephew visits. I could probably guess what you sing in the shower."

Unbidden, a fantasy flitted through my mind: *London in the shower with me. Soaping my back. Turning me for a kiss. Kissing me lower, then...And lower...* I felt heat gather in my core, race upward, knew my face must be scarlet.

Thrusting my chair back, avoiding her eyes, I scooped up our plates. London followed with the breadbasket, the butter dish. I didn't face her again until my cheeks were cool. "If you don't have to study, I could stay for a movie."

"Great. I'll straighten the kitchen while you check Netflix. Find something funny, okay?"

Which was perfect. Right then I absolutely couldn't have risked anything with a hint of romance. So I scrolled through dozens of options—all of which seemed to have an amorous aspect. I finally settled for a Jeff Dunham special and cued it up, but London was still banging around the kitchen. As the scent of melting butter wafted into the living room, I plucked a chunky photo album from a stack on her coffee table. And who but London—whose favorite word was "tangible"—would own actual albums?

If I teased her about that, she'd just say: "I like real things, Ali—handling something from a precise place and period. I like the sense of age, of passing time. You don't get that with digital storage." A memory of the wyldwomyn rose up—that gang of happy hippies. No wonder London fit in so well with them...

I flipped open the book. And there it was: our entire childhood, arranged in chronological order. London and me in diapers, grinning at one another through the chain link fence that separated our backyards. London, stepping off the school bus on our first day of kindergarten, with me close behind. Both of us duded up for Halloween—me as Miley Cyrus during her sparkliest teen years, and London as Justin Bieber.

Eighth grade graduation followed, with London displaying a first-place plaque from some essay contest. Then dozens of hideous high school photos. Going solo to dances. Sharing pizza with our first loves—me making googly eyes at Hal Hudson, while London pretended she wasn't totally bonkers over Kirsti Sullivan. Even though their clandestine infatuation had lasted forever, had almost splintered *our* friendship. I didn't figure out London's fascination with Kirsti until senior year. And I didn't follow in their footsteps until I was a college freshman.

When London entered the living room, I snapped the album shut and tried to regroup. But I was having trouble getting past visions of Kirsti in her arms, of their first exploratory attempts at sex, of the pair becoming progressively more adept on sleepovers and campouts. Thoughts I'd never allowed myself to think back in the day.

London plunked two beers and a bowl of popcorn on her coffee table, then dropped down beside me. When we reached for handfuls of the buttery stuff, I brushed her fingers. The same fingers that had made love to highbrow Kirsti Sullivan. For years. Why couldn't I get that thought out of my mind? Kirsti was long gone from our lives, attending college on the East Coast, last I knew. Like London and me, she was probably closing in on a master's degree. And London never, ever mentioned her. I didn't even know if they'd parted amicably. Or if they'd suffered from that separation. Or whether she was still in love with Kirsti. A permanently broken heart might explain why London was a loner throughout college. But I didn't know, had never even wondered. *Self-absorbed much?* a silent, sardonic voice inquired.

I tried to concentrate on Dunham's "Dead Terrorist" routine, but memories of Kirsti intruded. When the show was finally over, I picked up that album and tapped a picture. "Where's Kirsti now? Do you ever hear from her?"

"Not since she ditched me just before heading to Boston."

"She was an idiot."

"No. She wasn't. Kirsti realized I could never commit to her, and she had enough self-respect to walk away." London drained her beer bottle, set it down with an emphatic thunk. Then she stared into my eyes, daring me to ask the obvious.

"What does that mean?"

"Kirsti knew I was hung up on someone else—and always had been. In the beginning, I guess she hoped that would change— maybe I did, too. Ultimately, we both concluded it wouldn't."

My heart was pounding, my stomach clenching. I looked away, afraid we were on the cusp of a revelation that would alter our friendship forever.

London touched my hand, then whispered, "Just because it's *good*, Ali, doesn't mean it's *bad*. You don't always have to choose a loser."

There it was again: London's uncanny ability to divine my every thought. Which pissed me off. "If you're so smart, tell me what I'm thinking right now."

It turned out that wasn't even a challenge. London leaned in, her lips met mine, and suddenly I was swamped by a tidal wave of chemistry. I wrenched free, breathless and panicky. When I snatched up my bag, fumbled for my keys, London waited patiently. Then, inexplicably, every fear evaporated, and I couldn't have said what

I was running from. Because London was smart and funny and sexy. But most important, she was a true friend. She'd never hurt or humiliate me. And all at once I saw that I'd loved her forever. *Goddamn! London was right again!*

"I'm so dumb," I moaned.

"Not," she said, slipping my keys from my hand, dropping them in my purse. "You're the best thing ever—just a tad distractible in the presence of shiny objects."

"Maybe you could sharpen my focus." I raised her hand to my breast.

She levered me off the futon and led me to her bedroom, which was scarcely more than an alcove, almost filled by an expansive bed. Like everything that London touched, the space was orderly and inviting. In place of a headboard, a vintage poster of Janis Joplin smiled down upon us. London nodded at the photo. "I think she'd approve." And then she kissed me again. I'd thought Nicola Sevier knew her way around my libido, but London put the woman to shame.

I broke away to unfasten her shirt, then gazed in wonder at her matchless body. The gently defined musculature. The sweet, subtle curve of breast. Tufts of pale hair nestled in her armpits—a surprising discovery, and unexpectedly dear. Perhaps an homage to the wyldwomyn? And, oh! That softly rounded stomach sloping downward to an enticing unknown. Impetuous as always, I unzipped London's Levi's, stripped off my shirt, kicked out of my slacks.

We came together like lovers long separated, with a hunger that rocked us both. As I licked and lapped and sucked and thrust, London was reduced to words of one syllable: *"Yes! Ali! That! You!"*

And when she returned the favor, I could only cry, *"More! Please! Now!"*

We exhausted ourselves, then exhausted ourselves again. London's final assault on my virtue triggered sensations unlike any I'd experienced. I was upside down, inside out, electric, melting, out-of-body, nothing *but* body, the very definition of ecstatic. When I finally regained my powers of speech, I said, "What in hell was *that?*"

She kissed my throat, tweaked a yearning nipple, blew in one ear before answering. "It's called the butterfly rotation. Not to be confused with the singularity spiral. And we have yet to explore the tristeria phenomenon."

"You're making that up, right?"

London propped herself on one elbow and grinned down at me, her blue eyes sparkling. "I'm *very* well read—and it's amazing how much you can learn during downtime at the library."

Which didn't really answer my question. But I was certain that further research would clarify the matter. Pulling her closer, I said, "I'd love to be your study buddy, Ms. Woodruff."

London rolled atop me. Slipping one thigh between my legs, she slid it rhythmically against my important parts. "The position is yours. Permanently."

BLACK OUT

Ronica Black

The raw, earthy scent draws me out to my patio despite it being after eleven and nearly pitch black. The power is out due to the storm, and I'd rather watch the water dance on the lake than watch a flame dance on a candle. I sit in a lounger, cross my bare feet, and stare into the glassy lake water, mussed by the smattering of the falling sky. Distant candlelight on other patios looks like hazy moons in the monsoon mist, and tethered boats make odd sounds as they sway against the docks. My neighbors are no doubt turning in for the night, or, like me, they are sitting and staring, enjoying a summer storm.

I sip the wine in my glass and cringe but drink it anyway. Writers are supposed to have vices, and I have yet to find one that fits. Still, I try to enjoy the occasional buzz it gives me. Tonight, however, I'm buzz free and razor sharp, senses on key, libido on fire. My large house is empty save my dog, who associates rain with a bath and avoids both at all costs. She's looking at me through the window, a worried look on her face. I read somewhere that dogs live in the present. That they don't feel fear and don't worry. Bullshit.

She barks, ears back in alert. She stands and so do I, depositing my wineglass on the table. Thunder breaks and she goes crazy, running through the house. I step through the back door and nearly shiver at the cold remaining from the air conditioner. My skin is damp from the mist, and I catch the faint scent of Coppertone from my earlier excursion on the golf course. I need a long, cool shower and an hour or two at my laptop, but I'm procrastinating, one of three things I'm really good at.

Mama Jo is still barking as I move through the dim house. I find her at the front door, little butt wiggling. I shush her and look out the window. A woman is there, one I soon recognize as my neighbor, Cindy or Sidney, or something along those lines, blond hair wet and sticking to her tanned skin. I back away from the window and whisper at Mama Jo to be quiet. Cindy or Sidney? Cindy or Sidney? Fuck, I can't remember. I'm terrible with names, great with faces. Just never good with both.

I think about pretending to be asleep or not at home. But she looks desperate and alone in the dark, and I can't help but wonder what she wants. I'm nervous, not just because I'm unsure of her name, but because she's gorgeous and I've been trying like hell to watch her from afar while remaining aloof. Ridiculous, I know, but she's married with kids, and me, I've been known to be a right shit and not care about such things. Married straight women seem to be my specialty. And frankly, that is another one of the three things I'm very, very good at.

I unbolt the door, shooing Mama Jo back, and pull the door open. My neighbor wipes the water from her forehead and smiles, and things inside me begin to shoot off like fireworks.

"Hi, sorry to bother you. Sidney, from next door." She motions toward her home, pushes back wet hair, and smooths down the front of her khaki shorts. Her T-shirt is white and soaked, and damn it if I can't see her black lacy bra. Her nipples are thick and hard, showing her chill. I blink, try to fixate on the dark chocolate of her eyes, and try to control my insides. She continues, her nerves showing with her words. "I uh, well, I can't seem to find a flashlight that works, and all my candles are up on this shelf in the closet and I can't reach them even if I could see them."

I hear her, it makes sense and computes, but I don't move. Or speak. Mama Jo barks as if to wake me, and I jerk and force an embarrassed smile. I pull the door open farther and unlock the security door. "Of course, come on in. I'm sure I have one or two around here somewhere."

She thanks me, laughs a little, and steps inside. She moves past me and I inhale her. She smells like a scented bath and her skin glistens as if it's been soaked in oil. I lock the door behind us and head for the living room, but she hesitates.

"Um, I can't really see. I'm afraid I'm completely blind in the dark."

I stop, turn, and before I know it, I'm taking her hand, which is warm and soft. It makes my skin flush with heat, and I swear I can hear her breath catch at the contact. I try to ignore it and busy myself making small talk as I lead her through my home. We come to the kitchen, where I have a single candle lit. I release her to dig through a cabinet where I find more candles and matches. I light another one on the counter, and the room comes alive with a soft glow. She smiles as if relieved, moves her gaze from mine, and sits at a bar stool.

"No fan of the dark?" I light another candle and place it on the coffee table in the adjoining living room. The house is now dancing and breathing with soft light. Mama Jo jumps on the couch and relaxes like my guest, puffing out a breath of air as she settles down.

"No, not at all." She seems embarrassed. "Childhood fear, I'm afraid."

I dig through my junk drawer, searching for a flashlight. Damn if I can find one.

"Where are your kids?" I can't help but wonder. Her two small daughters are often attached to her hip. In fact, the only time I see them without her is when they are delivering cookies and casseroles to my front door, hopping up and down with excitement. Apparently, being single in a family neighborhood is cause for worry, and everyone equates it with near starvation.

"They're with their dad tonight." She's staring into the candle as if it's telling her story to her.

"Oh. Why didn't you go?" I'm kneeling now, looking in the lower cabinet. I can't see her, but I hear her intake of breath and hesitation.

"We're, uh, separated now."

I stop moving containers of cleaner around. How did I not notice this? And why is it making my heart beat faster now that I know?

"I'm sorry." I don't dare stand, for I'm absolutely sure she will see the raging desire building within me. For weeks I've watched her from a distance, saying hello whenever we meet. In the early morning, I run and she walks. On the road I drive my golf cart to run my errands and she passes me in her yellow convertible. On the golf course I drink with my buddies to help my terrible slice and she often smiles and waves as she plays behind us with her friends. On the water, I fly fish from my dock while she cruises slowly by in her boat, bikini top and surf shorts.

Just when I think I'm ahead of the curve and I know I'm purposely going to run into her, she surprises me by appearing before my planned moment. Now it's the mailbox. She's often sifting through her mail as I approach my box, key in hand, eyes squinting in the sun, taking a much-needed break from my writing corner. It seems she's everywhere, and now she's separated, and what's worse, she's in my house on a dark, rainy night.

I ignore the two flashlights I find in the cabinet and stand slowly. I glance at her, meet her quick gaze, and look away, but not before I'm once again moved by the angle of her jaw and the slash of her cheekbone. I know she is a photographer, but I wonder if anyone has ever photographed her. I don't have a clue about cameras or lighting or anything remotely close to photography, but I damn well know I'd love to take her picture, blow it up, and hang it on my wall.

"Don't be," she eventually says. "It's been a long time coming."

I press my lips together, unsure what to say. I decide to lie about the flashlight but I don't want to, afraid she'll leave regardless.

"I have no idea where my flashlight is," I say. "Probably in my car, and for sure the heat has drained the battery."

She sighs. "That's fine. Thanks for looking."

"You're welcome to as many candles as you need." I have a

dozen or so in the cabinet. And suddenly I'm concerned about my scented candle obsession. "I like my house to smell good."

She laughs a little. "It does smell good."

I cross to the candle cabinet and begin removing lids for her to smell. "I have all kinds."

"Actually, if it's okay with you...I'd prefer to hang out here."

I turn, holding a candle that promises to smell like a thunderstorm. "Oh."

She stands, walks to me, and takes the candle. She's looking into my eyes, pulling me in like a magnet. "I don't want to be alone."

She holds the candle to her nose and inhales. "Mmm, I like that one. But I like the way you smell better."

I find myself blinking in disbelief. I fight for breath while she returns to the stool and slides on. "There's something about the smell of suntan lotion and sweat that gets to me. Just makes me want to lick it."

I let out a noise of half laughter, half shock. She looks at me and smiles, but it's different this time. It's less friendly. Less innocent.

It's hungry.

I move to my couch and sit. The pressure on my clit sends it throbbing, along with my heart. I shift, scoot back, and try to look casual. I cross my legs but my clit prevents it. Her words keep replaying in my mind, and I try to remember the last time anyone had their mouth on me.

"You don't mind if I stay, do you?" She turns on the stool and stares me down. "I know it's late, but I know you're a bit of a night owl."

I feel my eyebrows raise. "No, I don't mind. I, uh, was just going to do some work, but honestly I've been putting it off."

"You're a writer," she says. "Pamela told me." Pamela lives on my other side, and she knows everything about everybody. It didn't surprise me that she'd told Sidney about my profession.

"Yes." I burn, knowing the next question. She is going to ask me what I write. To anyone else I can declare what I write, no problem. But to a beautiful woman, gay or straight, it isn't as easy.

"You write lesbian romance," she says, flooring me.

I rub my palms on my cotton shorts. "Mm-hmm."

She nods. "Do you like it?" She fingers her shirt, makes a face like she's uncomfortable.

"Yeah, it's…I don't know…"

"Fun?" She grins. "Can I take this off? I'm freezing."

I nod, frozen. Then, manners taking over my libido, I rise to get her a dry one. "I have a few small ones that might fit you." I head for the bedroom, heart pounding. What's happening here? Is she flirting? Coming on to me? Does she know what she's doing?

No, of course not. She just doesn't realize that she's not hanging out with a straight girlfriend. She's not trying to get to me. To turn me on.

I rummage through my dresser drawer and find a small tee. I turn to return to the living room but I see her glowing with candlelight in my doorway. She's holding a candle, wearing her black lace bra and matching panties. Her body is unbelievable. Tanned and toned. Petite but strong.

"I hope you don't mind," she says. "But wet clothes are no fun."

I hold out the T-shirt, speechless.

She enters the room. Places the candle on the dresser. Takes the shirt from my hands. She places it, too, on the dresser.

"For a writer, you don't say very much."

She reaches out, touches my face. I let out a shaky breath, breathe back in and then come alive.

"Sometimes words are useless." I place my hands on her hips and tug her closer. There's no mistaking it now. And I can't stop the freight train of feelings rushing through my body even if I wanted to. She makes a noise of approval and collides into me. I meet her open mouth with mine and we devour one another like long-lost, starving beings. Our tongues seek and thrust and I can't get enough of her, can't pull her close enough. My fingers dig into her full ass and I lift her with her legs straddled around me. She moans, kisses me deeper, knots fingers in my hair, and grinds her hot crotch against my abdomen. She's hungry for it, begging for release.

I take her to the bed, push her onto her back. Her legs cling to me and she's thrusting as if she can't help herself, wanting me to fuck her.

"Please," she says. "I want you so bad." She runs her hand down her body and rubs herself through the fabric of her panties. "I've never...Please touch me. Oh God, I feel like I'm going to explode."

I push her hand away, remove my own shirt, and lower to kiss her deeply. I press my body against her aching flesh and tease her with the pressure. She moans into me and I throw my head back and cry out as she runs her nails down my bare back.

"Don't toy with me," she says. "I can't take it."

She releases the grip of her legs and lightly kicks me away. Then she scrambles back on the bed, lies on a pillow, and spreads her legs.

"I know you want this," she says. "I see you watching me while trying so hard not to."

She runs her hand down to her panties again. "Come put your mouth on me." Her fingers tug the lace aside and I can see how pink and slick she is in the dancing light. "Make me come. Make me come so hard."

I feel my mouth salivate and I crawl unto the bed. I kiss her thigh, moving up slowly. Impatient, she tugs on my hair and digs nails into my shoulder.

"Fucking do it," she says, and her demand goes right to my clit and I nearly come in my shorts.

I lick up her inner thigh and snake my tongue into the peeking flesh, sending her bucking. I withdraw, wrap my fingers around her panties, and yank them down and off. She's panting now and playing with herself. Her dark eyes are flashing with desire and her abdominal muscles are tensing.

I want to feed from her. Take her in my mouth and suck so hard she comes out of her skin. But I'm getting off on the dirty talk and I don't want her to stop.

"Hurry," she says.

"I don't want to," I say. "I want to take my time, take you in slowly." Playing a woman's body long and slow is the third thing I'm really, really good at. But she wants none of it, and though I love a woman talking dirty in bed, I'm not ready for her. She sits up, grabs my face, and kisses me. She owns me with her tongue and then pulls away, biting my lower lip in the process. I make a noise of protest, of slight pain, but there isn't time to complain, for her hand has dug down into my shorts and found me, wet and hungry. She strokes me—I tremble and she laughs. Then her fingers frame my engorged clit and squeeze.

"Give it to me," she says. She bites my lip again. "Now." She squeezes harder, then strokes, and I make noises I don't recognize as coming from me.

"Fucking do it or I fucking play you."

She lies down again and removes her hand from my center. Both of her hands then knot in my hair and she's pulling me to her, raising her hips to meet my mouth. I give in, so turned on I'm ready to spontaneously combust. I take her flesh like I'm dying and suck so hard she screams. I laugh, pleased at her response, and begin to bob as I suck, giving her a little tongue as I pull back each time.

She scratches my back, scalp, and shoulders as she writhes beneath me, crying out, thrusting, and squeezing her eyes closed. When she comes she goes hoarse, sits straight up, holds my head to her until I'm nearly smothered.

"Fucking hell," she rasps, pulsing against me one last time before releasing me to collapse back on the bed. My ears are ringing and I struggle for breath, but I manage to laugh and roll to my side. In an instant she's on me, pushing me to my back and straddling me.

"You like that?" she asks.

"Yeah," I breathe.

She massages my breasts and pinches my nipples. "You're fucking something else," she says. "I knew you would be."

She reaches back, finds my flesh and begins to milk me. "You see, I've been wanting you for a while now. Watching. Waiting. Learning all I can about you. And then when Pamela told me about your books...I could hardly control myself."

I jerk against her, so close I can hardly concentrate on her words.

"I made sure I ran into you as much as possible. Waiting...for you to notice."

"I did notice," I say.

She stops her hand. Teasing me. "Why didn't you say anything?"

I lift my hips. "Like what? You're married."

She grins. "I was afraid that was what was stopping you." She milks me again, bringing me right to the edge. "It's important to you, that I'm not with him?"

I buck, grip her hips. "Yeah—yeah."

She stops and I groan.

"What about kids? You know I have the kids."

"Love the kids," I say. "Please."

"I don't love him," she says. "I haven't for a long time. You believe me?" Her eyes are dark and serious and her upper lip trembles.

I touch her face, trace her jaw with my fingertips. "Kiss me," I say.

She bends, kisses me. Softly, then deeper, and then fierce.

She pushes herself back up, grinds her flesh against my abdomen, and reaches back to find mine. She strokes me as she moves, and we both pant and moan and sweat in the low light. She closes her eyes and quickens, opens them and asks if I'm going to come.

I say yes and she explodes atop me and I buck up into her hand and nearly knock her off. We lock hands and she plays me, harder, faster, until I'm screaming and writhing and shoving back into my pillow. And just before my waves of orgasm dissipate, she moves down my body and finds me with her hot mouth. New waves come, bigger, stronger, and I shatter into her, my fingers lost in her hair. When I eventually still, she looks up at me, grins, and climbs to me.

She rests her slick body on mine, looks into my eyes.

"I have a confession to make," she says. "I'm not really afraid of the dark."

I laugh. "Really? Well, since we're telling the truth, I have plenty of flashlights."

She kisses me, bites my lower lip softly. "Mmm. Bad girl."

"I only lied after you said you were separated."

"I see."

In the distance a ringing sounds, and Mama Jo barks and trots down the hall toward the bedroom. Sidney looks at me for a moment as if she's questioning the noise and then her eyes widen and she shoves herself away and runs down the hall. I hear her answer her phone.

I can't hear what she says, but I know the news isn't good. Mama Jo jumps on the bed, circles, and lies down.

"She's leaving," I say.

Sidney appears in the doorway. "I need to go."

"I know." I still can't help but stare at her.

"One of my girls had a nightmare. She wants to come home."

I sit up, watch the candlelight dance against her beautiful form. "I understand."

She comes to me, slowly. She kisses me so soft, so deep, I know she doesn't want to go.

"Come to dinner tomorrow," she says. "Please."

I nod.

She smiles and holds my face. "Thank you," she says.

"For what?"

"For giving me what no one ever has before."

"You're kidding."

She shakes her head. A tear falls. "I didn't know it could be so good."

I wipe her tear. "Oh, honey, it can be really, really good. That was only a taste."

She laughs and the power kicks on. Mama Jo barks and jumps from the bed.

Sidney pulls away. "See you tomorrow."

"Tomorrow," I say, watching her disappear from the room. I slip on my shirt, walk to the door, and lean against the wall as I watch her dress from down the hall. I meet her at the front door.

"I would kiss you again but I don't think I'd be able to tear myself away from you," she says.

I pull her close, breathe in her neck and hair. I feel her shudder against me.

"Go," I say, pulling away, afraid I, too, will lose control. She opens the door and steps into the drizzle. I watch her jog to her home in the weak streetlight. Then I close the door, lock it, and head back into the living room. I grab my laptop and open the door to the back patio. I sit in my lounge chair and stare out at the water, now playing with porch lights. I glance at the wine, but I don't want it. I want to taste her for as long as I can.

I settle in and think about closing my eyes. But I know it is useless, sleep will not be coming tonight. Instead, I open my laptop and begin doing what I do best...telling a story.

DOG DAY OF SUMMER

Kris Bryant

You know it's time. I told you about this last night." Summer carried the buckets of warm water out to the backyard and walked slowly toward Max, the stray she'd found dumped at the Sugar Creek Animal Clinic last week. Nobody else at the clinic could get near him. Summer decided right then and there that she was his person. After tricking him into her car with treats and soft scratches behind his ears, she drove them to her two-bedroom home with a backyard big enough for a medium-sized dog to enjoy. Max paced the house the entire night, settling down on her bed when dawn broke. Her fractured sleep was punctuated by soft whimpers and sharp smells she didn't think should come from another living thing. "I promise to be gentle about this, but if you are going to sleep in my bed, you have to be clean." Max's ears lay flat against his head the closer she got to him. "No, no, no. We have to do this, buddy." Summer followed Max's sideways glance and noticed the side gate was open. Before she had a chance to react, her neighbor, the one who zoomed her motorcycle up and down the street at all hours of the day and night, the same neighbor whose grass was in desperate need of trimming, picked that exact moment to roar up the driveway, scaring both of them.

"Are you kidding me?" Summer yelled. Max ran for the partially opened gate, blowing through it without slowing down. "This is just great. Max! Max, come back here." She dropped the washcloth and sponge and ran after him. Unsure of which way he went, she ran down the block one way, turned around, and headed in the opposite direction, passing her neighbor, who stood there at the end of the driveway. Never mind that her neighbor looked fantastic in her tight faded Levi's and her tight black T-shirt. Or how toned her arms were as they casually held the motorcycle helmet close to her trim waist. Regardless of how attractive her neighbor was, Summer was pissed.

"Excuse me. What just happened here?" The neighbor pushed back the dark curls that fell across her forehead and stood directly in Summer's path. Summer had no choice but to stop.

"Your obnoxiously loud bike scared my dog, and he ran off," she said.

"I'm sorry. I didn't mean to scare you both. Hang on. I'll help you catch him if you want. I just need to throw my stuff down inside." Knowing two sets of eyes were better than one, Summer reluctantly gave a curt nod. She tried not to watch her neighbor's long legs as they climbed the stairs two at a time. Tried. It was hard to not to admire how those jeans clung to her body. They left little to Summer's sexually frustrated imagination. She turned her head when her neighbor headed back her way. "Look, I really am sorry about your dog. What's his name?"

"Max. He's a stray. I've been working with him at the clinic for a week and brought him home for the first time last night. He doesn't know his way around our neighborhood. What happens if I don't find him? What happens if he gets hit by a car? He must be so scared." Summer felt strong, warm hands on her bare arms and looked up at her neighbor. The green eyes staring back at her showed concern and compassion, neither of which she'd seen in a very long time.

"We will find him. Whatever it takes. Is that your truck?" Summer nodded. "It might be easier to drive around to find him." They quickly headed to the compact truck that was parked on the street. Summer slipped into the driver's seat and her neighbor crammed her long body into the passenger side.

"You can adjust the seat back. I had it forward because Max was sitting there. You'll probably get dog hair all over your clothes."

"I'm not worried. I have to do laundry tonight anyway. Is Max chipped? I mean, if somebody finds him, will they know how to get him back to you?"

"He's not chipped." Summer could hear the panic in her voice. "But he is wearing a collar with all of my contact information. I'm going to have him chipped once he trusts me." She rolled down her window and yelled for him. "Max! Come here, boy." When she looked to the right, she noticed her neighbor texting somebody and not looking out of the window for Max. "Are you seriously not helping me right now?" Those beautiful green eyes flashed angrily at Summer.

"I'm letting my little brother know that I'm with you. He heard the front door open and was worried that somebody else was in the house. He's laid up with a broken leg and doesn't get around the greatest."

Summer turned her head in embarrassment. "I'm sorry. I'm really not usually this rude. Let me start over. Hi, I'm Summer," she said.

"Call me Hart."

"Your name is Hart?" Summer asked in surprise.

"Well, it's what I go by," she said. At Summer's questioning look, Hart elaborated. "It's my last name. I've been going by it my whole life. Besides, it beats my first name."

"Do I dare ask?" Hart glared at her. "Okay. That's a no."

"We should head to the park a few blocks over. I bet he went there. Open space, grass, food. I know if I was a dog, that's where I would go," Hart said. Summer headed that direction, both women on the lookout for one forty-pound black-and-tan pup on the run.

"Yeah, we saw a dog that looked like that run by us about ten minutes or so." The old man waved his cane behind him, narrowly missing his wife. Summer thanked him and whipped her truck into the parking lot. She grabbed Max's leash, and she and Hart headed out on foot in the direction the man pointed.

"How did your brother break his leg?" Summer asked. She struggled to keep up with Hart's long stride. "And how do you walk so fast in those boots? They must weigh ten pounds." Summer was rewarded with a beautiful sideways smile. She was surprised at the fluttering she felt inside her chest.

"They aren't that heavy, and I only wear them when I ride." Hart slowed her step so that Summer could catch up. "My brother got T-boned while driving my car a few weeks ago. The car? Totaled. My brother? Wrecked. That's why I'm stuck driving my Harley. I'm really sorry I'm so loud. As soon as I get the insurance check, I will get a car. A quiet one."

"How's your brother doing?" Summer asked.

"Physically, he's healing nicely. Emotionally, Jamie is a typical teenager. I can't tell if it's teenage angst or teenage hormones. He's up one minute, down the next. I have a hard time keeping up," Hart said.

Summer liked the way Hart's curls fell into her face and how she constantly pushed them back behind her ear. The back was shaved close to her neck, but the front was long. Her skin was smooth, and even though it was sun-kissed, Summer could see the bluish purple smudges under Hart's green eyes, indicating that sleep was not a friend. She was hit with an overwhelming urge to be kind to her, even take care of her. Hart's boyish charm was sexy and stirred feelings in Summer that she had suppressed months ago.

"Enough about my family. Tell me about yours. Is it just you and Max, or is there somebody else?"

Summer put her hand against her stomach to settle the fluttering again. Was Hart making chitchat, or was there genuine interest in that question? "My girlfriend and I broke up about six months ago, so it's just me. Well, and now Max."

She gasped when she felt Hart's hand rest on her shoulder. The touch was unexpected and excited her instantly. "Look, Summer. Is that him? Is that Max?" Summer followed Hart's point and started running in that direction.

"Max! Come here, boy," she said. Max looked up from his lunch of leftover chicken and brownie crumbs. He eyed Summer warily, and she slowed down so as to not scare him again. "Let's go home, okay? No bath today. We can skip it." She motioned Hart to hang back and knelt down, holding out her hand to him. He licked up something Summer hoped was potato salad but wasn't quite sure. She inched her way forward and kept her voice even and calm. She was only a few feet in front of him when he started wagging his tail slightly. "Yeah, boy. It's me. How about we go home and eat something better than this?" She inched closer. He moved back a few steps.

"Um, Summer?" Summer waved off Hart, motioning her to be quiet. "No, really. You need to look at me." Summer turned quickly to her, only to shoot Hart a miffed look. She looked back at Max and gently rubbed her fingers together to get him to pay attention to her. It was at the exact moment when she leaned forward to try to pet Max that a small raccoon jumped out of the trash can, eyes wild, paws up, ready for a fight. Summer let out a scream and fell backward, landing half in discarded barbecue and half in something wet. She scooted as far away from the garbage cans as she could, and stopped when she smacked into Hart's legs. The raccoon stood up on his hind legs and chattered at them, waving his body back and forth. Max took off like a bullet. The raccoon squeaked out his anger and, after eyeing both women suspiciously, bounced off into some bushes, a half-eaten hot dog clutched in one of his paws.

"Did that just really happen? Isn't it bad when you see raccoons in the daylight? I mean, aren't they dangerous?" Summer asked in complete disbelief.

"I tried to tell you."

Realizing she was still clutching Hart's leg out of fear, Summer slowly let go and smoothed down the crumpled jeans she had gathered in her fist. Hart reached down to help her up, slowly, liking the feel of Summer against her body.

"And what the hell did I land in?" Summer looked down at the stains on her shorts and tried her best to knock some of the garbage off. "How bad is it?" Hart raised her eyebrows and quickly looked away to hide her smile. "Crap."

"Well, at least we found him and know what direction he went,"

Hart said. She found a relatively clean napkin, handed it to Summer, and set the garbage cans upright while Summer cleaned up.

"Across the park is the elementary school. If we can't find him in the park, maybe he went there," Summer said. She tossed the napkin in the trash and headed after Max, leaving a wide berth around the bushes that housed the angry raccoon.

"Should we go back for the truck?" Hart asked.

"Now that we know he's here, I don't think we should waste time backtracking. I mean, if you need to go, I understand," Summer said.

"No. I'm the reason you're in this mess to begin with, so let's keep going," Hart said. "Why is Max so skittish?"

"I work at the Sugar Creek Animal Clinic, and I showed up for work one morning and somebody had him chained up out back to our fence."

Hart heard the anger in Summer's voice and automatically touched her forearm for comfort. "There are a lot of assholes in our world for sure. But now he has you."

"If we find him." Summer sulked.

"I promise we will. Maybe he just sees this as an adventure. I'm sure he knows you will take good care of him. Last night was your first night together, right?"

"Yes. It took him forever, but he finally settled down early this morning. He's completely filthy, so I decided if he's going to be on my bed and on the furniture, he's going to need a bath," Summer said.

"Especially after digging through the trash. When we catch him, I'll even help you give him a bath," Hart said.

Summer liked the way Hart stressed the word "when."

"And if he doesn't like me, I'll stand guard at the gate so he can't get out. If he's nervous and starts running around the yard, you can nail him with the hose." For the first time that day, Hart saw Summer smile and decided she was going to make her smile again and again because it was a beautiful sight. Summer was the kind of girl that Hart wasn't normally attracted to. She was at least six inches shorter than Hart with long light brown hair and blue eyes.

She was femme and sensitive and probably needed more attention than Hart could give, but that didn't stop Hart from appreciating her neighbor's sharp curves and red, full lips.

"I figured it would be easier outside than in a tub. I can just see Max escaping the bathroom and getting the entire house wet," she said.

"How long have you lived in your house?" Hart asked. Hart had purchased the house next door to Summer almost three months ago, and today was the first day she'd seen her neighbor. Jamie had moved into her tiny apartment by the university after their parents died five years before, and they made it work. It was an adjustment, and therapy helped, but buying the house really gave Jamie the stability he craved. Hart's hospital shifts were unpredictable, but her boss worked with her to maintain some sort of consistency for her brother's sake.

"I lived with my grandmother, and when she passed away, I inherited the bungalow. I love it. You moved in a few months ago, right?" Hart nodded. "I'm sorry I haven't come over to introduce myself sooner." Hart shrugged. With her crazy schedule at the hospital, she understood more than anybody how life got in the way of manners.

"You probably would have only met Jamie. I'm not home a lot. He's always wanted a dog. I'm sure he will love Max. Once he's healed up, he'll probably beg to take him for walks," Hart said.

"I hope so. Max is still super skittish around other people. I hope that I can calm him down enough to train him." Summer's voice was not hopeful.

"I'm sure he will be fine after a few weeks. Is he still young?" Hart asked.

"Probably only a year old. We aren't quite sure," she said. They reached the end of the park, and if it wasn't for Hart's firm grasp on Summer's waist, Summer would have walked right into traffic just to get to the elementary school across the street.

"Look, I feel bad enough that I scared your puppy off. Last thing I need to do is have to get you to a hospital, sew you up, and still try to find Max. One stressful task at a time, please," Hart said.

She loosened her grip and slid her hand down to Summer's wrist, keeping her safely back on the curb until the cars cleared the street. If she slid her hand just a few inches more, their fingers would touch. Hart flushed at the thought, the blossoming heat welcoming and confusing all at once. She really did not have time for a girlfriend. Work was brutal. Her sex life was sparse at best. Quick releases in the shower, or if she really needed human touch, she would call Lori, the pharmaceutical representative, to have dinner and fast sex in her car or in one of the on-call rooms. It was a nice set-up for both of them, but it had been several months. Yet standing next to this beautiful, petite woman, Hart was rethinking her "wham bam thank you ma'am" attitude. Summer was the type of woman you wined and dined and treated with respect. Suddenly, that didn't sound like such a bad thing.

"I'll head to the back of the building and meet you in the playground if you want to circle the front of the school. That way if he runs to the back, he's trapped," Hart suggested. Summer agreed and they split up. Hart hopped the fence and quietly walked to the back of the empty school. When she rounded the corner, she stopped in surprise. Max was under the slide eating something. Did this dog eat everything?

"Max. Hey. Hi. I'm Hart. I live next door to your mommy," she said. Max stopped chewing and looked at her. He stood up when she got within fifteen feet. Hart was afraid he was going to bolt again, so she froze. Where was Summer? Max was getting restless, and Hart knew he wasn't going to stick around much longer. She had to make a decision. She could try to get him into the little alcove by the back door and trap him until Summer arrived with his leash. She stretched out her arms and walked toward him, hoping to make herself seem bigger. He darted to the left, but Hart was quick and blocked him. He turned and tried to race around her, but failed. Finally, after a bit of back-and-forth dodging, Max ran into the alcove per Hart's plan. She followed him and tried her best to calm him as he paced in the enclosed area. Hart prayed Summer would show up soon with the leash. Where was she? "Max. Buddy. It's okay. Settle down." Much to her surprise, he sat. Feeling confident and somewhat the alpha dog now, Hart stepped closer. Max laid his ears back against his head and wagged his tail. Hart felt confident that he was going to stay put, so she moved closer to him. The second she was within reach and touched his collar, he spun out of her grasp and twirled her so she crashed against the chain link fence. As she bounced off it, she heard a giant rip in her jeans. "Son of a—" Hart looked behind her and saw her back pocket dangling down, her boxer briefs bared to the world. She sighed. She'd picked a really bad day to wear her sushi-themed underwear. Not only was the world going to see it, but her sexy neighbor would, too. Realizing it was futile to fix them, Hart left the ripped jeans alone and turned her attention back to Max who, surprisingly, was sitting down watching her. She swore he was smiling. He broke eye contact with her and turned his head when Summer called out his name. Max trotted out of the alcove and dashed past Summer as she rounded the corner of the school. She lunged for him, but he darted past her, his adventure far from over.

"Why does he keep running away? What happened to you?"

"You don't even want to know what just happened. I honestly think he's playing with us," Hart said. She tried to keep her backside hidden from Summer, but it was hard when half of her jeans were hanging down.

"Let me try to help." Hart turned around and let out a growl when she heard Summer stifle a laugh. "It's not that bad." Hart lifted her eyebrow at Summer. "Okay, it is, but jeans with a jagged rip are sexy. Um, we should go."

Hart couldn't stop from smiling. Summer was adorable when she was flustered.

"Can we stop quickly and grab something to eat?" Hart hated interrupting their search and rescue mission, but she hadn't eaten since yesterday. "Something quick. We can stop at a gas station and I can pick up some peanut butter crackers or chips."

"We can drive through somewhere. I'm sorry. I wasn't thinking," Summer said. They had been driving around for the last three hours without a trace of Max. It was past dinnertime, and in an hour it was going to be too dark to see. Summer didn't want to think about it. She didn't want to think about Max all alone, in the dark, holed up in a bush somewhere. No water, no food—well, not the kind she wanted him to eat. She didn't want anybody to have him, either, because if somebody had him, they should have called by now. And if they didn't, then that made them assholes for stealing somebody's dog.

"Just somewhere quick," Hart said. "It's not like my eating habits are fantastic. Me and the vending machine at the hospital are BFFs."

"Do you not cook? Does your brother cook?"

"He's actually quite the little chef. He just hates to clean."

Summer darted into the nearest fast food restaurant. Their dinner of cheeseburgers and Cokes was eaten on the go. They drove past the park twice, the elementary school, the grocery store, and circled the neighborhood over and over. They stopped evening walkers, kids on bikes, and people who were getting out of their cars to ask if they had seen Max.

"What am I going to do, Hart? We haven't seen Max in hours, and it's dark." Summer pulled her truck over and stared at Hart. Hart reached out and rubbed Summer's back in tiny circles to calm her. Summer chalked up her racing heart to anxiety over the lateness of the hour, not the warmth and closeness of Hart.

"If we don't find him tonight, I'll help you in the morning before my shift." Hart moved her hand up to Summer's shoulder and gave it a gentle squeeze. She kept her hand there and brushed her fingers softly against Summer's skin. It was completely inappropriate after knowing her less than a day, but it felt right. Summer didn't move. As a matter of fact, Hart swore Summer caught her breath and briefly closed her eyes when Hart moved her fingers to brush a few strands of hair away from her own neck. "Are you tired of driving? Do you want me to?"

"Let's just go home. It's too dark to see anything anymore. I just hope he's somewhere safe and hidden from people."

"I'm sure he knows how to take care of himself for one night,"

Hart said. She moved her hand from Summer's warmth, instantly missing the connection. She didn't want the night to end, but tonight did not seem like the right time to hit on her.

Summer headed for their street, driving slowly in case they saw him. She parked in front of her house and rested her head against the steering wheel. When she turned her head to look at Hart, she shrieked. "Max!" Hart turned and saw Max sitting on the porch, wagging his tail as if the last ten hours hadn't been solely about him and his shenanigans around town. Summer yanked open the car door and raced up the steps, forgetting that she might scare him again. He greeted her with kisses and didn't try to escape. Hart closed the front gate in case he tried to make a run for it again. "Where have you been? You scared me. Don't ever do that again." She was rewarded with warm kisses all over her face.

"You owe me a new pair of jeans, bud," Hart said. She, too, was rewarded with tail wags. "Did you enjoy your one and only day of freedom?" She crouched down by him, and he sniffed her hand. He nudged her and she reached out to pet the top of his head.

"You're the only other person who has been able to touch him," Summer said. "He really likes you." They both babied him for a bit before Hart decided she needed to get home to check on Jamie.

"I'm so happy he showed up. It was nice hanging out with you today, Summer." She gave Max one more scratch behind the ears and stood.

"Thank you so much for helping me. Hey, Hart? Do you really have to go? At least let's have a beer." Summer heard the pleading in her voice and hoped it wasn't obvious to Hart that she wanted her to stay. Hart rewarded her with a lopsided smile.

"That sounds great. Let me just check on Jamie and see what he's up to. All day without me was either a blessing or a curse. And I should probably change my clothes." She looked at her ripped jeans again and feigned distress. "These were my favorite."

Summer nodded with approval. "They do look good on you." Realizing what she had just said, she flushed and cleared her throat. "Um. Just come on by."

Summer held on to Max's collar as she opened the front door.

Realizing she had about ten minutes or less, she quickly gathered up the morning paper and her coffee mug. She raced to the bathroom and groaned when she saw herself. She was a hot mess. After turning on the shower, she grabbed a clean T-shirt and pair of shorts. Her shower was under two minutes, but worth it. At least she was clean and no longer smelled like garbage. "This is going to happen to you sometime soon," she said to Max, who suddenly wouldn't leave her side. Summer swore he nodded at her. Both of them jumped at the knock at the door. She took one last look at herself and, after taking a deep breath to calm the butterflies, opened the door.

"Hi," Hart said. She handed Summer a stack of movies. "I didn't know if you wanted to watch a movie or what kind of movies you even like, so I brought over several." Hart grinned sheepishly at Summer.

"There's a little bit of everything here, except horror."

"My brother is watching *Thongs of the Undead*. It sounds worse than it is. I think. I hope. I can always go grab that if you really want to see a horror flick," Hart said.

Summer laughed. "No, thanks. I need something light and fluffy after today." She handed Hart a beer and sat on the couch next to her. Their knees touched, but neither one moved away. Max nudged both of them before he curled up on the floor in front of them. "Here's to a crazy day with a happy ending." They clinked their bottles together and focused on the romantic comedy on the television. After about twenty minutes, Summer felt her eyes start to close. She wasn't ready for this day to end, not with Hart sitting next to her. She could feel her body heat and wanted the connection to last.

"Summer. Wake up." Summer blinked as she felt a warm hand on her shoulder gently shaking her. She was confused because the television was sideways and she was trying to get her bearings. When she realized she was resting her head in Hart's lap, she quickly sat up.

"I'm so sorry," she said. She scurried away from Hart and tucked herself into the far corner of the couch.

"Nothing to be sorry about. I just need to get home. It was

actually nice having you close to me." Hart stood up and reached out for Summer's hand. She pulled her up from the couch and held her hand while they walked across the room. Hart turned to face Summer at the front door. "Even though I'm to blame for Max taking off, I would do this day again just to spend time with you."

Summer was very aware of Hart's warm hand in hers, their fingers entwined. She nodded and caught her breath when Hart leaned down to place a soft kiss on her lips. It was sweet and patient. Summer felt herself sway into Hart and put her hand on Hart's waist to keep her balance.

"Maybe we can do this again without having to chase Max everywhere," she said after they broke apart.

"I'd like that," Hart said. She touched Summer's cheek gently and closed the door behind her. Summer leaned up against it and sighed. Today ended up being a good day. Not only did she find her dog before it got dark, but she got the girl, too.

THE PERFECT BLEND

Rion Woolf

Not long after I heard the familiar rumble of Riley's Jeep in the driveway, she pushed open my front door. "Kate?"

"In the kitchen!"

I took a drink of cool water and wiped my brow with the edge of my food-crusted apron. The Ohio mid-July humidity was stifling despite the air conditioner blasting away. Soon Riley appeared at my side with a six-pack of cold beer and her charming boyish grin that held the power to break so many hearts.

"Thank God you're here." I grabbed a sweaty bottle. "No matter what I do, I can't get this recipe right."

Riley laughed as she glanced around the kitchen. The sink overflowed with dirty pans and utensils. The stovetop and granite counters that I usually kept spotless were coated with spills and splashes. I looked no better than my messy kitchen. Batter had caked on my hands and forearms. My long hair, usually kept in a tidy bun when I cooked, was loose with wild wisps of curly blond. I groaned with frustration and rubbed my temples, pushing off the edges of a panic attack.

"You look like you can use a hand," Riley said.

"Please." I was always grateful for my best friend's help and that familiar wash of relief her presence brought with it. "I'm not sure we can finish the order by morning, though."

"Of course we can." Riley tied a clean white apron around her slim waist.

She was always the confident one, and she'd been that way since we randomly met when we sat next to one another on our first day of culinary school. She'd given me a friendly wink as the head chef prattled on about how we'd entered the finest and most demanding time of our lives in *his* classroom. "This is going to be a breeze," Riley whispered. Her certainty, even then, had the ability to quiet my self-doubt and slow my anxious racing heart.

Since I'd last seen Riley, she'd buzzed the sides and back of her hair. With her long dark bangs tucked behind an ear, I noticed how much the new haircut brought out the strength of her face, the boldness of her chin and cheekbones, and the fine scattering of dark lashes over her olive green eyes.

"Team Culinary Creations!" Riley jokingly showed off her biceps until I laughed.

True, Riley and I were a business team. We'd started Culinary Creations four years ago, a business that catered desserts to private parties from my small kitchen. Although we both graduated from culinary school with honors, I was generally better at the baking and displaying of food, while Riley was much better at dealing with customers and the business end of things. Together we created Culinary Creations after we moved to my hometown of Columbus. Riley had said she needed a new beginning in a new city, and I'd needed a return to the familiar.

"What's the order?" Riley asked, rolling up her white sleeves, the crisp cuffs against her strong, summer-tanned forearms.

I threw my hands up in dramatic despair. "The Ambrosia Tart."

Riley laughed and joined me at the counter. "What was it Chef Debbie used to call this dessert in our cooking lab? Moody? Unpredictable?"

"She nailed it." I handed the recipe over to Riley. "We need two hundred fifty of these bad bitches by ten a.m. for a wedding lunch."

"There's a trick to this dessert," Riley said. "It's all about balance, right? We've got to find that perfect spot between sweet and tangy."

"I've been trying to find that perfect spot all day." I took a pull on my cold beer. Riley read through the recipe and checked over the mounds of mandarin oranges and pineapple I'd spent so much time peeling, sectioning, and crushing. Over the sweet smell of the fresh fruit, I caught the familiar scent of Riley's Polo aftershave. It smelled powerful and inviting, reminding me of our early culinary school days. Back then Riley's workstation was next to mine where she'd been by my side no matter how hard the recipe.

Riley, it seemed, had always been there to help me in one way or another these past few years. Her jokester personality was also full of compassion, and we'd quickly become friends. I learned that she had been a full-time firefighter before coming to culinary school, and those cool green eyes of hers had seen so much fire, so much pain. Cooking, she told me, was all about making people smile. She'd returned to school looking for a balance in her professional life between all that pain and pleasure. I imagined that Riley was an excellent firefighter, not just because of her muscular strength, but also because she was one of the most observant people I'd ever met. She noticed every time my breathing ratcheted up along with all of my frequent escapes to the bathroom. When I finally told her about my debilitating anxiety disorder, she promised to help me in any way she could. Riley, a caretaker at heart, kept that promise by staying close and frequently reminding me to breathe. I was so grateful for my best friend and tried not to get jealous over the women that circled around her like flies on sugar. Riley, I told myself, was meant to be my great friend and nothing more. I'd been attracted to her, with all those muscles of a well-disciplined athlete, but I knew I wasn't the kind of girl Riley was looking for. I was a soft, introverted reader who rarely left home.

I'd gone into the business of cooking because I'd found it had a strong calming effect on my soul; when I became engrossed in a recipe, my mind finally quieted and I was able to gain some resemblance of control of my body that so often felt completely out of my control. Most days it was simply a matter becoming fully engaged with a recipe to get me through the moments of sheer terror. Tonight, Riley helped me back into the Ambrosia Tart recipe, and I soon forgot all about the panic that had caused me to call her in the first place. We worked together in the kitchen as the Indigo

Girls cycled through repeat on my iPod. I melted mounds of sweet marshmallow while Riley set up rows of my hand-molded graham cracker shells with flowery edges. Soon the recipe came together.

I caught a glimpse of the oven clock: after midnight. "So much for your Friday night," I said. "Sorry, Riley."

She shrugged. "Work comes first, right?"

In so many ways, Riley was my opposite; she liked to comb all the clubs from Wednesday through Saturday nights where a string of women followed, swooned, and argued over her. And rightly so. Riley was one of the most handsome women I'd met, and given her part-time career as a firefighter, she was nothing short of flaming hot. Add in that she could cook the meanest and fluffiest farmer's omelet in the state of Ohio, and you had a gorgeous and talented butch to wake up to in the morning.

My anxiety didn't allow for many relationships in my life, and I'd only been with one woman, my high school sweetheart, Anna. Unlike Riley, I wasn't made for one-night stands. I didn't have the ability to "meet and play hard," as she called it, and then move on to the next woman. Still, I liked to hear about Riley's adventures in the lesbian world, and she always said her playing would end the minute the love of her life recognized her.

I spooned out creamy marshmallow to build a small, fluffy base into each shell. Riley followed, layering in the crushed pineapple. We worked together this way for a few hours, me filling in the sweet as Riley followed with the tart.

"You doing okay?" she asked. "I know we see each other a lot, but we don't really get the chance to talk."

"Yeah, mostly." I rubbed my tired eyes.

"Still missing Anna?"

Anna was the familiar I'd moved back to Columbus to be with, and it was only recently that my body didn't stiffen at the mention of her name. It had been two years since we were over, and Anna's presence sometimes lingered around my house like an unwelcome ghost. "Not really."

"Honestly?"

I nodded. "We got together so young," I said. "I was holding on to what we had out of some sort of loyalty, but she never really understood my need to feel safe. I can't be with someone who doesn't get that."

Riley understood my need for safety. After Anna and I split, I'd regressed, and my anxiety and panic kept me at home even more than usual. Riley had been the one to tell me it was time for some help. When I finally decided to take Riley's advice, she sat in the therapist's waiting area while I was in session and left the office with me, reminding me how good this would be for my health. With a relatively low dosage of anti-anxiety medication and talk therapy, anxiety attacks came on less frequently and I was getting out of the house more. I felt stronger than I had in a long time.

"I'm glad you're finally over Anna," Riley said.

"I don't miss her, but I do miss being with a woman, you know?"

"Life can be lonely," Riley agreed and teased me with the bump of her hip against mine. "It's only been two years, Kate. About freaking time to get back out there, huh?"

I had to agree—it was about freaking time. I desperately missed a woman's touch, her tender kiss, and the excitement of her fingertips trailing down my navel. And for the first time in a very long time, my imaginings of these actions didn't include Anna.

"What about you? How are things going with…what's her name again?"

Riley laughed. "It doesn't matter. Whoever you're thinking of, it was short-lived. Besides, I'm interested in something more long-term these days."

I almost dropped the spoon. "Seriously? I never thought I'd see the day."

Riley's eyes twinkled at me with her grin. "That day is here, Kate. It's exhausting, you know? All the playing and the dyke drama that goes with it. I need something stable, something real."

I wasn't completely surprised by Riley's sudden need for stability. She'd recently had her thirty-seventh birthday and had been rethinking a lot in her life. Suddenly an image flashed across my mind, a picture of the two of us entwined with our bare legs entangled in sheets. The clear image caused my breath to catch inside my throat and threw a sharp spike in my heartbeat.

"You okay?" Riley came closer to me.

I nodded. "I'm just tired of messing with this stupid dessert."

Riley stood so very close to me; I was sandwiched between her and the counter. She reached over and cupped my face in her hand. "You have some marshmallow on your cheek." She caressed my skin with her thumb. I leaned into her, feeling the folds of her warm palm with her gentle touch.

"Kate..." Riley started. "I..."

Her cell phone interrupted us, the chime way too loud in the small kitchen, and I jumped with surprise. I turned away when she answered the phone, and went back to work. While Riley's touch ignited everything inside me, I feared she had been on the brink of telling me she only wanted me for a night and nothing more. Sure, she'd said she was looking for long-term, but that didn't mean *I* was that woman. Riley had her choice from just about any woman, why would she pick someone like me?

"Sorry." She slipped her phone in her back pocket. "Where were we?"

"Finishing up with the cream and sprigs."

While I spooned the handmade whipped cream into the cups, Riley hesitated but eventually followed with thin slices of orange and rosemary sprigs. She placed them in a semicircle, a spray of orange with a touch of green. For the first time, I noticed the delicacy of her strong hands and felt the pull toward her taut, muscular body. I wanted to slip my hand into hers, I wanted to feel the warmth of her skin against mine, and I wanted those strong hands all over me.

Whoa. Where were these feelings coming from? Maybe it was the heat or closeness of her body to mine. Whatever it was, I needed to get my mind back on business. But there was something *different* about Riley tonight, something I couldn't quite place.

"We're done," Riley finally said. She high-fived me, but didn't release my hand.

"I couldn't have done it without you." I didn't trust myself to look Riley in the eyes, unsure where my desire would take me.

"Team Culinary Creations. The perfect blend," Riley teased. She wound her fingers between mine as she pulled me closer. My heart slammed in my ears as my breath quickened.

"Tell me what you're thinking," she whispered.

My body screamed for her touch, and I was too tired to be anything but honest with her. "I can't be another one of your women," I said. "It would break my heart."

"Seriously? One of my women?" Riley asked incredulously. "Kate, it's been four years and I've always been at your side. Waiting."

Now it was my turn to be incredulous. "Waiting. For me?"

Riley nodded, her forehead nearly touching mine.

"How long have you felt this way?"

"Since we the day we met," Riley said. "There was always Anna, though, so I never said anything."

I thought about that undeniable pull I'd felt toward this strong woman before me. There had always been this fierce loyalty between Riley and me, along with a strong desire I'd forced myself to ignore. I'd wanted her, I realized, from the very beginning.

"I'm afraid I won't make you happy. I'm afraid of so much in this world." The truth-filled admission brought tears to my eyes.

"I'm a firefighter, remember? I'll keep you safe." Riley pulled me into a hug, her strong hands caressing my back. When we parted, her lips lingered near mine, the heat between us nearly unbearable. "Besides, how could you make me anything other than happy?" She reached for a long sundae spoon. "You make a killer whipped cream."

I giggled as she filled her mouth full of the white fluff and then held out the remaining cream on the spoon for me. Closing my mouth over the cool metal, I let the sweet mixture explode against my tongue.

I reached for a mandarin orange and slowly fed it to Riley. Her tongue teased my fingertips as the juicy pleasure ran down my fingers.

"Have we found it?" Riley asked. "That perfect blend between the sweet and tangy?"

"I think so."

"Thankfully, you're messy in the kitchen." Riley pointed out a string of marshmallow that had wound itself from my mouth down my chin. "Let me help you with that."

Riley's warm lips slowly kissed away the gooey dessert. I shuddered as her lips slipped down the line of my neck. She kissed and licked away the sticky marshmallow from my skin as the crisp odor of oranges and pineapples engulfed us.

"I'm not going anywhere, Kate." She gave me her boyish grin that I couldn't resist. "I've just been waiting for you to notice."

"I've noticed," I said, near breathless.

Riley reached for the nearby bowl. "We've got quite a bit left over," she said with a playful smile. "I love the whipped cream, but it tastes so much better off you." She dunked her finger and spread the cream across my mouth. "And I'm starving."

Then Riley kissed me, soft and hard all at once, both of us so very hungry for more.

WELCOME TO THE NEIGHBORHOOD

Aurora Rey

Gina drummed her fingers on the kitchen counter. She hadn't felt this inept since that time in eleventh grade when Tracy Malone kissed her while they were studying for the chemistry final. Tracy'd been as pretty as she was smart, and Gina had harbored a colossal crush on her for the better part of a year. That kiss left her both exhilarated and fumbling.

Since then, Gina had figured it out. She wouldn't consider herself a master of romance or anything, but she'd learned how to flirt. She'd even managed a couple of epic seductions in college and grad school. She liked to think of herself as savvy, confident without being cocky.

Until Kel Monroe moved in next door. One day, her life had been going along just fine and the next, she turned into a blushing, blathering idiot. At least she did anytime she happened to come within fifty feet of Kel. And given how close together the houses were in her neighborhood, that happened quite a bit.

It was demoralizing. It was wrong. It was—

The knock on the front door interrupted Gina's internal rant. She opened it, relieved to see Olivia standing on her front porch. Olivia had been in the Cornell English Department for exactly three days when Gina discovered she was both queer and a femme. That had been less than two months ago, and they were now, to be a bit clichéd, besties.

Gina glanced over toward Kel's house, a gorgeous Craftsman that was much nicer than her Victorian duplex rental, then ushered Olivia inside. "Did you see her?"

"Who?"

"Kel. Obviously. Jeez. Pay attention, woman."

Olivia rolled her eyes. "I was being facetious. I know who you're talking about. She's the only thing you've talked about in the last week and a half."

Gina might have argued the point if it weren't true. "So did you see her?"

"I did. I parked up the street so I'd have to walk by her house. She was in the driveway with someone who looked to be delivering a lawn mower."

"And?"

Olivia lifted a shoulder as if conceding something. "And from what I can tell, she's seriously hot."

"I told you." Gina's voice rose with exasperation. "What am I going to do?"

"Have you talked to her?"

"Not beyond exchanging names and a couple of passing hellos."

"Why not?"

"Because I haven't figured out what to say."

"Gina, you're an English professor. You figure out what to say for a living."

"But this is different."

Olivia's eyes got huge. "Oh, my God. Are you a wallflower?"

"No!" Gina crossed her arms. "Who even uses that word anymore?"

"I do. And you're deflecting." It was Olivia's turn to cross her arms. "So, what's the problem?"

"If I knew that, I'd be asking her out instead of wringing my hands with you." Gina hated being so awkward, especially in front of Olivia. Hopefully, Olivia would have some words of wisdom and the embarrassment would be worth it.

"I'd bake."

"Excuse me?"

Olivia's expression grew serious. "If you want an excuse to talk to her, bake. Show up with something delicious to welcome her to the neighborhood."

Gina made a face. "That's such a straight girl thing to do."

Olivia planted her hands on her hips. "I find that exceedingly offensive. Not to mention wrong. Baked goods have landed me several dates. And the upside is that, should the conversation go horribly, you can let it stand as a neighborly gesture and nothing more."

"Huh." Olivia's suggestion was the last thing in the world Gina would consider, but it might work. "That actually makes sense."

"I'm pretty smart, you know."

"There's only one problem."

"What's that?"

"I can't bake."

Olivia looked at her like she'd grown a second head. "Like, at all?"

Gina glowered. "I am an independent, academic, lesbian woman."

"Honey, I am, too. That doesn't mean you shouldn't know how to whip up something sweet and seductive."

"Honey," Gina drawled in an exaggerated version of Olivia's Georgia accent, "I whip up plenty of sweet and seductive. I just don't do it with sugar and flour."

"Maybe you should give it a try."

Gina considered. She didn't have anything to lose. And it wasn't like she had any better ideas. "I might. Are you willing to be my coach?"

Olivia beamed. "I'd be happy to."

They spent the next twenty minutes debating what to make and drafting a grocery list. Despite Gina's initial hesitation, Olivia convinced her that cookies were not childish, but rather perfectly ambiguous. "They show effort without being presumptuous," she insisted. "You might have made them special for her or they might be extras from something else."

"I had no idea there'd be so much strategy involved."

Olivia rolled her eyes. "That's because you're an amateur."

They went to lunch as planned, then the store. There was no sign of Kel when they left or when they returned. Gina didn't want to keep Olivia from any other plans and offered to do the baking some other time. Olivia, in turn, accused her of chickening out and assured her she had nowhere else to be.

Gina pulled out mixing bowls and measuring cups that she'd bought but never used, and they got to work. In just under two hours, they produced two dozen of Olivia's signature chewy triple chocolate cookies. As far as Gina was concerned, they looked like they belonged in a bakery case. "I can't believe we made these."

"You made them. I helped."

"That's generous, but I'll take it." They sampled one that looked less than perfect, after which Gina concluded, "I don't know about Kel, but I'd go to bed with me."

"Me too."

Gina raised a brow. "Dr. Bennett, are you propositioning me?"

Olivia laughed. "I love you, but you're not my type. I'm going home now. You should go deliver these while they're fresh."

"You know," Gina mused, "I feel markedly more confident."

Olivia offered her a smug smile. "You're welcome."

Olivia left and Gina took a moment to fuss over the arrangement of the cookies on the plate, then another moment to fuss with her hair. Knowing she was stalling, she picked up the plate, squared her shoulders, and headed out the door.

Much to her relief, Kel had reappeared and was fiddling with what appeared to be a brand-new John Deere lawn mower. Gina started up the front walk, admiring the view of Kel's ass as she bent over the motor. She paused when Kel stood and yanked the starter rope. The mower made a pained coughing noise. Kel yanked three more times, each time eliciting a worse noise from the machine.

All the nervousness she'd been harboring melted away. "What on earth are you doing to that poor, defenseless lawn mower?"

Kel looked up, scowling. The snug gray T-shirt and smear of dirt across her cheek made Gina's heart race. "The mower started it. I think I bought a lemon. Hey, are those for me?"

The rapid progression of the conversation made her smile. "I'm sorry it's giving you trouble, and yes, these are for you. I wanted to officially welcome you to the neighborhood."

"That's nice. Thank you."

The smile Kel offered dispelled any notions Gina had about baking being a straight-girl tactic. "I've been meaning to stop by. I'm sorry it took so long."

"Can I offer you something to drink?"

Gina hesitated, or at least, feigned hesitation. "I don't want to keep you from what you're doing."

Kel looked at the mower shook her head. "Clearly, I wasn't doing much of anything."

Maybe this wouldn't be so hard after all. "In that case, I'd love a drink."

"Right this way." Kel led them through the house to the kitchen. "I'm still stocking my kitchen, I'm afraid. I can offer you water, Pepsi, or a beer."

"I'll have a beer if you are."

"Oh, I'd say we're safely at beer o'clock. I've also yet to get a sofa. Shall we sit on the deck?"

They talked until the sun went down and the air began to take on a chill. They talked about jobs and hometowns and favorite movies and reasons for moving to Ithaca. Eventually, Kel offered to make dinner. Gina never expected things to go so well. She'd have to find a way to thank Olivia.

They threw some vegetables and skewers of shrimp on the grill. Kel opened a bottle of wine and they moved inside to the antique dining room table Kel had inherited from her grandmother. They polished off three of the cookies. Even after eating, they lingered at the table.

"Did you prime it?" Gina asked.

"Excuse me?"

"I was thinking about your poor lawn mower. Did you prime it before you tried to start it?"

Kel frowned. "I don't know what that means."

Gina looked at her. "Have you never used a lawn mower?"

"I just moved here from the city. I've never had reason to use a lawn mower."

Gina resisted the temptation to tease her. It had only been a couple of years since she'd moved up from Brooklyn, and she'd had plenty of her own debacles with yard work. "There's a little button on the side of the motor. You have to push it a few times before you start it. The engine is cold, so you have to prime it to get it to start."

Kel smiled at her, easy and slow. "You know, I don't know much about lawn mowers, but I'm familiar with the concept."

The look on Kel's face, combined with the subtext of her words, made Gina's insides go hot and full of yearning. She returned the smile. Two could play at that game. "It's like being neighborly. You want to ease into it with a little something sweet."

Kel leaned forward on the table, bringing her face within a foot of Gina's. "Is that so?"

Gina shifted slightly but didn't break eye contact. She licked her lips in anticipation. "It is."

"Is that what you're doing here? Easing into it?"

"Something like that." Gina would swear she could feel the heat radiating from Kel. Maybe it was her own temperature ratcheting up a notch.

"What about right now? Am I easing in too far? Too fast?"

Gina swallowed. Was Kel about to kiss her? It sure as hell felt like Kel was about to kiss her. "Not at all."

Kel leaned in a little more, her lips mere inches from Gina's. "How about now?"

Gina's eyes flicked down to Kel's mouth, then back to her eyes. They were so close Gina could detect the subtle flecks of mahogany in her otherwise dark brown irises. Gina parted her lips to respond, but no words came. She offered the slightest shake of her head instead.

Kel closed the remaining distance between them and covered Gina's lips with hers. The kiss seemed to end before it began. Gina opened her eyes and found Kel looking at her intently. Gina smiled, then leaned in for another taste.

The move emboldened Kel, who took the kiss deeper and took the lead. When Kel's tongue slid over her bottom lip, Gina shivered. Kel pulled back, searching her face. "Are you okay?"

Gina nodded, perhaps a little more emphatically than was necessary. Kel offered her a half smile and stood. Gina feared the spell had been broken. But she wasn't ready to be done. All she could think about was more—more of Kel's mouth, more of her ebony skin, more of the longing that threatened to consume her.

Fueled by that desire, she stepped closer to Kel and placed her hand on Kel's chest, just below her collarbone. "Thank you for dinner."

"Thank you for the cookies."

Despite the banality of the conversation, the huskiness in Kel's voice gave Gina courage. Just one more kiss, one more taste to take home and tide her over. She placed her hand on Kel's arm, surprised by how muscular it was.

"You're welcome. I..." Gina engaged in a rapid-fire internal debate about whether to take things to the next level, or whether it was too soon.

She must have trailed off, because Kel looked at her with a mixture of expectation and desire. "Yes?"

The word felt like both a question and an invitation. Instead of speaking, Gina leaned in and kissed Kel again. She ran her hand up Kel's arm to her shoulder. Because they were now standing, she was able to move her whole body closer. One of Kel's hands moved to the small of Gina's back, the other into her hair.

The kiss went on and on. Gina snuck her hands under the hem of Kel's shirt. Kel's hand roamed up and down Gina's back, making its way to her side and, eventually, her breast.

Kel eased back and looked into Gina's eyes. "Stay?"

It was Gina's turn to offer a slow smile. She said simply, "Yes."

Kel took her hand and led her upstairs. The bedroom had the feel of someone just moved in—bare walls, boxes stacked in the corner. But there was a big beautiful bed, and it was made, so Gina had no complaints. The reality of what she was about to do sank in. "I don't usually..."

Kel stopped and turned to look at her. "Me either. If you'd rather not—"

"No, I definitely want to. I think I needed to say this isn't my usual way of doing things."

Kel smiled. "Well, we're in agreement, then."

"Okay. Good. Now where were we?"

Kel leaned in and gave her a slow, teasing kiss. "Here, I think."

"Ah, yes," Gina whispered.

"And here." Kel made a trail of kisses down Gina's neck to her collarbone, pausing to run her tongue along the groove.

"Right." Gina grabbed the hem of Kel's shirt and lifted it over her head. She ran her fingers over the smooth, dark skin of Kel's stomach, her chest. In return, Kel took hold of Gina's sundress, working the fabric up her torso. Gina lifted her arms and the dress joined Kel's shirt on the floor. Kel kissed her again and, without breaking contact, led them to the bed.

Despite the newness, it wasn't awkward. Their bodies seemed to fit together. Gina marveled that Kel seemed to know just how to touch her, both to excite and to satisfy. At first, it felt like they were driven by urgency, a need to give and to take. What followed was something slower, more of a lazy exploration, that lasted until the early morning.

When she got home the next day, Gina realized she'd missed two texts and a call from Olivia. She dialed her friend and, after saying hello, apologized for making her worry. "I just got home," she confessed.

"Home from next door?" Gina couldn't tell if the pitch in Olivia's voice came from excitement or disapproval.

"Home from next door."

"You had sex?" Olivia's voice went even higher.

"Why do you sound so shocked? You're the one who said baked goods were seductive."

"It was a figure of speech."

"Well, the cookies opened the door and I figured I'd walk right on through."

"I'm impressed. A little jealous, maybe, but impressed. Are you going to see her again?"

"God, I hope so."

❖

"I love that you want to recreate your first night together," Olivia said as she scraped dough from the sides of the bowl and turned the mixer back on. "I think you might be in the running for most romantic proposal."

Kel paced back and forth in Olivia's small kitchen. "It doesn't have to be the most romantic, it just has to make her say yes."

"Well, I can't pretend to speak for her, but I have a good idea of how she feels about you. I'm pretty sure she's going to say yes and I'm pretty sure it's going to have nothing to do with cookies."

Kel continued to pace. "I hope you're right."

Back at the house, Kel hid the cookies on top of the fridge and got the rest of dinner ready. She resisted the desire to make something fancy, wanting everything to be the same as the first night she and Gina had spent together.

When Gina pulled into the driveway, Kel stood scowling at the lawn mower. Gina got out of the car and frowned. "Are you mowing the lawn? I thought we were going to dinner."

Kel smiled. "I thought we'd stay in."

"Oh. I'm not starving, so if you want to mow the lawn, then go ahead."

"No, I was just looking at it." Gina looked at her like she'd gone a little bit crazy, but Kel took her hand and led her around to the back deck. "I'm going for something here."

Kel handed Gina one of the beers she'd set out a few minutes before. Gina took one, but the puzzled look remained. "What is that exactly?"

"I'll give you one more hint." Kel went through the sliding glass door to the kitchen and emerged with a plate piled with shrimp and vegetables.

A smile spread across Gina's face. "It's our first date."

"Hard to believe it was a year ago."

"A really good year. This is sweet. Thank you."

"Baby, you ain't seen nothing yet." Kel grilled up the food and they ate at her grandmother's table, just as they'd done that first night. When they were finished, she fetched the cookies. "I hope you don't mind that I took the liberty of procuring these."

Gina laughed. "You thought of everything. Where did you get them?"

"I couldn't find anything close at Ithaca Bakery, so I enlisted Olivia's help. I wanted it to be just right."

"And to think, when I brought you those cookies, I only had my sights set on getting you into bed."

"Well, they worked."

"For the record, I hadn't actually planned to get you into bed that first night."

"Oh, sure, you say that now."

"I don't regret it. I'm only saying I didn't plan it."

"Either way, it was an incredible night. It was also the beginning of the best year of my life."

Gina's smile softened. "I couldn't agree more."

"Just like that first night was the first of many, I'm hoping this first year is, too." Kel's heart pounded in her chest. Telling herself she shouldn't be nervous did little to help.

"Well, I'm not going anywhere if you aren't."

"I'm not. Except somewhere exotic for a honeymoon, maybe." Before Gina could come back with a witty reply, Kel slid from her chair onto one knee. She took Gina's hand in hers. "I love you, Gina. I want to spend all my nights and all my days and all my years with you. I want a family and a forever and everything that comes with being your wife. Will you marry me?"

Gina's eyes filled and Kel prayed they were the happy sort of tears. "Yes. Yes to everything."

Kel thought she'd known joy in her life, but nothing compared to the feeling in that moment. She made to get up and realized the ring box still sat in her pocket. "Shit."

Gina's face registered alarm. "What? What's wrong?"

She pulled out the box, opened it. At Olivia's suggestion, she'd gone with an antique instead of something new—a single diamond in an intricate setting of pink gold. Kel took it out and slipped it on Gina's finger. "You're not supposed to propose without a ring."

"It's beautiful," Gina said, "but I would have said yes without it."

Kel chuckled. "I can't believe I forgot about it. No one tells you how stressful proposing is."

Gina smiled. "Well, the good news is you shouldn't ever have to do it again."

Kel smiled, letting that reality sink in. She hadn't expected Gina to say no, but having her say yes added something official, something certain, to the prospect of their future. "Right. Since this is hopefully your only one, too, I'm sorry it wasn't perfect."

"It was pretty great. As far as I can tell, there's only one thing missing."

Kel's mind raced. Other than the ring, she didn't have anything in her back pocket, or up her sleeve, for that matter. "What's that?"

"If we're recreating our first night together…"

"Oh," Kel let the word hang, "that. I'd never forget that."

Kel took Gina's hand and led her upstairs. The hesitation of that first night, the feeling of recklessness, was long gone. It its place, the confidence and desire that only comes after being with someone a while. Rather than diminished, Kel found the passion intensified by the added layers of knowing each other so well, of wanting a future together.

Later, when they lay in the afterglow with limbs twisted together, Gina said, "I feel like I should call Olivia and thank her for the cookies."

"I know. It was very sweet of her to help me make them for tonight. I think they were pretty close to the ones you made for me."

Gina buried her face in Kel's neck and began to laugh. When she lifted her head and locked eyes with Kel, there was mischief in her eyes. "About that."

"What?"

"I didn't actually make the cookies that first night."

"What?"

"I had a massive crush on you and didn't know how to make the first move. The cookies were Olivia's idea. And she'd say she helped me, but she totally made them."

"You seduced me under false pretenses."

"My pretenses weren't false, only my abilities in the kitchen."

Kel shook her head. "Were you ever going to tell me?"

Gina shrugged. "I kind of thought you'd figured it out given that I haven't baked anything since."

Gina often brought home treats from the various bakeries and restaurants and ice cream shops in town. Kel had figured it was more a time and convenience thing than anything else. "Huh. I guess I hadn't noticed."

"You know, for a lawyer, you always think the best of people."

"Thanks?" Kel shook her head. "Any other deep dark secrets you want to share?"

Gina considered. Kel feared for a second that a more serious bombshell might be looming, but then she smiled. "No, I think that's the worst of it."

Kel kept her face serious. "I suppose that's a relief."

"Will you still have me?"

Gina looked at her with those big brown eyes, and Kel felt her heart swell for the second time that day. Kel leaned in and kissed her. "I'll take you any day of the week, Morelli."

Gina's eyes sparkled and she laughed again. "That's good, because I'm all yours."

NEIGHBORS

Elizabeth Black

The seventeen floors of the Calvert Beach Apartments stretched out like a pale, sleeping fat man at the edge of the dirty beach. The sand may have been pristine when the place was built in 1957, but by 2009 it had marbleized into swirls of dirt, oil, grease, Styrofoam coffee cups, and dog shit. A real tourist haven.

Annie had settled into apartment 15-E on the day she moved in. She didn't own much: a queen-sized mattress and box spring on a frame. Several pots and pans she picked up at a yard sale. Her computer, fax, phone, printer, and copier. A TV/VCR/DVD player and stereo, stacks of videotapes, DVDs, and CDs, the mandatory can't-live-without-it coffeemaker, and a few other possessions she had accumulated over the years.

In many ways, her life was in the same condition as her belongings. She took so much of herself for granted that she barely noticed her own existence. She didn't purchase anything new because she felt quite comfortable with what she already owned.

Everything looked lived-in and safe. A new, shiny item would jar her sense of security. She didn't like adjusting to anything new and unusual. Some people might consider her a touch dull and conventional, but Annie didn't care. She preferred to live her life on a predictable and even keel.

Sometimes the most steadfast people need a little jarring now and then to remind them that they're alive.

Seven weeks after moving into her apartment, her routine was set. She freelanced for computer firms that specialized in creating websites for businesses. She met with clients on Mondays and Tuesdays, and she rounded out the rest of the week doing the computer work. Occasionally, if the weather was nice and if the ozone level was not so high that she was forced to breathe with the assistance of an oxygen tent, she'd blow off Friday and take a long weekend. She'd always wanted to live near the beach. This pitiful strip of it was less expensive than the coastal towns. Even though Calvert Beach sometimes looked like the local sewage dump, it was home. Her peaceful and quiet existence was set.

Then Charlotte and Angelina moved in.

While she brushed and flossed her teeth one morning, she heard the scraping of large furniture being dragged across the wooden floor in the apartment next door, amid bursts of cursing and laughter when something wouldn't budge properly. Lots of bellowing and thumping and door-slamming for several hours. By noon, the stereo on the other side of that very thin wall blasted Lords of Acid. It was a good thing she didn't have any clients on this particular Tuesday. How the hell was she supposed to get any work done with all that racket?

She wanted to knock on the door and ask them to turn down the stereo, but the last thing she wanted to do was get on the bad side of her new neighbors on their first day in the building. So she rummaged through her refrigerator, found some chocolate chip cookies she had baked the previous evening in a fit of domestic bliss, and tossed them onto a chipped china plate. Good idea—give the new folks some munchies to get on their good side and then tell them the stereo bass was so intense it was jostling the perfume bottles on her bedroom dresser.

The rhythm thundered in her ears when she opened her apartment door. If it was going to be like this every day, she didn't know how she was going to survive. She walked to Apartment 15-D, held her breath, and knocked on the door.

No answer. The stereo was too loud. She knocked harder, so hard her knuckles stung.

A deadbolt clicked. Biting her lip to stave off her nervousness, she looked at the cookies staring up at her with chocolate chip eyes. She could have sworn they were laughing. Her knuckles blanched from gripping the plate.

The door opened. Annie raised her eyes.

Two identical faces stared at her, bright and flushed with excitement. The women couldn't have been any more than twenty years old. Both were tanned. Both had shoulder-length, bushy black hair. Upturned hazel eyes hinted at Asian ancestry. Both were mirror images of each other.

Twins?

Not quite. More like doppelgangers. Harbingers of change. Never before had she seen a couple of vamps like out of those old movies she watched late at night.

One of them grinned.

"Hi. Are you our neighbor?"

Annie snapped out of her reverie. "Yes. Name's Annie," she shouted over the stereo. "I live over there." She tilted her head toward her apartment. "I brought a welcoming gift for you." She held out the plate and smiled sheepishly. She felt awkward because she was never very good at this sort of thing.

"Oh, you're so sweet!" one of them gushed. "Come on in. The place is a mess 'cause we just moved in, and we have no idea where we're going to put all this stuff, and we have so much to do, and I just gotta find something for you to drink, since you were nice enough to bring us homemade cookies! That is *so* kewl! I *love* chocolate chips…"

She chattered on. Her voice was lost over the din of the stereo.

"I can't hear you!" Annie shouted.

The noisy one leaped to the stereo and turned the volume down to a dull roar.

"I'm Charlotte, and that's my best friend Angelina. Lina for short. Don't ever call her Angie. She thinks that's a high school hooker cheerleader name, and she hates it. We've been best friends for so long that we even look alike. We finish each other's sentences."

She stopped chattering long enough to munch on a cookie.

Annie watched as her tongue flicked at the cookie crumbs on her lips. She licked her index finger, wrapping her full lips around her fingertip. She scooped chocolate from a long, red fingernail with the tip of her pointed tongue.

Annie could have sworn she was doing it for her benefit.

Both women flitted about the room like moths. They rarely sat still for long.

"Hey, these are good cookies. I hope the water stays warm for a few more weeks. We like to swim. How long have you lived here? Is this a nice place?"

Charlotte's high-pitched, staccato jabbering reverberated against the walls like the chirping of a mad chipmunk.

"Place is decent enough. The beach could use a bath, but the water is usually clean," Annie said. Her voice sounded deep, mellow, and calm; a placid sea in the midst of the whitewater frenzy that crashed in the room. "I've been here for a month and a half. I work out of my apartment."

Charlotte's eyes widened. At least, Annie *thought* she was Charlotte. Keeping track of these two was more difficult than that acorn in the three cups trick. The women were in constant motion around the room. They moved boxes. One of them grabbed a fistful of CDs and dumped them on the couch. The other dug drinking glasses out of another box. They were like two hummingbirds in search of nectar.

Charlotte, the talkative hummingbird, flitted to Annie. She held a glass in one hand.

"Oh, that is *so* kewl!" she squealed. "I'd love to work at home. You don't have to wear real clothes if you work at home. You can get yourself settled without feeling like you're living out of a suitcase all the time. We always get covered in paint and gook where we work. We go out of town a lot. We have to go again on Saturday for a few weeks. Hotels are nice at first, but they get dull after a while. Would you like a cola or something? We'd give you coffee, but the coffeemaker is in one of these boxes."

"No thanks. I have to get back to work." Annie shuffled back and forth. She glanced about the room. This apartment appeared to be a mirror image of her own. The bathroom was positioned opposite hers. Annie assumed that there were two bedrooms, but she couldn't see that far down the hall. One bedroom shared the same thin wall as her own. The stereo also shared the same thin wall.

"Um, could I ask you to keep the stereo down? I can't concentrate with the music so loud."

"Hey, no problem. We're just used to lots of noise. What kind of work do you do?"

"Computer work. Internet advertising for businesses."

"Sounds neat," Charlotte said in between bites of her third cookie. The deadpan tone of her voice made it obvious that she didn't think Annie's work sounded neat at all.

"We're set painters."

Annie had wondered if Lina had a voice. She obviously did.

"Broadway shows. Movies. TV. We're in between gigs right now, so we're just hanging out until the next round." Lina slumped in an armchair with her long, tanned legs dangling over one side. Her shorts rode up the crack of her ass. Annie could never wear anything like that. She wished she could, but exhibitionism wasn't one of her strong points. She watched Lina swing her slender, toned legs. The shorts rode up her crotch. Black pubic hairs teased her from between the swinging legs as if they peeked out from behind the denim long enough to say "boo!"

"Hey, when you finish working, come over. We'll pop some popcorn and watch a movie...or something."

"I'll have to see. Maybe. I better go. Gotta get back to work. See ya."

She suddenly felt very hot.

There was no one in her life at the moment. Why is it that when you can't get laid, you can't think about anything else? Everything reminds you of a steaming fuck. Sometimes she got so horny she resorted to using inanimate objects to get off. The washer during the spin cycle. Her 1988 Winter Olympics Coca-Cola bottle. That exit ramp off the highway with the five sets of rumble strips.

These two were cute, and their teasing could not have been more obvious. The last time she'd been laid was almost a year ago.

Sex with that guy was nothing to rave about. Her relationships had always been with men. She had preferred women, but the opportunity had never before presented itself. Now here it was, playing peek-a-boo from behind a strip of denim.

She was scared to death.

Charlotte and Lina walked her to the door. Both women stood a little too close. Annie noticed that they were several inches shorter than she. They gazed upward at her with quizzical and amused expressions. Charlotte giggled. Lina kicked Charlotte lightly on the shin and grinned broadly. Annie smelled brown sugar, molasses, and chocolate chips on their breath. Her thighs felt wobbly.

She wanted to get back to her quiet, boring apartment as quickly as possible.

After they said their good-byes, Annie went home and locked the door. She spent the rest of the day working but kept one ear focused on her new neighbors. She laughed when several times Charlotte (it had to be Charlotte) would get a bit too noisy and Lina would loudly shush her. Since Annie worked in total silence, she could hear them quite clearly.

She worked undisturbed most of the next day. Charlotte and Lina arranged bric-a-brac in their apartment. They were fairly quiet about it. She was rather touched that they were considerate of her working next door. Granted, they made more than enough noise. After all, how quiet could mad chipmunks be?

The door slammed shut at about eleven a.m., and she heard two sets of feet scurry down the hall to the elevator, accompanied by staccato giggles and diffused conversation. Charlotte's and Lina's chattering faded and then there was silence. Annie was relieved. All that boundless energy wore her out.

At exactly two p.m., as she stretched her aching back, the elevator went *ding*. Sonorous laughter echoed up and down the narrow hallway as Charlotte and Lina ran toward their apartment. However, they didn't stop at their front door. They stopped at Annie's door and knocked so loudly that the door shook in its hinges.

Charlotte and Lina gaped at her when she opened the door.

Both wore skimpy swimsuits. They were covered with sand. Their huge breasts nearly spilled from their bikini tops. Annie caught a glimpse of a brown areola peeking out from beneath Lina's top. It looked like her pubic hair had taught her tits how to say "boo."

Charlotte wore the most ridiculous pair of sunglasses she had ever seen. They were an electric blue horn-rimmed eyesore studded with rhinestones at the corners. Only someone with Charlotte's exuberant personality could ever get away with wearing something so outlandish. Annie saw her own bemused expression in the mirrored lenses and almost laughed out loud.

Charlotte looked her up and down through the sunglasses. "How come you're not dressed? You always sit around in a bathrobe?"

She must have seen Annie's annoyed curl of the lip because she quickly changed the subject.

"Hey, we're going back to the beach. Wanna come?"

"Well, I don't want to be a bother..." She wanted to go but didn't have the energy. By mid-afternoon she was usually too tired to do much of anything.

"It's no bother. You look like you've been cooped up in here too long, and it's gorgeous outside. Hey, the sand machine came by early this morning and cleaned the gunk up from the beach. It doesn't look like a biohazard anymore."

"Get on a bathing suit. We'll be by in about fifteen minutes," Lina ordered quietly as both women walked sideways toward their apartment. Annie gaped at the bronze halo that teased her from beneath the bikini top one last time before Lina turned to unlock the door.

They didn't give Annie a chance to refuse, which was probably good because she did need to get out of her apartment. She had finished most of her work for the day. It wouldn't hurt to take a break. Sometimes it took all her energy to walk to the grocery store, let alone take an evening on the town. Since she didn't like to go anywhere alone, she rarely went out. Not knowing many people, she didn't have any friends.

Now she had two new ones.

She felt a little uneasy because the women seemed to push themselves on her too quickly. Annie suspected they did that to everybody. Besides, going to the beach could be fun.

Could lead to other things, too. Annie smiled over that delightful thought, even though it still scared her to death.

In the month and a half since she had moved to Calvert Beach, she had gone swimming only twice. Would this third time be more enjoyable because she would share her time with those two whirlwinds? Which bathing suit should she wear? The black one-piece that she usually wore, or the neon visual assault she bought on a whim six years ago while in Florida? She opted for dazzling. As she gazed at her reflection in the mirror, dressed to look like a tropical fish on acid, she wondered at the changes taking place in her body and in her mind. She felt as if she was on a roller-coaster ride, and she didn't want to get off.

The water was warmer than she had anticipated, and the beach was clean. Nary a Styrofoam coffee cup in sight. Must have been the company. The three of them swam and caroused in the sand and surf until dusk. As they conversed, their bodies intermingled and entwined; a touch here, an embrace there. Very tentative, but becoming more bold as the tide came in.

At dusk, Annie and her new friends returned to their apartments to get cleaned up. Annie's mind spun as she dried her hair after her shower. Was she ready to dive in and become involved with Charlotte and Lina? She acknowledged the reasons she held back. She was afraid of letting go. Afraid of succumbing to their fever-dream way of living. Afraid of the sexual attraction she felt toward them, especially Charlotte.

While her thoughts churned, there came a knock on the door. Charlotte grinned when she saw Annie's bathrobe, but she made no snide comments this time. She asked if Annie would like a trial run as a computer artist for the indie film she was about to work on.

As soon as Charlotte left, Annie made her decision.

She tossed off the bathrobe and threw on shorts and a T-shirt. No underwear. Freedom from underwire, nylon, and elastic felt luxurious. No more schlepping around her apartment in a dingy bathrobe. Something curious was happening to her. Her inhibitions were dissolving like the sugar in her fifth cup of coffee that morning. She held her new friends responsible. They were having quite an effect on her.

She did not turn them down when they invited her into their apartment. Charlotte sat on the couch next to Annie. She sat very close.

"I'm so glad you decided to go swimming with us. That was fun."

Annie looked into her eyes. They were the color of warm honey, and they crinkled at the corners when she smiled. Lamplight skipped across them like pebbles tossed atop ocean waves. Charlotte touched her fingers to Annie's cheek. Her touch felt electric, almost as electric as those silly sunglasses she'd worn earlier that day. Annie's mouth dried and her heart pounded. She held her breath. A strange, warm feeling was coming over her. Her pussy threatened to melt and leak out all over her sneakers.

Charlotte rose and walked over to the balcony. Annie let out her breath with relief. She watched as Charlotte pulled back the vertical blinds and opened the balcony door. The sound of crashing waves exploded into the living room. The beat of the waves nearly matched the thumping of Annie's heart. She stared at Charlotte. The glare from the balcony's halogen light poured into the room. She could see the outline of Charlotte's strong legs and the curve of her ample hips through the thin linen of her minidress. Charlotte was beautiful. Annie recrossed her legs, which were beginning to cramp.

"Here's the wine," Lina announced as she entered the room with a bottle and three small glasses. She poured a small amount of wine into all three glasses. Annie held hers by its delicate stem. The glass, with its red liquid, looked like a fragile, bloodied swan. She sipped. Her taste buds curled at the dryness of the wine.

"Is it good?" Charlotte asked as she glided across the living room. "Lina picked out this one. We've never had it before. Wanted to try something new. Have you ever wanted to try something new just to try it?"

"Yes," Annie said, not certain whether she was answering the first question or the second. She realized she was probably answering both.

Charlotte had taken her seat to Annie's left, and Lina stood by the stereo. Both women eyed her with curious expressions on their open faces. Lina beamed a wide grin at her and sipped her wine.

"Are you two always together?" Annie asked.

"Since age four." Charlotte's honey-sweet breath warmed her ear. "We go everywhere together. We share everything, too."

Lina turned her head, smiled and nodded. Her body was more muscular than Charlotte's. Annie noticed her broad shoulders, full breasts, and tight thighs as she twisted her lithe body toward the couch. Annie realized in that instant that Lina's stance was a pose. Lina was flirting with her. She then took her place on the floor at Annie's knees.

Annie looked into Charlotte's eyes and felt herself falling down an abyss. A voice inside her head whispered, *Do it. Let go.*

"You two really share everything?"

"Yes, everything." Charlotte's mouth was inches from Annie's. She could feel the heat emanating from her body.

The scent of Godiva and Black Opal wafted around Annie's head, and made her feel dizzy. *Such delicious scents make me feel so aroused.* Five thin fingers alighted on her left breast, and Charlotte's hand squeezed hard. Her fingers gripped like tiny vises. Charlotte's hands were very strong from years of rendering and painting, and Annie felt the result of that power. *If she can grasp me with such emotion, imagine how strong she would feel if I gave in to her every demand.* As Charlotte's thumb gently circled around her left nipple, her hand stretched to its full length. Her fingers played with Annie's right nipple while her thumb flicked the left one.

All that action with one hand.

Charlotte kissed her. Her lips were full and swollen; tender and warm. Annie slid her tongue slowly along the length of Charlotte's lower lip, feeling the cracks and crevasses embedded in her soft skin.

She'd never done anything like this before, and she liked it. A lot. All that free-floating anxiety over...nothing.

Charlotte's tongue flicked at her lips the same way she'd licked those cookie crumbs the day before. As Annie explored Charlotte's mouth with her tongue, she tasted dark chocolate and red wine. Her head spun with arousal. No man had ever made her react the way these two women did. Annie gave her will over to both of them. Lina unfastened her belt buckle and unzipped her shorts. Annie lifted her butt so that Lina could remove them. The breeze felt cool against her trembling skin.

Annie felt Lina's hands massage the taut, nervous muscles in her thighs until they had relaxed. *It feels so good to let go. I've been alone for too long, and these two sexy women make me feel alive again.* Charlotte had already unbuttoned Annie's blouse. Charlotte leaned back, stood up, and smiled. She looked at Annie with an amused expression.

Annie didn't want Charlotte to stop what she was doing. Charlotte caught the look and smiled slowly. She unbuttoned her linen minidress and let it fall to the floor. She wore no underwear. Charlotte was not a small woman, despite her short stature. Her body was full and muscular; broad-shouldered, broad-hipped. Her bulk was supported by two very powerful legs; thoroughbred's legs. Her hands were big, strong, and blue-veined from years of artistic work. They were capped by chrome-lacquered nails, painted blood red. Lina had told her that before they moved to the new place, Charlotte had painted them the same shade of blue as a '63 Chevy. Annie considered Charlotte's hands the most beautiful part of her body. She could easily cover an octave and a half on a piano, which came in very handy in bed. She knew those hands could crush a windpipe if necessary, by the look of them. Yet Annie knew that those hands could also caress with more gentleness than she had ever experienced in her entire life. *I'll let those strong hands take over my body and do whatever they like.*

Charlotte's huge breasts made her waist look smaller than it probably was. Despite their size, her breasts did not sag. Her left one was slightly larger than the right. *I want to touch her, so why am I hesitating? Oh, to reach out and press my hands against her warm skin!*

Since Annie did not move first, Charlotte took over. *I want her to make all the moves. Let her run the show. Let her dominate me.*

Charlotte moved back toward the couch and pressed Annie's shoulders against the fabric. She knelt to her right and thrust her breasts into her face. Giving in to her arousal, Annie grasped both huge breasts in her hands. They were heavy, like balloons filled with beach sand and ocean water. She squeezed them gently and pressed her lips to the left one. The hard nipple was as thick as an eraser. *Oh, my, they are perfect!* Annie sucked harder and flicked her tongue back and forth across the nipple until it was brick red and grew to the size of a cork. Charlotte threw her head back and moaned.

Two firm hands gripped Annie's knees and spread her legs. She scooted her butt down until her cheeks hung over the edge of the couch. Lina's mouth teased the downy underside of Annie's thighs and soon found her moist pussy. A long tongue flicked roughly at her clit. *Oh my, she knows just what to do to make me melt!* Ready to burst, Annie's legs tensed as she relished the feel of Lina's tongue along her clit. Charlotte kneaded Annie's breasts. Her head was thrown back; mouth open wide, gasping for air. Her firm breasts bounced with each quickening breath. A rosy flush flowed from Charlotte's tanned face to her hard nipples. Lina's fingers were buried in Annie's pussy, and her thumb manipulated her clit. Her bicep bulged with her hand motions. *All those muscles are so sexy, and I want more!* Charlotte reached out one hand and ran her fingers through Lina's hair. Lina's face was flushed and moist. Annie had been too busy to notice that Lina had removed her clothing.

As Lina tongued her clit, Charlotte massaged her own breasts, lifting each one as she pressed her fingers into her skin. She stared Annie directly in the eye and slid her right hand down to her pussy. Long fingers manipulated her clit and slid inside. Charlotte arched her back, tossed her head, and moaned with pleasure. Her body stiffened as Lina's tongue drove passion home, and Charlotte cried out in both pain and pleasure at her own release. At the sight of the woman's orgasm and Lina's expert tongue doing its magical work. Annie's own passion burst forth and she writhed on the couch, overwhelmed by her own pleasure. Her orgasm crested and then waned, and she collapsed in a heap against the couch.

Lina then leaped up and nuzzled Charlotte's breasts. She slid her lips along the curve of her jaw. When their mouths connected, they shared the same breath. The two nearly ate each other.

Annie watched in awe. It was like observing a person making out with a mirror.

They stopped at the same moment and looked at her. Something had passed between them that she did not catch. The two probably communicated by mental telepathy.

Charlotte and Lina resumed their places next to Annie and at her feet. They enjoyed the quiet for several minutes. The pounding pulse in Annie's throat tapered to a soft beat. She felt Charlotte's hot fingers in the palm of her hand.

"You two really have to leave this weekend?" Annie asked.

"Yup," said Lina. "We're nomads."

A wave of sadness drifted over her. "I'm going to miss you."

Charlotte bolted into a seated position and poked Annie's left breast with one sharp fingernail. "Why don't you come with us? It's only a week. Have you taken a vacation yet?"

Annie laughed. "What's a vacation? I haven't had one in four years."

"Then it's settled. This is so easy. Going with us shouldn't be a big deal at all."

"You two sound like every day of the year is a vacation."

Charlotte's laugh tinkled like a glass wind chime. "We never pass up a great trip to the beach. Too bad we'll spend most of the time working. Maybe we can tack on an extra week down there just to goof off. Can you make it? Please?"

Who could resist those doe eyes? Annie happily accepted. She had definitely spent the last few years loading herself with many unnecessary rules. Not anymore. The day before leaving, she ran to a local boutique and bought a few tropical-toned sundresses, blouses, tank tops, and shorts. No more underwear. She piled all of her scrappy bras and panties into a plastic bag and tossed them in the trash. She felt so lightweight with joy that she feared she'd float to the ceiling if she stood too quickly.

Upon arriving on location for the movie shoot, they moved into a small apartment that overlooked sea cliffs. Windswept ocean breezes frizzled Annie's thick red hair, which she wore loose and down her back in one long wave. No more braids and French twists. She wanted a mane.

As the three of them unpacked their belongings and turned up the stereo (Kitaro, at Annie's request), there came a loud knock at the door. The three of them looked at each other and laughed. They bolted en masse to the front door and opened it.

A woman in her late thirties leaned on the door frame, looking quite exhausted. A seven-year-old girl danced in uninhibited circles in the hallway. The woman wore no wedding ring. Probably divorced. Annie looked from the woman's weary face to the small chipped plate of Oreo cookies she held in her hands. Charlotte giggled in her ear. Annie felt a finger wiggling against the crack of her ass. She kicked Charlotte lightly on the shin.

Annie looked directly into the woman's eyes and gave her a big, warm smile.

"Hi. Are you our neighbor?"

BLACK SHEEP

Nell Stark

I never gain weight over the holidays. It's not for lack of trying—I have a soft spot for Christmas cookies, eggnog, and mountains of mashed potatoes—but since coming out to my family a few years back, I've had to exercise like a maniac just to stay sane for the one week a year when I'm under their roof again.

So here I am, rounding the corner onto my parents' street at the end of an hour's jog, panting and sweaty despite the snow-scented air. Each breath spikes the bottom of my lungs in sharp, burning pricks that make me feel alive and strong. I don't want to stop running, but I promised I'd be home in enough time to help Mom with dinner. Or rather, to chop veggies while listening to her rave on and on about this one guy student she has, "the kind of man I want you to marry," she'll say, even though I've told them over and over and over that I'm gay and I'm not sorry, and it's not their fault or mine, it just *is*—

I'm only dimly aware of a car passing on my right, but it catches my eye as it turns into the driveway next to the house that's supposed to feel like mine but no longer does. The Jacobsens moved in a few years after we did, but seeing as their son was my age and their daughter as old as my younger brother—well, they became "part of the family" right away. I begin to speed up because I really don't want to have to face down Mrs. J and her naive, solicitous questions, but then the door opens and out steps the kid. Meredith. Who isn't really a kid anymore, seeing as she's clearly just driven back from

State after her exams, what with the big duffel and overflowing basket of dirty laundry taking up almost the entire backseat.

When she sees me, she gives a shy little wave, but the eager smile on her face stops me from merely returning the gesture and blazing by. I pull up next to the car, quick breaths steaming.

"Hi, Sabrina," she says, swiping a few strands of dark hair out of her eyes. She's looking up at me, of course—like she's looked up at me thousands of times, with that sweet little grin that lets me know I'm still her hero—but all of a sudden, my 'dar starts pinging like I'm down in the hold of the goddamn *Red October*. I'm caught totally unawares, the sensation so strong that the skin on my arms actually starts to crawl. I'd probably take a step back if her car weren't in my way—but as it is, I just blink a little and finally manage, "Hey, Mer."

Her eyes narrow slightly, and I wonder if I did something strange during that second of complete astonishment. But when she doesn't say anything, I shrug and point at the car. "Want some help with your stuff?"

"Sure," she replies, opening the door and dragging out the bag. As she's rustling up her laundry, I catch sight of a cute little pair of bright purple panties—just a scrap of lacy material, really—that wouldn't cover much of anything. My eyebrows try to climb into my hairline, because while I've known for years that Mer loves purple—purple hats, Popsicles, gumballs, sweaters, you name it—the fact that she now owns *lingerie* is just way too much to handle. Especially on top of the vibes she's somehow giving off.

But that's impossible. Meredith Jacobsen can't be gay. No way, no how. Clearly, my system is going haywire—probably a side effect of having to "straighten up" for the holidays.

"How's school?" I ask as I lug her bag toward the door. "And lax?" Because Mer is a damn good lacrosse player, despite her relatively petite stature—so good, in fact, that State recruited her and put her on the second string right away. I know all of this from my mother, who gives me regular updates on the golden girl next door just to make me feel guilty. She can't stand it that little Meredith, who always looked up to *me*, actually turned out "better."

You just wish she were queer, I tell myself, taking care to step over the patches of ice on the driveway. *It'd make you feel vindicated.*

"But I had a wicked hard psych final," Mer is saying as I tune back in. I nod sympathetically and heave her bag up on the front porch while she fumbles for her keys. She fits one into the lock, pushes open the door, and beckons me inside.

"Lacrosse is great, though," she enthuses as I carefully set the duffel down on an immaculate hardwood floor. Her smile is still shy when she turns to face me again. "So, um, do you know what you're doing after graduation?" Her eyes suddenly widen in alarm. "Or am I not supposed to ask that question?"

"It's okay." Having to reassure her restores my confidence. I cross my arms and lean against the doorjamb. I may be the black sheep of my own family, but this kid still thinks I walk on water. "I've applied for a few teaching positions at private high schools, and to a master's program in case that doesn't work out."

"Sounds like a good plan." Meredith rocks back and forth on her feet and jingles the change in her pocket in a clear display of nerves. She's dressed in a hooded gray sweatshirt, jeans, and sneakers, but somehow doesn't look grungy in the slightest. Maybe it's her hair—a perfect ponytail except for a few loose strands that frame her oval face. "You'd teach English?"

"Yeah. And coach girls' soccer, hopefully."

"Nice!" she exclaims, grinning and nodding. Suddenly, she seems very young. "That's cool."

"Yeah." I tilt my head toward the door. "Well, guess I'd better head home."

"Oh, sure," she says, and lets me out. "Thanks for the help, Sabrina."

"See you tomorrow," I tell her, flashing my trademark Endearing Grin as I step over the threshold. When she blushes, I get gobsmacked all over again by screaming gaydar. At least this time, I'm ready for it.

Despite the cold, I walk slowly across our adjoining side yards. There's some mighty weird shit going on in my brain, and all of a sudden, my head actually starts to hurt. I need a vacation—a *real* vacation, not this farce of one. It's exhausting to walk around "my" house on pins and needles, knowing that my parents and brother think I'm some kind of lost soul. Exhausting to have to think over every single word I say lest I offend them. I'm tired and angry way, way down deep, and all I want to do is get back to campus, curl up in my bed, and sleep for a month.

My car is right there, parked in the driveway. I could do it—just get in now and leave all of this behind. I could. But then again, it's only been two years. Lots of families take longer than two years to reach some measure of acceptance—or so I've heard, anyway. I can be patient, at least for a little while. I can show them I love them and respect them, even though that means continuing to hide my true self from my entire hometown. If I just stick it out until they finally realize this isn't a phase...well, maybe things will start to get better.

I force my feet to walk around the house, and let myself into the kitchen. Time for those damn vegetables. At least the chopping will be cathartic.

❖

When the doorbell rings, Mom is still angry that I'm refusing to wear a skirt for Christmas Eve dinner. She huffs a long sigh, smooths the skirt of her immaculate dress, and pirouettes gracefully on one heel to go greet the neighbors.

"Saved by the bell," I mutter under my breath. What I *am* wearing is black slacks and a pink oxford shirt with the cuffs rolled up to mid-wrist. I look hot and butch and I know it. So does Mom, and it bugs the hell out of her.

I scrub one hand through my hair and settle my butt against the kitchen counter. The sound of my brother pounding down the stairs almost manages to drown out the squeal of Mrs. J's high-pitched voice—but not quite. I start to sigh...but then Mer walks into the room and my breath gets all snarled up in the back of my throat. She's wearing a short black skirt, black pumps, and a long-sleeved gold top that's made out of some kind of shimmery material. It pulls just a bit across her breasts—and that's it, that's when I know I've gone off the deep end, because I'm standing here under the fluorescent lights of my mother's kitchen, ogling Meredith Jacobsen's breasts on Christmas Eve.

She hesitates when she sees me, then flashes one of those shy little smiles. "Merry Christmas, Sabrina."

"Same to you," I say, noting the hoarseness in my voice. Hoping I haven't betrayed my arousal, I turn to the fridge. "Get you a drink?" I ask over my shoulder.

"Sure. What are you having?"

"Beer." I sneak another look at her and can't help wondering if she's wearing those tiny purple panties under that skirt. The mental image makes my skin prickle, and I have to fight the urge to rub my arms.

Her eyes flick toward the foyer where the rest of her family is lingering, then back to me. She shakes her head. "Mom'll never let me get away with that," she murmurs. Her voice is low and tight—frustrated.

I don't even stop to consider ethics. She sounds like I feel right about now—sick to death of having to pretend. Somehow, I'm not surprised. "Quick," I tell her softly, "grab the rum. Cupboard down and to the left."

I snag a red and green plastic cup from the counter as she fishes the bottle out from the liquor cabinet. Our fingers brush as she hands it over, and I let the left corner of my mouth quirk in a grin. She watches the doorway for me as I pour a generous amount into the cup before stashing the bottle again—and I'm just topping it off with Coke as the rest of her family enters the kitchen.

I hand her the cup, making sure to reconnect with her fingers in the process. Her nails are the same color as her shirt. They glitter. "There you go, Mer."

"Thanks, Sabrina." She winks at me behind her father's broad back.

I turn to face the guests, tilt my head a little, and become Politeness Incarnate. "Merry Christmas, Mr. and Mrs. Jacobsen. Merry Christmas, Derek. What can I get you all to drink?"

It only takes me a few minutes to get Mr. and Mrs. J settled with a scotch and glass of white wine, respectively. Derek drinks beer, same as me. He's tall and handsome, with dark hair that matches the color of his suit and a few freckles splayed across his patrician nose. I should be in love with him, but I'm not. We're the same in more ways than he knows, and sometimes I wish I could tell him—because I can just see us, sharing a pitcher down at the local pub, arguing over which female celebrity is the fairest of them all. Getting drunk and saying too much about how women are so goddamn fucking *beautiful*. He used to be my best friend, and I miss him like hell. But I don't dare say a word.

I take a long pull off my beer as Mrs. Jacobsen asks me about my love life. "So, Sabrina," she begins, perching on the edge of a stool. "Don't be shy, now, and tell us about your boyfriend."

My eyebrows arch involuntarily. *What the fuck has my mother told this woman?*

"Boyfriend?" I ask carefully. Trying to remain nonchalant. Trying to resist the abruptly overwhelming impulse to chug my beer.

Across the room, Meredith is frowning at her mother. My own mother is frowning at me. Derek is rolling his eyes, and Sammy— my younger sibling—looks like a deer caught in headlights. The fathers are expressionless.

"There *must* be some dashing, athletic young man who has caught your eye," Mrs. J continues, her voice rising in pitch as she imagines my passion for such a creature. "Perhaps a captain of one of the men's teams?"

I relax as I realize this is just a flight of fancy rather than something she's been fed. Smiling sweetly at her, I shake my head and assume a sheepish grin. "Sorry to disappoint, Mrs. J—I've been far too busy with soccer and classes and applications to think about a relationship."

"And hey, don't you think it's time for the annual foosball match?" Derek cuts in, shooting me a sympathetic look. "Guys versus lose—I mean girls?" He's smirking, but not unkindly. In fact, I almost want to kiss him for rescuing me from his mother's interrogation. Almost.

"Step into my parlor," I reply, gesturing to the basement door. I turn to Mrs. J as the guys clomp down the stairs, and shrug. "Please excuse us," I tell her. "Looks like Mer and I have some egos to knock down a few pegs."

Just then, Meredith glides past—and for some reason, her breasts brush against my upper arm as she begins the descent into the basement. I stop breathing until the touch of her hand on mine jolts me out of my shock. "Hey, let's go," she urges from a few stairs below. As I watch, she reaches up, twines her fingers with mine, and tugs. "They're getting all warmed up down there!"

"Yeah," I manage to reply as she drags me down.

❖

I watch the checkered plastic ball dribble to one side of Derek's spinning defender and into the tiny goal. On my left, Meredith twirls around and war-whoops loudly. I look up into Derek's disbelieving face and grin as Sammy turns away from the table, groaning in disgust.

"Happy holidays, boys," I tell them smugly, sticking my hands into my pockets after a high five with Meredith. "Three years in a row now—you really should start practicing."

"Yeah, yeah, yeah," Derek grumbles good-naturedly. He looks down at his watch and lightly punches Sam in the arm. "Game's on in five, man—we should head upstairs." He turns, first to his sister and then to me. "You guys coming?"

My mouth opens, but Mer beats me to the punch, her nose wrinkling in a slight frown. "I'm not really in the mood," she announces, then looks at me. "Want to put in a movie or something?"

I shrug, but my pulse starts to trip-hop at the thought of Meredith and me, lying entwined on the futon while some film plays softly in the background. I grab the side of the foosball table to keep my hands from trembling visibly. It's beyond time for another drink. "Sure, yeah," I say aloud. "Fine with me."

"Suit yourselves," Derek replies, and leads Sammy up the stairs. The door closes behind them.

We're alone.

I take a step closer to her and peer into the bottom of her cup. "You're empty," I tell her. "Want another?"

The grin she turns on me is less shy than it was earlier in the night, and her cheeks are pinker. "Think you can sneak down two of those?" she asks, pointing to the empty beer bottle dangling from my left hand.

I smirk. "Not a problem. How 'bout you pick the movie?"

She nods and moves away as I take the stairs two at a time. I could try to be real quiet about opening the door, but that wouldn't do anything except *draw* attention. It took coming out to myself to realize that the key to doing anything truly sneaky is to act like it's not sneaky at all. So I walk right past the kitchen table where my mother and Mrs. Jacobsen are having a tête-à-tête, and snag four beers from the fridge. They don't even look up as I pass them on the way back, but I *do* hear my mom saying something about how nice Meredith looks and wondering whether maybe she dressed that way for Sam.

It's really, really hard not to bust up laughing, but I manage. Barely. After all, maybe Mom's right. I still don't have any hard evidence—just this feeling in the pit of my belly that Mer isn't flirting with Sammy at all.

That she's flirting with me.

I'm careful to close the door behind me before descending the stairs. "What are we watching?" I ask, carefully depositing the beers on the table. When Meredith's eyebrows arch in surprise, I grin, flick open one bottle, and hand it to her. "Figured we might need seconds in a little while."

"You're good," she murmurs before taking a long swallow.

I sit back on the futon and put my feet up on the scuffed coffee table. *You have no idea*, I think as she settles in—close to me, but not touching—and tucks her legs demurely to one side. I reach down to hit play on the remote, and immediately recognize the opening music of *The Matrix*.

"Good choice," I say, deftly twisting the cap off my own beer. I clink the base lightly with hers, then sit back to enjoy the film.

I really do love this movie—especially how it starts. Carrie-Anne Moss as Trinity, kicking the ever-loving shit out of the bad guys... and man, that outfit doesn't hurt, either.

"God, she's hot," Mer whispers as Trinity launches herself into the air and breaks through a window to escape the Agents on her tail.

For a few seconds, her comment doesn't really register—maybe because I'm thinking the exact same thing. But as awareness sinks in, I immediately lose all interest in the movie. Meredith is sitting there looking at me and blinking—a half-defiant, half-scared expression on her face.

"Damn," I mutter, staring into those wide, hazel eyes. "I knew it." Grinning, I shift so that my knee is touching hers. "When'd you come out?"

She swallows. "T-thanksgiving. You?"

"Two years ago." The warring expressions on her face give way to surprise.

"Two years?" she exclaims. "I never even...I mean..."

I shrug. "Mom didn't want anyone to know. Especially not your family." I can feel my smile changing flavor, transforming into the half snarl that's come so easily since writing that letter back in sophomore year.

"Same here," Mer replies, leaning forward. "My mom—she keeps telling me it's just a phase, you know?" But she sort of laughs, then, and touches my knee with two hesitant fingers. "Just today, she asked why I couldn't be more like you."

I laugh too—a real laugh from deep inside—and find myself covering her hand with mine. "How obedient of you," I murmur as her index finger curls around mine. "So, who brought you out?"

Meredith rolls her shoulders in a long shrug, and I can't help but sneak a quick glance at her breasts again. They would fit perfectly into my hands.

"A sophomore on the team." She meets my eyes, then, her pupils huge and dark. Electromagnets. "We broke up during finals week."

"Sorry," I murmur. I'm leaning forward, slowly but inevitably. Caught.

"It's okay," she whispers, just before our mouths meet. The taste of rum clings to her lips. I suck gently—first the top, then the bottom—before finally slipping my tongue inside to tangle slowly with hers. She groans, low and deep. As the kiss goes on and on, I dare to cradle her face in my palms.

When I finally pull away, she's breathing hard. Her eyes are dark pools ringed with green and gold, and her expression is hungry.

"You're a good kisser," I tell her, trying catch my own breath. And then it leaves me entirely as she shifts to straddle my lap in one smooth movement. Her breasts bob lightly at my eye level.

"Holy shit," I mutter, grabbing hold of the futon cover so I won't touch her. "Uh, Mer…"

"Iwantyou," she says, all in a rush. She's biting her lower lip, and her face is flushed—but I can tell that she means it. Or, well, that she *thinks* she does.

"You're a little buzzed," I say gently, bringing my hands up to caress her forearms. She's so fucking hot as she hovers above me, but…well, damn it, this is the girl next door. The kid who hero-worships me. I've always sort of taken care of her, from a distance, and I don't want her to regret anything. Ever.

She shakes her head and grins, stroking the right side of my face with one hand as the other begins to unbutton my shirt. When I grab hold of her wrist, she shakes her head again. "I know what I'm doing, Sabrina," she tells me. For a moment, her fingers still as she tilts her head to one side. "Do you have a girlfriend?"

"No." I have to actively fight the urge to let my hands follow the curve of her arms—to slide up her biceps and then down to cup her breasts.

"Then let me." She brings her head down to mine again, and I can't help it—I allow her to kiss me. Her. Meredith Jacobsen. Who has apparently turned into a femme top during her first three months of college. I can't help the low moan that surfaces from the depths of my chest. Her fingers are remarkably agile, and she manages to unbutton my entire shirt without ever stopping the kiss.

"You ever have that feeling where you're not sure you're awake or still dreaming?" I can barely hear Keanu Reeves's voice over the buzzing in my ears, as her hand slips inside to caress my right breast through my sports bra.

Oh yeah, Neo. Right here, right now. At her touch, I feel my entire body tighten—and then she pulls away from me, gasping quietly.

"God, Sabrina—"

In that split second of clarity when her hands are no longer in contact with my body, I make my bid for control. I may be literally on the bottom at this point, but I can work with that. Her skirt is already riding high on her thighs, and before she can return her fingers to my breasts, I've got a hand on each leg just above the knee and am quickly pushing *up* against the offending fabric.

She sucks in a breath and grabs for my shoulders. Fortunately, the movement brings her breasts within range of my mouth. "Take off your shirt," I rasp as my thumbs massage her inner thighs.

"Sabrina—" she says again, almost as though she might protest.

I take the opportunity to slide my fingers a fraction of an inch closer. "Do it."

She pulls off her shirt and hikes up her bra without another word, and I capture the tip of one breast with my mouth, letting my teeth graze her skin as I hollow my cheeks. She groans, long and low, her hips thrusting helplessly against me. The motion brings my thumbs directly against the junction of her thighs, and I gasp at the sensation of lace against my fingertips. I lift her skirt enough to catch a glimpse of purple beneath the black, and my pulse ratchets up so fast that I get a little dizzy. *No fucking way!*

I want nothing more than to spend a good ten minutes teasing her as I work the lingerie down her toned legs, but we're in my basement, and our parents are upstairs, and the slow seduction will just have to wait. Instead, I sweep the thin material aside. She's so soft and warm and wet...for *me*.

Awe. That's what I'm feeling—this strange sort of awe that I've never experienced before. Ever. It's almost overwhelming, but as I caress her lightly and thrill to her quiet, encouraging moans, the need to see her come apart above me overshadows every other emotion. I slide one thumb down and *in*—shallowly, because I don't want to hurt her. I massage her firmly with the other, tracing the exquisite softness of her lips until my finger brushes the ridge of her clitoris.

Her hips buck again, and she cries out softly. "Shhh," I tell her, circling the swollen knot of nerves with slow, steady strokes. This time, she whimpers. My thumb slides gently in and out, marking counterpoint. Stroke, thrust, stroke thrust—I tease her other breast with my tongue as I increase the speed of my fingers—and suddenly she's shaking above me, quivering as the climax jumps like a spark from my fingertips through every cell of her body. Head thrown back, throat muscles taut, breasts jutting toward me... I forget to breathe for a few seconds, she's so damn beautiful. Unrestrained.

As the sensation finally wanes, she leans forward to cushion her forehead against my shoulder. I continue to touch her lightly until the aftershocks have passed and I'm sure that she's sated. Gently, I readjust her underwear and slide my hands out from under her skirt. She raises her head to look at me, and her eyes are dark and hazy. I smile, despite the insistent pressure between my own legs.

"You're beautiful, Mer."

"And you're a-amazing," she murmurs hoarsely. She looks about ready to fall asleep—and I'm just about to suggest that we spoon—when all of a sudden she slides partially off my lap to the left and cups me with her right hand.

"Fuck," I groan, bucking helplessly against her. "Oh *God*—"

And at that moment, the basement door opens. "Girls?" calls my mother. My blood literally freezes as I hear her take a step down. "Time to come upstairs—dinner's almost ready!"

"Okay, Mom!" I manage to shout over the movie. "Be there in a minute!"

I hold my breath until I hear the door close behind her, and then I'm slumping into the futon, head whirling in relief. "Fuck," I say again. "That was too *fucking* close!"

But Meredith won't be deterred. Her fingers move against me, and somehow, my desire pushes its way past the panic. "Help me," she whispers, her breath warm against the shell of my ear. Her fingers glide in firm circles, subtly shifting as she tests each vantage point, and—

"Oh, yeah," I gasp suddenly. My legs fall open even farther. "Just li—like that."

As much as I wish I could feel her against my skin, the friction created by the silky material of my slacks is incredibly arousing, and it only takes a few seconds before I'm surging up off the futon, hips thrusting wildly as I come fast and hard.

I lean my head back and fight for breath as she peppers kisses across my neck. Meredith Jacobsen and I just had sex in the basement on Christmas Eve. Unbelievable.

"C'mon," she urges, pulling her shirt back over her head. "We have to get up there."

I blink and sit up straighter, nerveless fingers fumbling with the buttons on my shirt. When she hands over my mostly full bottle of beer, I grin in thanks. She downs her own in a few long swallows, and I can't help but admire the pale column of her throat. I'd like to kiss her there—to bring the blood rushing to the surface of her skin.

"All right," she says decisively as she sets the empty beer down hard on the coffee table. "Think I'll be able to make it through the rest of the night now."

I laugh and let her pull me up off the couch. My hip bumps hers as we make our way up the stairs, and I find myself sliding my arm around her waist, just to feel her. Her. Meredith. The kid next door who finally grew up.

"What are you doing tomorrow?" I ask as we reach the top of the stairs. Reluctantly, I move my hand from her waist to the doorknob.

"Church, then opening presents, then family brunch," she says. She's got that look in her eyes, again—half-defiant, half-scared. "After that, nothing much."

As insanely hot as our hook-up was, I want what's supposed to come afterward, too—the cuddling, the laughter, the reassurance. More. I want more, and I want her to know it. "I'm sure I'll get some ultra-feminine clothing items that I'll need to return at the mall tomorrow afternoon," I say. "Want to come with? Maybe we can get dinner and...take the scenic way home."

The smile that curves her lips is slow and promising, and I find myself wondering what else that sweet mouth can do. The thought sends a tingling warmth all the way into my toes.

"You're on," she murmurs. She rests one hand over mine, then looks up at me.

Together, we open the door and step out into the kitchen.

CONTRIBUTORS

SANDY LOWE began her publishing career in Sydney, Australia, and is now senior editor at Bold Strokes Books.

STACIA SEAMAN is an award-winning editor of multiple anthologies, including the Lambda Literary Award winner *Erotic Interludes 2: Stolen Moments* and IPPY gold medalist *Erotic Interludes 5: Road Games.*

GEORGIA BEERS is a Lambda, Foreword Book of the Year, and Goldie Award–winning author of lesbian romance who lives in upstate New York. When not writing, she loves movies, TV, baking, reading, and walking with her dog. You can visit her and find out more at www.georgiabeers.com.

ELIZABETH BLACK writes erotic fiction, dark fiction, and horror. Her stories have been published by Cleis Press, Xcite Books, Circlet Press, and others. She lives on the Massachusetts coast with her husband, son, and three cats. The ocean calls to her every day, and she responds.

RONICA BLACK was born in North Carolina but has spent most of her life in the Phoenix area. She loves animals, art, film, creating, reading, and writing.

KRIS BRYANT lives in Kansas City, MO. She enjoys photography, writing, reading, and spending time with her family, friends, and the true love of her life, her westie Molly. Kris can be reached at krisbryantbooks@gmail.com, @KrisBryant14, and krisbryant.net.

BETH BURNETT is an author, a teacher, and a women's empowerment coach. A grad student, she also teaches self-love classes and serves on the board of GCLS. In her spare time, she reads, writes, and hikes with her geriatric rescue dog. She is at work on her fifth novel.

LEA DALEY has written fiction and poetry while raising children, claiming a lesbian identity, earning a BFA in painting, teaching preschoolers and college students, surviving the death of her only daughter, and heading a nonprofit agency that serves low-income working families. Her debut novel, *Waiting for Harper Lee*, was a Goldie Award finalist and received a Lavender Certificate from the Alice B Readers Appreciation Committee. Her second book, *FutureDyke*, won a Goldie Award and was a Lambda Literary Award finalist.

An English literature graduate with a passion for LGBT heritage, ANNA LARNER is the author of the lesbian romance *Highland Fling*.

LISA MOREAU has a bachelor's degree in journalism from Midwestern State University (TX) and has taken creative writing courses at Santa Monica College, CA. She has two books published, *Love on the Red Rocks* and *The Butterfly Whisperer*. Lisa lives in Los Angeles.

GISELLE RENARDE is an award-winning queer Canadian writer. Nominated Toronto's Best Author in NOW Magazine's 2015 Readers' Choice Awards, her fiction has appeared in over 200 anthologies, including *Best Lesbian Romance* and the Lambda Award–winning collection *Take Me There*. Giselle's juicy novels include *Anonymous*, *Cherry*, *Seven Kisses*, and *The Other Side of Ruth*.

AURORA REY (aurorarey.com) is a college dean by day and lesbian romance author the rest of the time. She grew up in south Louisiana and lives with her partner in Ithaca, NY. Baking is her favorite form of seduction.

NELL STARK is an award-winning author of lesbian romance, published by Bold Strokes Books. Her 2010 novel *everafter* (with Trinity Tam) won a Goldie for paranormal romance. In 2013, *The Princess Affair* was a Lambda Literary Award finalist. Nell lives in New York City with her wife, son, and dogs.

M. ULLRICH has always called New Jersey home and currently resides by the beach with her wife and three boisterous felines. By day, M. Ullrich works in the optical field and spends her time off writing. She also happens to be fluent in three languages: English, sarcasm, and TV/movie quotes.

MISSOURI VAUN spent her childhood in Mississippi. Her roots in the rural South have been a grounding force. Vaun spent twelve years working as a journalist in places as disparate as Chicago and Jackson, MS. Her novels are heartfelt, earthy; speak of loyalty and our responsibility to others.

KARIS WALSH is the author of lesbian romances including Rainbow Award–winning *Harmony* and *Sea Glass Inn*, and a romantic intrigue series about a mounted police unit. She's a Pacific Northwest native, and when she isn't writing, she's spending time with her animals, playing her viola, or hiking in the state park.

LANEY WEBBER is a GCLS Writing Academy graduate and also a member of the Vermont League of Writers and Romance Writers of America.

BREY WILLOWS is the author of the Afterlife Inc series and has been editing lesbian fiction for nearly a decade. Under another pen name she has published stories in *Me and My Boi, Order Up, Don't Be Shy, Women of the Dark Streets, Where the Girls Are,* and several others. She lives with her partner and fellow author in the UK.

SHERI LEWIS WOHL lives in northeastern Washington State and happily writes surrounded by unspoiled nature. She tries to capture a bit of that beauty in her work, though no matter how hard she tries to write *normal*, it doesn't work. Something of the preternatural variety always sneaks in.

ALLISON WONDERLAND (aisforallison.blogspot.com) has contributed to nearly forty collections of lesbian literature, including Bold Strokes' *Girls on Campus* and *Myth and Magic*. In addition to storytelling, Allison is involved in the performing arts and, as a volunteer with organizations that serve survivors of domestic abuse, helping others make new starts.

RION WOOLF writes and lives in Ohio. Her erotica stories have appeared in anthologies such as *Girls on Campus, Dirty: Dirty,* and *Shameless Behavior: Brazen Stories of Overcoming Shame.*

Books Available From Bold Strokes Books

Complications by MJ Williamz. Two women battle for the heart of one. (978-1-62639-769-9)

Crossing the Wide Forever by Missouri Vaun. As Cody Walsh and Lillie Ellis face the perils of the untamed West, they discover that love's uncharted frontier isn't for the weak in spirit or the faint of heart. (978-1-62639-851-1)

Fake It till You Make It by M. Ullrich. Lies will lead to trouble, but can they lead to love? (978-1-62639-923-5)

Girls Next Door, edited by Sandy Lowe and Stacia Seaman. Bestselling romance authors tell it from the heart—sexy, romantic stories of falling for the girls next door. (978-1-62639-916-7)

Pursuit by Jackie D. The pursuit of the most dangerous terrorist in America will crack the lines of friendship and love, and not everyone will make it out from under the weight of duty and service. (978-1-62639-903-7)

The Practitioner by Ronica Black. Sometimes love comes calling whether you're ready for it or not. (978-1-62639-948-8)

Unlikely Match by Fiona Riley. When an ambitious PR exec and her super-rich coding geek-girl client fall in love, they learn that giving something up may be the only way to have everything. (978-1-62639-891-7)

Where Love Leads by Erin McKenzie. A high school counselor and the mom of her new student bond in support of the troubled girl, never expecting deeper feelings to emerge, testing the boundaries of their relationship. (978-1-62639-991-4)

Forsaken Trust by Meredith Doench. When four women are murdered, Agent Luce Hansen must regain trust in her most valuable investigative tool—herself—to catch the killer. (978-1-62639-737-8)

Letter of the Law by Carsen Taite. Will federal prosecutor Bianca Cruz take a chance at love with horse breeder Jade Vargas, whose dark family ties threaten everything Bianca has worked to protect—including her child? (978-1-62639-750-7)

New Life by Jan Gayle. Trigena and Karrie are having a baby, but the stress of becoming a mother and the impact on their relationship might be too much for Trigena. (978-1-62639-878-8)

Royal Rebel by Jenny Frame. Charity director Lennox King sees through the party-girl image Princess Roza has cultivated, but will Lennox's past indiscretions and Roza's responsibilities make their love impossible? (978-1-62639-893-1)

Unbroken by Donna K. Ford. When Kayla and Jackie, two women with every reason to reject Happily Ever After, fall in love, will they have the courage to overcome their pasts and rewrite their stories? (978-1-62639-921-1)

Where the Light Glows by Dena Blake. Mel Thomas doesn't realize just how unhappy she is in her marriage until she meets Izzy Calabrese. Will she have the courage to overcome her insecurities and follow her heart? (978-1-62639-958-7)

Her Best Friend's Sister by Meghan O'Brien. For fifteen years, Claire Barker has nursed a massive crush on her best friend's older sister. What happens when all her wildest fantasies come true? (978-1-62639-861-0)

Escape in Time by Robyn Nyx. Working in the past is hell on your future. (978-1-62639-855-9)

Forget-Me-Not by Kris Bryant. Is love worth walking away from the only life you've ever dreamed of? (978-1-62639-865-8)

Highland Fling by Anna Larner. On vacation in the Scottish Highlands, Eve Eddison falls for the enigmatic forestry officer Moira Burns despite Eve's best friend's campaign to convince her that Moira will break her heart. (978-1-62639-853-5)

boldstrokesbooks.com

Bold Strokes Books

Quality and Diversity in LGBTQ Literature

victory
EDITIONS

Drama

MATINEE BOOKS

SCI-FI

E-BOOKS

MYSTERY

erotica

BSB
SOLILOQUY

EROTICA

YOUNG
ADULT

BOLD
STROKES
BOOKS

LIBERTY
EDITIONS

Romance

W·E·B·S·T·O·R·E

PRINT AND EBOOKS